T0279648

The Girls

More Belt Revivals

Poor White by Sherwood Anderson

Main-Travelled Roads by Hamlin Garland

The History of the Standard Oil Company by Ida Tarbell

The Damnation of Theron Ware by Harold Frederic

Stories from Ohio by William Dean Howells

The Artificial Man and Other Stories by Clare Winger Harris

The Marrow of Tradition by Charles W. Chesnutt

The Shame of the Cities by Lincoln Steffens

One of Ours by Willa Cather

The Fastest Bicycle Rider in the World
by Marshall W. "Major" Taylor

The Girls

Edna Ferber

Introduction copyright © 2023, Kathleen Rooney

All rights reserved. This introduction or any portion thereof may not be reproduced or used
in any manner whatsoever without the express written permission of the publisher except for
the use of brief quotations in a book review.

First Belt Publishing Edition 2023
ISBN: 978-1-953368-49-2

Belt Publishing
13443 Detroit Avenue, Lakewood, OH 44107
www.beltpublishing.com

Book design by Meredith Pangrace
Cover by David Wilson

Contents

Introduction

What could be simpler than the game Old Maid, a basic affair where cards are matched in pairs and the player stuck with the unmatched card at the end is the loser? The implications of the game and its name could hardly be clearer: to end up as an unmarried, childless woman is to lose out on all that life has to offer—to be a prim, fussy person, sexless and repressed and pitied by others.

Even now, in the twenty-first century, when more adults, both men and women, are going through life unattached by matrimony than ever before, women who never marry still find themselves pegged—sometimes by peers, sometimes by family, and almost always by pop culture—as odd or eccentric at best, pathetic and rejected at worst. Not winners.

Which is why, a century after its initial publication, Edna Ferber's deft, affectionate 1921 novel *The Girls* refreshes us with its exuberant focus upon not one but three old maids. From the very first page, Ferber breezes us into the lives of her titular women:

> It is a question of method. Whether to rush you up to the
> girls pell-mell, leaving you to become acquainted as best you

can; or, with elaborate slyness, to slip you so casually into their family life that they will not even glance up when you enter the room or leave it; or to present the three of them in solemn order according to age, epoch, and story. This last would mean beginning with Great-Aunt Charlotte Thrift, spinster, aged seventy-four; thence to her niece and namesake Lottie Payson, spinster, aged thirty-two; finishing with Lottie's niece and namesake Charley Kemp, spinster, aged eighteen and a half—you may be certain nobody ever dreamed of calling her Charlotte. If you are led by all this to exclaim, aghast, "A story about old maids!"—you are right. It is.

Ferber, who never married and had no children herself, even dedicates *The Girls* to her dear friend Lillian Adler, another old maid and fellow spinster, albeit one "who shies at butterflies but not at life." That latter phrase, "but not at life," turns out to be thematically crucial, for this is absolutely a book about old maids, but it is not the dreary narrative a reader might first expect.

These three women, though unwed and child-free, are not isolated but enmeshed in their families, friendships, and surrounding communities. Granted, to greater or lesser extents, each finds herself within a sexist and claustrophobic societal atmosphere in which any little act of self-assertion can feel like a leap from a precipice. Yet Ferber is not interested in cautionary tales of shrinking violets, favoring instead women who, out of necessity or desire or both, discover that meaningful work and recognition outside the home can unlock the door to a meaningful life.

Early on, while living in Chicago during the Civil War and in its immediate aftermath, practically under house arrest by her parents after a perceived romantic indiscretion, the eldest Charlotte—lively and passionate yet suppressed by her respectability-obsessed Victorian mother—finishes sewing a phenomenal quilt, one that "became quite famous; a renowned work of art." Visitors, the narrator tells us, ask Charlotte about its progress, "as a novelist is sounded about an opus with which he is struggling or a painter his canvas," prompting the quilter to explain, "This one has a purple satin center, you see. I always think purple is so rich, don't you? Then the next row will be white uncut velvet. Doesn't it have a sumptuous sound! Next blue velvet and the last row orange-colored silk." This precious object and its method of composition—patches and colors that repeat and intersect to create a bigger pattern—resurface throughout the book, becoming an analog for Ferber's nimble and elegant assembly of her own saga. Moving back and forth through time, she highlights the rhymes in the lives of the elderly Aunt Charlotte, the middle-aged Lottie, and the galoshed and rebellious young flapper, Charley. It is the similarities and differences among these three women and their love for one another that provides the thread that binds the narrative.

Quilts, historically considered to be the product of women's work, have almost always been viewed as a lesser art form than the traditionally male-dominated pursuits of painting, sculpture, and even literature, as Ferber, a so-called "woman novelist," was well aware. And she uses Aunt Charlotte's quilt as a recurring reminder of the perils of undervaluing not just women's labor but women themselves. When at last Charlotte completes her masterpiece, "lined with turkey red and bound with red ribbon," she lets her friends persuade her to exhibit it at the fair, where it takes first prize. "A day of great triumph for Charlotte Thrift," the narrator sums up, adding that "the prize was a basket worth fully eight dollars."

In her review of Eliza McGraw's 2014 book, *Edna Ferber's America*, Lori Harrison-Kahan observes how the author was scorned both for being a woman and for being a Jew, noting that "a chorus of critical voices, most of them male" dismissed Ferber's "crowd-pleasing plots as well as her hyperbolic, though accessible, writing style." F. Scott Fitzgerald refused even to "read her wildly popular stories, derisively labeling her one of the 'Yiddish descendants of O. Henry.'" In his 1960 *Partisan Review* essay "Masscult and Midcult," Dwight Macdonald offered his notorious assessment of middlebrow writers, stating that their work "really isn't culture at all" but "a parody of High Culture"; he placed Ferber at the top of his "list of writers who should not be taken seriously."

One hopes that these men, if they were still alive, would be embarrassed at having made such fatuous statements. Regardless, these guys were missing out. Ferber's writing is a delight, and now, with Belt Publishing's reissue of *The Girls,* more readers will get the opportunity see that.

This three-protagonist story relies on a masterful omniscience, which skips like a stone across Lake Michigan, hopping thrillingly from mind to mind. Set in 1916 but published in 1921, so too does the narration capitalize on the insights available to its slightly retrospective perspective. For instance, when a minor character says of World War I, "We're a peace-loving nation. . . . We simply don't believe in war. Barbaric," both the narrator and we know how tragically incorrect she is. Moreover, when the narrator mentions the struggle for suffrage, we are aware, as the women are not, that they will finally be granted the right to vote in 1920, after the novel ends but before it gets published. Ferber delivers this deep sociohistorical sweep with a deceptively light touch that enhances the novel's underlying seriousness while also keeping the plot moving along.

Near the book's surprising and satisfying conclusion, Lottie tells her kindred Charlottes about a man she met in Paris during the Great War. Of this man's most attractive quality, she declares, "They call it a sense of humor, I suppose, but it's more than that. It's the most delightful thing in the world, and if you have it you don't need anything else." Ferber displays this quality in abundance, as well as plenty of that "anything else." Because here's the thing: this book is *funny*, but with a genuine generosity of spirit that never reduces even its most ridiculous figures to total buffoons. The dominant outlook feels loving and compassionate. And its gentle mockery of its major and minor characters' blind spots and foibles blends with its profound understanding.

Ferber perfectly captures the unfulfilled feeling within so many conventional people and the petty tyranny a forcefully normal family member can exert over those in her orbit, from Great Aunt Charlotte Thrift's authoritarian mother to her sister, Carrie Payson, who is Lottie's mother. The latter, in addition to fairly running Lottie into the ground with her domineering demands, is "the sort of person who does slammy flappy things in a room where you happened to be breakfasting, or writing, or reading; things at which you could not express annoyance and yet which annoyed you to the point of frenzy."

Through a gradual accumulation of events and encounters, Ferber shows how a bit of resistance and freethinking, especially when they are supported by other female family members, can set off a series of earthquakes that can shift a household's—and a society's—entire geography. This trifecta of Charlottes proves that sisterhood is indeed powerful, maybe even more so when it comes from beyond your actual blood sisters.

Certainly, Ferber's approach—critical but forgiving to individual people and America at large—stems largely from who she was as a person and the way in which she moved through the world as a *feme sole*. A firsthand expert on the old maid lifestyle herself, Ferber was never known to have had a romantic or sexual relationship. But far from being a sad, sere figure whom life was passing by, she was vibrant, indefatigable, witty, and successful, a member of the Algonquin Round Table in New York and a winner of the Pulitzer Prize in 1924 for another wonderful Chicago novel, *So Big*. She saw that book eventually adapted into one silent picture and two talking ones. Her 1926 novel *Show Boat* was made into the famous 1927 musical, and *Cimarron* (1930), *Giant* (1952), and *The Ice Palace* (1958) were all adapted into films as well.

Born in 1885 in Kalamazoo, Michigan, to a Hungarian Jewish father and a German Jewish mother, Ferber lived a peripatetic youth throughout the Midwest, including Chicago for a year when she was three, Ottumwa, Iowa, from 1890 to 1897, and Appleton, Wisconsin, where she graduated from high school and became a reporter for the *Appleton Crescent* before moving to Milwaukee to write for the *Sentinel*. She returned to Chicago around 1910, where, similar to the Thrift girls, she lived with her mother and sister in furnished apartments and hotels on the city's South Side. There, as she later put it, "Chicago stories tumbled, one after another out of my typewriter. New Year's Eve in a Chicago Loop hotel . . . a woman buyer in a Chicago department store . . . a clerk in a cut-price shoe store. They were stories of working people, of the Little People, of those who got the tough end of life."

Although she had settled in New York by the mid-1920s, she returned to Chicago frequently and continued to draw upon its people and neighborhoods, including in *The Girls*, which, in its span from the Civil War to World War I, uses its three Charlottes to depict and critique the city's conventional, status-driven social circles.

Beset by anti-Semitism, especially in her early life, Ferber depicts that prejudice and others—including classism and anti-Blackness—unsparingly in *The Girls*. Many characters either engage in unthinking intolerance themselves or, due to the strictures of feminine deference, fail to subvert such biases, at least at first. Ferber's frank descriptions of class stratifications, ethnic divides, and sexism illustrate how these snobberies and preconceptions shape not only individual lives but the life of a metropolis.

At one point, Lottie drives downtown in the family's "ancient electric" to help her unusual-in-her-profession friend, Judge Emma Barton, rehabilitate a wayward girl. She catches "her breath a little at the spaciousness and magnificence of those blocks between Twelfth and Randolph. The new Field Columbian Museum, a white wraith, rose out of the lake mist at her right." Ferber notes that Lottie "always felt civic when driving down Michigan," which enhances the marvel we feel a few pages later when Ferber writes just as convincingly about "all that vast stratum of submerged servers over whom the flood of humanity sweeps in a careless torrent leaving no one knows what sediment of rich knowledge." With subtle characterization and wry sympathy of tone, Ferber shows in *The Girls* that the underestimated often have a richer life than anyone who fails to look closely might suspect, and that there are fates far worse than never marrying a husband and sacrificing oneself to a nuclear family.

The phrase "beloved woman" comes up over and over in this novel, referring to the radiance that a woman exudes when a man has chosen to treasure her above others. Each time this coveted glow appears, however, Ferber presents us with an occasion to wonder: Could a woman be beloved in other ways? Not disdained or taken for granted based upon her ability to be selected by a husband, but loved more broadly, respected for everything else inherent to her being?

Kathleen Rooney
March 2023

The Girls

To
Lillian Adler

Who shies at butterflies
But not at life

Chapter I

It is a question of method. Whether to rush you up to the girls pell-mell, leaving you to become acquainted as best you can; or, with elaborate slyness, to slip you so casually into their family life that they will not even glance up when you enter the room or leave it; or to present the three of them in solemn order according to age, epoch, and story. This last would mean beginning with Great-Aunt Charlotte Thrift, spinster, aged seventy-four; thence to her niece and namesake Lottie Payson, spinster, aged thirty-two; finishing with Lottie's niece and namesake Charley Kemp, spinster, aged eighteen and a half—you may be certain nobody ever dreamed of calling *her* Charlotte. If you are led by all this to exclaim, aghast, "A story about old maids!"—you are right. It is. Though, after all, perhaps one couldn't call Great-Aunt Charlotte an old maid. When a woman has achieved seventy-four, a virgin, there is about her something as sexless, as aloof and monumental, as there is about a cathedral or a sequoia. Perhaps, too, the term is inappropriate to the vigorous, alert, and fun-loving Lottie. For that matter, a glimpse of Charley in her white woolly sweater and gym pants might cause you to demand a complete retraction of the term. Charley is of the type before whom this era stands in amazement and something like terror. Charley speaks freely on subjects of which Great-Aunt Charlotte has never even heard. Words obstetrical, psychoanalytical, political, metaphysical, and eugenic trip from Charley's tongue. Don't think that Charley is a highbrow (to use a word fallen into disuse). Not at all. Even her enemies admit, grudgingly, that she packs a nasty backhand tennis wallop and that her dancing is almost professional. Her chief horror is of what she calls sentiment. Her minor hatreds are "glad" books, knitted underwear, corsets, dirt both physical and mental, lies, fat minds and corporeal fat. She looks her best in a white fuzzy sweater. A shade too slim and boyish, perhaps, for chiffons.

The relationship between Charlotte, Lottie, and Charley is a simple one, really, though having, perhaps, an intricate look to the outsider. Great-aunt, niece, grand-niece: it was understood readily enough in Chicago's South Side, just as it was understood that no one ever called Lottie "Charlotte," or Charley "Lottie," though any of the three might be designated as "one of the Thrift girls."

The Thrifts had been Chicago South Siders since that September in 1836 when Isaac Thrift had traveled tediously by rail, sound steamer, riverboat, canal boat, lake ship, and horse wagon from his native New York State to the unkempt prairie settlement on the banks of the sluggish stream that the Pottawatamie Indians called Che-ca-gou. Their reason for having thus named a city after the homely garlic plant was plain enough whenever the breeze came pungently from the prairies instead of from Lake Michigan.

Right here is the start of Aunt Charlotte. And yet the temptation is almost irresistible to brush rudely past her and to hurry on to Lottie Payson, who is herself hurrying on home through the slate and salmon-pink Chicago sunset after what is known on the South Side as "spending the afternoon."

An exhilarating but breathless business—this catching up with Lottie; Lottie of the fine straight back, the short sturdy legs, the sensible shoes, the well-tailored suit, and the elfish interior. All these items contributed to the facility with which she put the long Chicago blocks behind her—all, that is, except the last. An unwed woman of thirty-odd is not supposed to possess an elfish exterior; she is expected to be well balanced and matter-of-fact and practical. Lottie knew this and usually managed to keep the imp pretty well concealed. Yet she so often felt sixteen and utterly irresponsible that she had to take brisk walks along the lakefront on blustery days, when the spray stung your cheeks; or out Bryn Mawr way or even to Beverly Hills, where dwellings were sparse and one could take off one's hat and venture to skip, furtively, without being eyed askance. This was supposed to help work off the feeling—not that Lottie wanted to work it off. She liked it. But you can't act Peter Panish at thirty-two without causing a good deal of action among conservative eyebrows. Lottie's mother, Mrs. Carrie Payson, would have been terribly distressed at the thought of South Side eyebrows elevated against a member of her household. Sixty-six years of a full life had taught Mrs. Carrie Payson little about the chemistry of existence. Else she must have known how inevitably a disastrous explosion follows the bottling up of the Lotties of this world.

On this particular March day, the elf was proving obstreperous. An afternoon spent indoors talking to women of her own age and position was likely to affect Lottie Payson thus. Walking fleetly along now, she decided that she hated spending afternoons; that they were not only spent but squandered. Beck Schaefer had taken the others home in her electric. Lottie, seized with a sudden distaste for the glittering enameled box with its cut-glass cornucopia for flowers (artificial), its gray velvet upholstery and tasseled straps, had elected to walk, though she knew it would mean being late.

"Figger?" Beck Schaefer had asked, settling her own plump person in the driver's seat.

"Air," Lottie had answered, not altogether truthfully; and drew a long breath. She turned away from the curb. The electric trundled richly off, its plate-glass windows filled with snugly tailored shoulders, furs, white gloves, vivid hats. Lottie held a hand high in farewell, palm out, as the gleaming vehicle sped silently away, lurched fatly around a corner, and was gone.

So she strode home now, through the early evening mist, the zany March wind buffeting her skirts—no skirt: it is 1916 and women are knickerbockered underneath instead of petticoated—and the fishy smell that was Lake Michigan in March; the fertilizer smell that was the Stockyards when the wind was west; and the smoky smell that was soft coal from the IC trains and a million unfettered chimneys, all blending and mellowing to a rich mixture that was incense to her Chicago-bred nostrils.

She was walking rapidly and thinking clearly, if disconnectedly:

"How we lied to each other this afternoon! Once or twice, though, we came nearer the truth than was strictly comfortable . . . Beck's bitter . . . There! I forgot Celia's recipe for that icebox cake after all . . . Beck's legs . . . I never saw such—uh—tumultuous legs . . . gray silk stockings ought to be prohibited on fat legs; room seemed to be full of them . . . That's a nice sunset. I'd love to go over to the lake just for a minute . . . No, guess I'd better not with the folks coming to dinner . . . People always saying Chicago's ugly when it's really . . . Of course the Loop is pretty bad . . . Tomorrow'd be a good day to go downtown and look at blue serges . . . a tricotine I think . . . I wonder if Mother will want to go . . . I do hope this once . . ."

Here Lottie drew a deep breath; the kind of breathing that relieves stomach nerves. She was so sure that Mother would want to go. She almost always did.

Here we are, striding briskly along with Lottie Payson, while Great-Aunt Charlotte, a wistful black-silk figure, lingers far behind. We are prone to be impatient of black-silk figures, quite forgetting that they once were slim and eager white, young figures in hoopskirts that sometimes tilted perilously up behind, displaying an unseemly length of frilled pantalette. Great-Aunt Charlotte's skirts had shaped the course of her whole life.

Charlotte Thrift had passed eighteen when the Civil War began. There is a really beautiful picture of her in her riding habit, taken at the time. She is wearing a hard-boiled hat with a plume, and you wonder how she ever managed to reconcile that skirt with a horse's back. The picture doesn't show the color of the plume but you doubtless would know. It is a dashing plume anyway and caresses her shoulder. In one hand she is catching up the folds of her voluminous skirt, oh, ever so little; and in the other, carelessly, she is holding a rose. Her young face is so serious as to be almost severe. That is, perhaps, due to her eyebrows, which were considered too heavy and dark for feminine beauty. And yet there is a radiance about the face, and an effect of life and motion about the young figure that bespeaks but one thing. Great-Aunt Charlotte still has the picture somewhere. Sometimes, in a mild orgy of "straightening up," she comes upon it in its pasteboard box tucked away at the bottom of an old chest in her bedroom. At such times she is likely to take it out and look at it with a curiously detached air, as though it were the picture of a stranger. It is in this wise, too, that her dim old eyes regard the world—impersonally. It is as though, at seventy-four, she no longer is swayed by emotions, memories, people, events. Remote, inaccessible, immune, she sees, weighs, and judges with the detached directness of a grim old idol.

Fifty-five years had yellowed the photograph of the wasp-waisted girl in the billowing riding skirt when her grand-niece, Charley Kemp, appeared before her in twentieth-century riding clothes: sleeveless jacket ending a little below the hips; breeches baggy in the seat but gripping the knees. Great-Aunt Charlotte had said, "So that's what it's come to." You could almost hear her agile old mind clicking back to that other young thing of the plume, and the rose and the little booted foot peeping so demurely from beneath the folds of the sweeping skirt.

"Don't you like it?" Charley had looked down at her slim self and had flicked her glittering tan boots with her riding whip because that seemed the thing to do. Charley went to matinees.

Great-Aunt Charlotte had pursed her crumpled old lips, whether in amusement or disapproval—those withered lips whose muscles had long ago lost their elasticity. "Well, it's kind of comical, really. And ugly. But you don't look ugly in it, Charley, or comical either. You look like a right pretty young boy."

Her eyes had a tenderly amused glint. Those eyes saw less now than they used to: an encroaching cataract. But they had a bright and piercing appearance owing to the heavy brows, which, by some prank of nature, had defied the aging process that had laid its blight upon hair, cheek, lips, skin, and frame. The brows had remained jetty black; twin cornices of defiance in the ivory ruin of her face. They gave her a misleadingly sinister and cynical look. Piratical, almost.

Perhaps those eyebrows indicated in Charlotte Thrift something of the iron that had sustained her father, Isaac Thrift, the young easterner, throughout his first years of Middle-Western hardship. Chicago today is full of resentful grandsons and granddaughters who will tell you that if their grandsire had bought the southwest corner of State and Madison Streets for $2,050 in cash, as he could have, they would be worth their millions today. And they are right. Still, if all those who tell you this were granted their wish, Chicago now would be populated almost wholly by millionaire real estate holders; and the southwest corner of State and Madison would have had to be as the loaves and the fishes.

Isaac Thrift had been one of these inconsiderate forebears. He had bought real estate, it is true, but in the mistaken belief that the city's growth and future lay along the south shore instead of the north. Chicago's South Side in that day was a prairie waste where wolves howled on winter nights and where, in the summer, flowers grew so riotously as to make a trackless sea of bloom. Isaac Thrift had thought himself very canny and farsighted to vision that which his contemporaries could not see. They had bought North Side property. They had built their houses there. Isaac Thrift built his on Wabash, near Madison, and announced daringly that some day he would have a real country place, far south, near Eighteenth Street. For that matter, he said, the time would come when they would hear of houses thick in a street that would be known as Thirtieth, or even Fortieth. How they laughed at that! Besides, it was pretty well acknowledged by the wiseacres that St. Charles, a far older town, would soon surpass Chicago and become the metropolis of the West.

In books on early Chicago and its settlers, you can see Isaac Thrift pictured as one of the stem and flinty city fathers, all boots and stock and massive watch chain and side-whiskers. It was neither a time nor a place for weaklings. The young man who had come hopefully out of York state to find his fortune in the welter of mud, swamp, Indians, frame shanties, and two-wheeled carts that constituted Chicago had needed all his indomitability.

It is characteristic of him that until his marriage, he lived at the New Temperance Hotel (board and lodging $2.00 a week; clothes washed extra) instead of at the popular Saugenash Hotel on Market and Lake, where the innkeeper, that gay and genial Frenchman and pioneer, Mark Beaubien, would sometimes take down his fiddle and set feet to twinkling and stepping in the square dance. None of this for Isaac Thrift. He literally had rolled up his sleeves and got to work. Little enough use he made of the fine bottle-green broadcloth coat with the gilt buttons, the high stock, and the pale gray pantaloons brought from the East. But in two years, he had opened a sort of general store and real estate office on Lake Street, had bought a piece of ground for a house on Wabash (which piece he later foolishly sold) and had sent back East for his bride. That lady left her comfortable rooftree to make the long and arduous trip that duplicated the one made earlier by her husband-to-be. It is to her credit that she braved it; but she had a hard time trying to adjust her New England viewpoint to the crude, rough setting in which she now found herself. Her letters back East are so typical and revealing that extracts, at least, are imperative.

> The times are exceedingly dull in this city of Chicago; there is little business, no balls, no parties, some shooting, some riding, and plenty of loafers, and today, after the rain, a plenty of mud which completes the picture . . . The water here is first-rate bad and the only way we get along is by drinking a great deal of tea and coffee—two coffees to one tea . . . The weather has been very mild. There has not been snow enough to stop the burning of the prairies . . . If the waters of Lake Michigan continue to rise for a year or two more, Chicago and all the surrounding country will be covered with one vast sheet of water, and the inhabitants of this place must find a home elsewhere—and I, for one, will find said home farther East . . . Everyone admires my pretty things from New York; my cherry-colored scarf; my gingham dress with the silk stripe in it, my Thibet cloth cloak of dark mulberry color; and my fine velvet bonnet which cost only $3.50 in New York. It is prettier than any I have seen here. A milliner here said that it would have cost $8.00 in Chicago but I think that is exaggerated. The ladies here wear only one flounce to their skirts. Even my third best—the brown-and-white plaid merino—has three . . . The mud here is so bad that the men wear hip boots and we women must go about in two-wheeled carts that sink to the hubs in many places. There

are signs stuck up in the mud with the warning, "No bottom here" . . . Our new furniture has come. A beautiful flowered red and green carpet in the chamber and parlor. When the folding doors are open the stove will heat both rooms . . . They have most excellent markets in this place. We can get meat of every description for four cents a pound, such as sausages, venison, beef, pork—everything except fowls. Of fruit there is little. I saw some grapes yesterday in the market, all powdered over with sawdust. They had come from Spain. They made my mouth water . . . Every day great prairie schooners, as they call them, go by the house. They have come all the way from the East . . . I am terrified of the Indians though I have said little to Isaac. They are very dirty and not at all noble as our history and geography books state . . .

She bore Isaac Thrift two children, accomplishing the feat as circumspectly and with as much reticence as is possible in the achievement of so physical a rite. Girls, both. I think she would have considered a man-child indelicate.

Charlotte had been the first of these girls. Carrie, the second, came a tardy ten years later. It was a time and a city of strange contradictions and fluctuations. Fortunes were made in the boom of 1835 and lost in the panic of '37. Chicago was a broken-down speculative shanty village one day and an embryo metropolis the next. The Firemen's Ball was the event of the social season, with Engine No. 3, glittering gift of "Long John" Wentworth, set in the upper end of the dance hall and festooned with flowers and ribbons. All the worthwhile beaux of the town belonged to the volunteer fire brigade. The names of Chicago's firemen of 1838 or '40, if read aloud today, would sound like the annual list of boxholders at the opera. The streets of the town were frequently impassable; servants almost unknown; quiltings and church sociables noteworthy events. The open prairie, just beyond town, teemed with partridges, quail, prairie chicken. Fort Dearborn, deserted, was a playground for little children. Indians, dirty, blanketed, saturnine, slouched along the streets. "Long John" Wentworth was kinging it in Congress. Young ladies went to balls primly gowned in dark-colored merinos, long-sleeved, high-necked. Little girls went to school in bodices low-cut and nearly sleeveless; toe-slippers; and manifold skirts starched to stand out like a ballerina's.

These stiffly starched skirts, layer on layer, first brought romance into Charlotte Thrift's life. She was thirteen, a rather stocky little girl, not too obedient of the prim maternal voice that was forever bidding her point her toes out, hold her shoulders back, and not talk at table. She must surely have talked at table this morning, or perhaps slouched her shoulders and perversely toed in once safely out of sight of the house, because she was late for school. The horrid realization of this came as Charlotte reached the Rush Street ferry—a crude ramshackle affair drawn from one side of the river to the other with ropes pulled by hand. Charlotte attended Miss Rapp's school on the North Side though the Thrifts lived south. This makeshift craft was about to leave the south shore as Charlotte, her tardiness heavy upon her, sighted the river. With a little cry and a rush, she sped down the path, leaped, slipped, and landed just short of the ferry in the slimy waters of the Chicago River. Landed exactly expresses it. Though, on second thought, perhaps settled is better. Layer on layer of stiffly starched skirts sustained her. She had fallen feet downward. There she rested on the water, her skirts spread petallike about her, her toes, in their cross-strapped slippers, no doubt pointing demurely downward. She looked like some weird white river lily afloat on its pad in the turbid stream. Her eyes were round with fright beneath the strongly marked black brows. Then, suddenly and quite naturally, she screamed, kicked wildly, and began to sink. Sank, in fact. It had all happened with incredible swiftness. The ferry men had scarcely had time to open their mouths vacuously. Charlotte's calliope screams, so ominously muffled now, wakened them into action. But before their clumsy wits and hands had seized on ropes, a slim black-and-white line cleft the water, disappeared, and reappeared with the choking, struggling, frantic Charlotte, very unstarched now and utterly unmindful of toes, shoulders, and vocal restraint.

The black-and-white line had been young Jesse Dick, of the "Hardscrabble" Dicks; the black had been his trousers, the white his shirt. He swam like a river rat—which he more or less was. Of all the Chicago male inhabitants to which Mrs. Thrift would most have objected as the rescuer of her small daughter, this lounging, good-for-nothing young Jesse Dick would have been most prominently ineligible. Fortunately (or unfortunately) she did not even know his name until five years later. Charlotte herself did not know it. She had had one frantic glimpse of a wet, set face above hers, but it had been only a flash in a kaleidoscopic whole. Young Dick, having towed her ashore, had plumped her down, retrieved his coat, and lounged off unmissed and unrecognized in the ensuing hubbub. The rescue accomplished, his seventeen-year-old emotions found no romantic stirrings in the thought of this limp and dripping bundle of corded muslin, bedraggled pantalettes, and streaming, stringy hair.

Charlotte, put promptly to bed of course, with a pan at her feet and flannel on her chest and hot broth administered at intervals—though she was no whit the worse for her ducking—lay very flat and still under the gay calico comfortable, her hair in two damp braids, her eyes wide and thoughtful.

"But who was he?" insisted Mrs. Thrift, from the foot of the bed.

And "I don't know," replied Charlotte for the dozenth time.

"What did he look like?" demanded Isaac Thrift (hastily summoned from his place of business so near the scene of the mishap).

"I—don't know," replied Charlotte. And that, bafflingly enough, was the truth. Only sometimes in her dreams she saw his face again, white, set, and yet with something almost merry about it. From these dreams, Charlotte would wake shivering deliciously. But she never told them. During the next five years, she never went to a dance, a sleigh ride, walked or rode, that she did not unconsciously scan the room or the street for his face.

Five years later, Charlotte was shopping on Lake Street in her second-best merino, voluminously hooped. Fortunately (she thought later, devoutly) she had put on her best bonnet of sage green velvet with the frill of blond lace inside the face. A frill of blond lace is most flattering when set inside the bonnet. She had come out of her father's store and was bound for the shop of Mr. Potter Palmer where, the week before, she had flirted with a plum-colored pelisse and had known no happiness since then. She must feel it resting on her own sloping shoulders. Of course it was—but then, Mr. Palmer, when he waited on you himself, often came down in his price.

Chicago sidewalks were crazy wooden affairs raised high on rickety stilts, uneven, full of cracks for the unwary, now five steps up, now six steps down, with great nails raising their ugly heads to bite at unsuspecting draperies. Below this structure lay a morass of mud, and woe to him who stepped into it.

Along this precarious eminence, Charlotte moved with the gait that fashion demanded; a mingling of mince, swoop, and glide. Her mind was on the plum pelisse. A malicious nail, seeing this, bit at her dipping and voluminous skirt with a snick and a snarl. R-r-rip! it went. Charlotte stepped back with a little cry of dismay—stepped back just too far, lost her footing, and tumbled over the edge of the high boardwalk into the muck and slime below.

For the second time in five years, Jesse Dick's lounging habit served a good purpose. There he was on Lake Street, idly viewing the world when he should have been helping to build it as were the other young men of that hardworking city. He heard her little cry of surprise and fright; saw her topple, a hoopskirted heap, into the mire. Those same ridiculous hoops, wire traps that they were, rendered her as helpless as a beetle on its back. Jesse Dick's long legs sprang to her rescue, though he could not suppress a smile at her plight. This before he caught a glimpse of the face set off by the frill of blond lace. He picked her up, set her on her feet—little feet in cloth-gaitered side boots and muddied white stockings—and began gently to wipe her sadly soiled second-best merino with his handkerchief, with his shabby coat sleeve, with his coattail and, later, with his heart.

"Oh, don't—please—you mustn't—please—oh—" Charlotte kept murmuring, the color high in her cheeks. She was poised at that dangerous pinnacle between tears and laughter; between vexation and mirth. "Oh, please—"

Her vaguely protesting hand, in its flutterings, brushed his blond curly head. He was on his knees, tidying her skirts with great deftness and thoroughness. There was about the act an intimacy and a boyish delicacy, too, that had perhaps startled her into her maidenly protest. He had looked up at her then, as she bent down.

"Why, you're the boy!" gasped Charlotte.

"What boy?" No wonder he failed to recognize her as she did him. Her mouth, at the time of the rescue five years before, had been wide open to emit burbles and strangled coughs; her features had been distorted with fright.

"The boy who pulled me out of the river. Long ago. I was going to school. Rush Street. You jumped in. I never knew. But you're the boy. I mean—of course you're grown now. But you are, aren't you? The boy, I mean. The—"

She became silent, looking down at him, her face like a rose in the blond lace frill. He was still on his knees in the mud, brushing at her skirts with a gesture that now was merely mechanical; brushing, as we know, with his heart in his hand.

So, out of the slime of the river and the grime of Lake Street had flowered their romance.

Chapter II

A short-lived and tragic enough romance. It wasn't that the Dicks were rowdy or of evil repute. They were nobodies. In a day when social lines were so elastic as to be nearly all-inclusive, the Dicks were miles outside the pale. In the first place, they lived out "Hardscrabble" way. That definitely placed them. The name designated a mean, tumble-down district southwest of town, inhabited by poor whites. A welter of mud, curs, barefoot babies, slatternly women, shirtsleeved men lounging slackly against open doorways, acrid pipe in mouth.

Young Jesse Dick, sprung from this soil, still was alien to it; a dreamer; a fawn among wallowing swine; an idler with nothing of the villain about him and the more dangerous because of that. Isaac Thrift and his prim wife certainly would sooner have seen their daughter Charlotte dead than involved with one of the Dick clan. But they were unaware of the very existence of the riffraff Dicks. The Thrifts lived in two-story-and-basement elegance on Wabash near Madison and kept their own cow.

There was a fine natural forest between Clark and Pine Streets, north, on the lake shore. Along its grassy paths lay fallen and decayed trees. Here the two used to meet, for it came to that. Charlotte had an Indian pony which she rode daily. Sometimes they met on the prairie to the south of town. The picture of Charlotte in the sweeping skirt, the stiff little hat, the caressing plume, and the rose must have been taken at about this time. There was in her face a glow, a bloom, a radiance such as comes to a woman—with too heavy eyebrows—who is beloved for the first time.

It was, as it turned out, for the last time as well. Charlotte had the courage for clandestine meetings in spite of a girlhood hedged about with prim pickets of propriety: but when she thought of open revolt, of appearing with Jesse Dick before the priggish mother and the flinty father, she shrank and cowered and was afraid. To them she was little more than a fresh young vegetable without emotions, thoughts, or knowledge of a kind which they would have considered unmaidenly.

Charlotte was sitting in the dining room window nook one day, sewing. It was a pleasant room in which to sit and sew. One could see passersby on Madison Street as well as Wabash, and even, by screwing around a little, get glimpses of State Street with its great trees and its frame cottages. Mrs. Thrift, at the dining room table, was casting up her weekly accounts. She closed the little leather-bound book now and sat back with a sigh. There was a worried frown between her eyes. Mrs. Thrift always wore a worried frown between her eyes. She took wife-and-motherhood hard. She would have thought herself unwifely and unmotherly to take them otherwise. She wore her frown about the house as she did her cap—badge of housewifeliness.

"I declare," she said now, "with beef six cents the pound—and not a very choice cut, either—a body dreads the weekly accounts."

"M-m-m," murmured Charlotte remotely, from the miles and miles that separated them.

Mrs. Thrift regarded her for a moment, tapping her cheek thoughtfully with the quill in her hand. Her frown deepened. Charlotte was wearing a black sateen apron, very full. Her hair, drawn straight back from her face, was gathered at the back into a chenille net. A Garibaldi blouse completed the hideousness of her costume. There quivered about her an aura—a glow—a roseate something—that triumphed over apron, net, and blouse. Mrs. Thrift sensed this without understanding it. Her puzzlement took the form of nagging.

"It seems to me, Charlotte, that you might better be employed with your plain sewing than with fancywork such as that."

Charlotte's black sateen lap was gay with scraps of silk; cherry satin, purple velvet, green taffeta, scarlet, blue. She was making a patchwork silk quilt of an intricate pattern (of which work of art more later). "Yes, indeed," said she now, unfortunately. And hummed a little tune.

Mrs. Thrift stood up with a great rustling of account-book leaves, and of skirts; with all the stir of outraged dignity. "Well, miss, I'll thank you to pay the compliment of listening when I talk to you. You sit there smiling at nothing, like a simpleton, I do declare!"

"I was listening, Mother."

"What did I last say?"

"Why—beef—six—"

"Humph! What with patchwork quilts and nonsense like that, and out on your pony every day, fine or not, I sometimes wonder, miss, what you think yourself. Beef indeed!"

She gathered up her books and papers. It was on her tongue's tip to forbid the afternoon's ride. Something occult in Charlotte sensed this. She leaned forward. "Oh, Mother, Mrs. Perry's passing on Madison and looking at the house. I do believe she's coming in. Wait. Yes, she's turning in. I think I'll just—"

"Stay where you are," commanded Mrs. Thrift. Charlotte subsided. She bent over her work again, half hidden by the curtains that hung stiffly before the entrance to the window nook. You could hear Mrs. Perry's high sharp voice in speech with Cassie, the servant. "If she's in the dining room, I'll go right in. Don't bother about the parlor." She came sweeping down the hall. It was evident that news was on her tongue's tip. Her bonnet was slightly askew. Her hoops swayed like a hill in a quake. Mrs. Thrift advanced to meet her. They shook hands at arm's length across the billows of their outstanding skirts.

"Such news, Mrs. Thrift! What do you think! After all these years Mrs. Holcomb's going to have a ba—"

"My *dear!*" interrupted Mrs. Thrift, hastily; and raised a significant eyebrow in the direction of the slim figure bent over her sewing in the window nook.

Mrs. Perry coughed apologetically. "Oh! I didn't see—"

"Charlotte dear, leave the room."

Charlotte gathered up the bits of silk in her apron. Anxious as she was to be gone, there was still something in the manner of her dismissal that offended her new sense of her own importance. She swooped and stooped for bits of silk and satin, thrusting them into her apron and workbag. Though she seemed to be making haste, her progress was maddeningly slow. The two ladies, eying her with ill-concealed impatience, made polite and innocuous conversation meanwhile.

"And have you heard that the Empress Eugénie has decided to put aside her crinoline?"

Mrs. Thrift made a sound that amounted to a sniff. "So the newspapers said last year. You remember she appeared at a court ball without a crinoline? Yes. Well, fancy how ridiculous she must have looked! She put them on again fast enough, I imagine, after that."

"Ah, but they do say she didn't. I have a letter from New York written by my friend Mrs. Hollister who comes straight from Paris, and she says that the new skirts are quite flat about the—below the waist, to the knees—"

Charlotte fled the room dutifully now, with a little curtsey for Mrs. Perry. In the dark passageway, she stamped an unfilial foot. Then, it is to be regretted, she screwed her features into one of those unadult contortions known as making a face. Turning, she saw regarding her from the second-story balustrade her eight-year-old sister Carrie. Carrie, ten years her sister's junior, never had been late to school; never had fallen into the Chicago River, nor off a high wooden sidewalk; always turned her toes out; held her shoulders like a Hessian.

"*I* saw you!" cried this true daughter of her mother.

Charlotte, mounting the stairs to her own room, swept past this paragon with such a disdainful swishing of skirts, apron, and squares of bright-colored silk stuff as to create quite a breeze. She even dropped one of the gay silken bits, saw it flutter to the ground at her tormentor's feet, and did not deign to pick it up. Carrie swooped for it. "You dropped a piece." She looked at it. "It's the orange-colored silk one!" (Destined to be the quilt's high note of color.) "Finding's keeping." She tucked it into her apron pocket. Charlotte entered her own room. "*I* saw you, miss." Charlotte slammed her chamber door and locked it.

She was not as magnificently aloof and unconcerned as she seemed. She knew the threat in the impish Carrie's "*I* saw you." In the Thrift household, a daughter who had stamped a foot and screwed up a face in contempt of maternal authority did not go unpunished. Once informed, an explanation would be demanded. How could Charlotte explain that one who has been told almost daily for three weeks that she is the most enchanting, witty, beauteous, and intelligent woman in the world naturally resents being ignominiously dismissed from a room, like a chit.

That night at supper, she tried unsuccessfully to appear indifferent and at ease under Carrie's round unblinking stare of malice. Carrie began:

"Mama, what did Mrs. Perry have to tell you when she came calling this afternoon?"

"Nothing that would interest you, my pet. You haven't touched your potato."

"Would it interest Charlotte?"

"No."

"Is that why you sent her out of the room?"

"Yes. Now eat your p—"

"Charlotte didn't like being sent out of the room, did she? H'm, Mama?"

"Isaac, will you speak to that child. I don't know what—"

Charlotte's face was scarlet. She knew. Her father would speak sternly to the too-inquisitive Carrie. That crafty one would thrust out a moist and quivering nether lip and, with tears dropping into her uneaten potato, snivel, "But I only wanted to know because Charlotte—" and out would come the tale of Charlotte's foot-stamping and facemaking.

But Isaac Thrift never framed the first chiding sentence; and Carrie got no further than the thrusting out of the lip. For the second time that day, news appeared in the form of a neighbor. A man this time, one Abner Rathburn. His news was no mere old wives' gossip of births and babies. He told it, white-faced. Fort Sumter had been fired on. War!

Chicago's interest in the soldiery, up to now, had been confined to that ornamental and gayly caparisoned group known as Colonel Ellsworth's Zouaves. In their brilliant uniforms, these gave exhibition drills, flashing through marvelous evolutions learned during evenings of practice in a vacant hall above a little brick store near Rush Street bridge. They had gone on grand tours through the East as well. The illustrated papers had had their pictures. Now their absurd baggy trousers and their pert little jackets and their brilliant-hued sashes took on a new, grim meaning. Off they trotted, double-quick, to Donelson and death, most of them. Off went the boys of that socially elect group belonging to the Fire Engine Company. Off went brothers, sons, fathers. Off went Jesse Dick from out Hardscrabble way, and fought his brief fight, too, at Donelson, with weapons so unfit and ineffectual as to be little better than toys; and lost. But just before he left, Charlotte, frantic with fear, apprehension, and thwarted love publicly did that which branded her forever in the eyes of her straitlaced little world. Or perhaps her little world would have understood and forgiven her had her parents shown any trace of understanding or forgiveness.

In all their meetings, these two young things—the prim girl with the dash of daring in her and the boy who wrote verses to her and read them with telling effect, quite as though they had not sprung from the mire of Hardscrabble—had never once kissed or even shyly embraced. Their hands had met and clung. Touching subterfuges. "That's a funny ring you wear. Let's see it. My, how little! It won't go on any of my—no, sir! Not even this one." Their eyes had spoken. His fingers sometimes softly touched the plume that drooped from her stiff little hat. When he helped her mount the Indian pony, perhaps he pressed closer in farewell than that fiery little steed's hoof quite warranted. But that was all. He was over-conscious of his social inferiority. Years of narrow nagging bound her with bands of steel riveted with turn-your-toes-out, hold-your-shoulders-back, you-mustn't-play-with-them, ladylike, ladylike.

A week after Sumter, "I've enlisted," he told her.

"Of course," Charlotte had replied, dazedly. Then, in sudden realization, "When? When?"

He knew what she meant. "Right away I reckon. They said—right away." She looked at him mutely. "Charlotte, I wish you'd—I wish your father and mother—I'd like to speak to them—I mean about us—me." There was little of Hardscrabble about him as he said it.

"Oh, I couldn't. I'm afraid! I'm afraid!"

He was silent for a long time, poking about with a dried stick in the leaves and loam and grass at their feet as they sat on a fallen tree trunk, just as for years and years despairing lovers have poked in absentminded frenzy; digging a fork's prong into the white defenseless surface of a tablecloth; prodding the sand with a cane; rooting into the ground with an umbrella ferrule; making meaningless marks on gravel paths.

At last: "I don't suppose it makes any real difference; but the Dicks came from Holland. I mean a long time ago. With Hendrik Hudson. And my great-great-grandmother was a Pomroy. You wouldn't believe, would you, that a shiftless lot like us could come from stock like that? I guess it's run thin. Of course my mother—" he stopped. She put a timid hand on his arm then, and he made as though to cover it with his own but did not. He went on picking at the ground with his bit of stick. "Sometimes my father—if he's been drinking too much—imagines he's one of his own ancestors. Sometimes it's a Dutch ancestor and sometimes it's an English one, but he's always very magnificent about it, and when he's like that even my mother can't—can't scream him down. You should hear then what he thinks of all you people who live in fine brick houses on Wabash and on Michigan, and over on the North Side. My brother Pom says—"

"Pom?"

"Pomroy. Pomroy Dick, you see. Both the . . . I've been thinking that perhaps if your father and mother knew about—I mean we're not—that is my father—"

She shook her head gently. "It isn't that. You see, it's businessmen—. Those who have stores or real estate and are successful. Or young lawyers. That's the kind Father and Mother—"

They were not finishing their sentences. Groping for words. Fearful of hurting each other.

He laughed. "I guess there won't be much choice among the lot of us when this is over."

"Why, Jesse, it'll only last a few months—two or three. Father says it'll only last a few months."

"It doesn't take that long to—"

"To what?"

"Nothing."

He was whisked away after that. Charlotte saw him but once again. That once was her undoing. She did not even know the time set for his going. He had tried to get word to her and had failed somehow. With her father and mother, Charlotte was one of the crowd gathered about the courthouse steps to hear Jules Lombard sing the "Battle Cry of Freedom." George Root, of Chicago, George, whom they all knew, had written it. The ink was scarcely dry on the manuscript. The crowds gathered in the street before the courthouse. Soon they were all singing it. Suddenly, through the singing, like a dull throb, throb, came the sound of thudding feet. Soldiers. With a great surge, the crowd turned its face toward the street. Still singing. Here they came. In marching order. Their uniforms belied the name. Had they been less comic they would have been less tragic. They were equipped with muskets altered from flintlocks; with Harper's Ferry and Deneger rifles; with horse pistols and musketoons—deadly sounding but ridiculous. With these they faced Donelson. They were hardly more than boys. After them trailed women, running alongside, dropping back breathless. Old women, mothers. Young women, sweethearts, wives. This was no time for the proprieties, for reticence.

They were passing. The first of them had passed. Then Charlotte saw him. His face flashed out at her from among the lines. His face, under the absurd pancake hat, was white, set. And oh, how young! He was at the end of his line. Charlotte watched him coming. She felt a queer tingling in her fingertips, in the skin around her eyes, in her throat. Then a great surge of fear, horror, fright, and love shook her. He was passing. Someone, herself and yet not herself, was battling a way through the crowd, was pushing, thrusting with elbows, shoulders. She gained the roadway. She ran, stumblingly. She grasped his arm. "You didn't let me know! You didn't let me know!" Someone took hold of her elbow—someone in the crowd on the sidewalk—but she shook them off. She ran on at his side. Came the double-quick command. With a little cry, she threw her arms about him and kissed him. Her lips were parted like a child's. Her face was distorted with weeping. There was something terrible about her not caring; not covering it. "You didn't let me know! You didn't let me know!" The ranks broke into double-quick. She ran with them a short minute, breathlessly, sobbing.

Chapter III

It was a submissive enough little figure that they had hustled home through the crowded streets, up the front stoop and into the brick house on Wabash Avenue. Crushed and rumpled.

The crudest edge of the things they said to her was mercifully dulled by the time it penetrated her numbed consciousness. She hardly seemed to hear them. At intervals she sobbed. It was more than a sob. It was a dry paroxysm that shook her whole body and jarred her head. Her handkerchief, a wet gray ball, she opened, and began to stare at its neatly hemstitched border, turning it corner for corner, round and round.

Who was he? Who was he?

She told them.

At each fresh accusation, she seemed to shrink into smaller compass; to occupy less space within the circle of her outstanding hoopskirts, until finally she was just a pair of hunted eyes in a tangle of ringlets, handkerchief, and crinoline. She caught fragments of what they were saying . . . ruined her life . . . brought down disgrace . . . entire family . . . never hold head up . . . common lout like a Dick . . . Dick! . . . Dick! . . .

Once, Charlotte raised her head and launched a feeble something that sounded like ". . . Hendrik Hudson," but it was lost in the torrent of talk. It appeared that she had not only ruined herself and brought lifelong disgrace upon her parents' hitherto unsullied name, but she had made improbable any future matrimonial prospects for her sister Carrie—then aged eight.

That, unfortunately, struck Charlotte as being humorous. Racked though she was, one remote corner of her mind's eye pictured the waspish little Carrie, in pinafore and strapped slippers, languishing for love, all forlorn—Carrie, who still stuck her tongue out by way of repartee. Charlotte giggled suddenly, quite without meaning to. Hysteria, probably. At this fresh exhibition of shamelessness, her parents were aghast.

"Well! And you can laugh!" shouted Isaac Thrift through the soft and unheeded susurrus of his wife's sh-sh-sh! "As if I hadn't enough trouble, with this war"—it sounded like a private personal grievance—"and business what it is, and real estate practically worth—"

"Sh-sh-sh! Carrie will hear you. The child mustn't know of this."

"Know! Everyone in town knows by now. My daughter running after a common soldier in the streets—a beggar—worse than a beggar— and kissing him like a—like a—"

Mrs. Thrift interrupted with mournful hastiness. "We must send her away. East. For a little visit. That would be best, for a few months."

At that Isaac Thrift laughed a rather terrible laugh. "Away! That *would* give them a fine chance to talk. Away indeed, madam! A few months, h'm? Ha!"

Mrs. Thrift threw out her palms as though warding off a blow. "Isaac! You don't mean they'd think—Isaac!"

Charlotte regarded them both with wide, uncomprehending eyes.

Her mother looked at her. Charlotte raised her own tear-drenched face that was so mutely miserable, so stricken, so dumbly questioning. Marred as it was, and grief-ravaged, Mrs. Thrift seemed still to find there something that relieved her. She said more gently, perhaps, than in any previous questioning:

"Why did you do it, Charlotte?"

"I couldn't help it. I couldn't help it."

Isaac Thrift snorted impatiently. Hetty Thrift compressed her lips a little and sighed. "Yes, but why did you do it, Charlotte? Why? You have been brought up so carefully. How could you do it?"

Now, the answer that lay ready in Charlotte's mind was one that could have explained everything. And yet it would have explained nothing; at least nothing to Hetty and Isaac Thrift. The natural reply on Charlotte's tongue was simply, "Because I love him." But the Thrifts did not speak of love. It was not a ladylike word. There were certain words which delicacy forbade. "Love" was one of them. From the manner in which they shunned it—shrank from the very mention of it—you might almost have thought it an obscenity.

Mrs. Thrift put a final question. She had to. "Had you ever kissed him before?"

"Oh, no!" cried Charlotte so earnestly that they could not but believe. Then, quiveringly, as one bereaved, cheated. "Oh, no! No! Never! Not once . . . Not once."

The glance that Mrs. Thrift shot at her husband then was a mingling of triumph and relief.

Isaac Thrift and his wife did not mean to be hard and cruel. They had sprung from stern stock. Theirs was the narrow middle-class outlook of members of a small respectable community. According to the standards of that community, Charlotte Thrift had done an outrageous thing. War, in that day, was a grimmer, though less bloody and wholesale, business than it is today. An army whose marching song is "Where Do We Go From Here?" attaches small significance to the passing kiss of a hysterical flapper, whether the object of the kiss be buck private or general. But an army that finds vocal expression in the "Battle Cry of Freedom" and "John Brown's Body" is likely to take its bussing seriously. The publicly kissed soldier on his way to battle was the publicly proclaimed property of the kissee. And there in front of the courthouse steps, in full sight of her world—the Addison Canes, the Thomas Holcombs, the Lewis Fullers, the Clapps—Charlotte Thrift, daughter of Isaac Thrift, had run after, had thrown her arms about, and had kissed a young man so obscure, so undesirable, so altogether an unfitting object for a gently bred maiden's kisses (public or private) as to render valueless her kisses in future.

Of Charlotte's impulsive act, her father and mother made something repulsive and sinister. She was made to go everywhere but was duennaed like a naughty Spanish princess. Her every act was remarked. Did she pine, she was berated and told to rouse herself; did she laugh, she was frowned down. Her neat little escritoire frequently betrayed traces of an overhauling by suspicious alien fingers. There was little need of that after the first few days. The news of Jesse Dick's death at Donelson went almost unnoticed but for two Chicago households—one out Hardscrabble way, one on Wabash Avenue. It was otherwise as unimportant as an uprooted tree in the path of an avalanche that destroys a village. At Donelson had fallen many sons of Chicago's pioneer families; young men who were to have carried on the future business of the city; boys who had squired its daughters to sleigh rides, to dances, to church sociables and horseback parties; who had drilled with Ellsworth's famous Zouaves. A Dick of Hardscrabble could pass unnoticed in this company.

There came to Charlotte a desperate and quite natural desire to go to his people; to see his mother; to talk with his father. But she never did. Instinctively, her mother sensed this (perhaps, after all, she had been eighteen herself, once) and by her increased watchfulness made Hardscrabble as remote and unattainable as heaven.

"Where are you going, Charlotte?"

"Just out for a breath of air, Mother."

"Take Carrie with you."

"Oh, Mother, I don't want—"

"Take Carrie with you."

She stopped at home.

She had no tangible thing over which to mourn; not one of those bits of paper or pasteboard or linen or metal over which to keen; nothing to hold in her two hands or press to her lips or wear in her bosom. She did not even possess one of those absurd tintypes of the day showing her soldier in wrinkled uniform and wooden attitude against a mixed background of chenille drapery and Versailles garden. She had only her wound and her memory, and perhaps these would have healed and grown dim had not Isaac Thrift and his wife so persistently rubbed salt in the one and prodded the other. After all, she was little more than eighteen, and eighteen does not break so readily. If they had made light of it, perhaps she would soon have lifted her head again and even cast about for consolation.

"Moping again!"

"I'm not moping, Father."

"What would you call it then?"

"Why, I'm just sitting by the window in the dusk. I often do. Even before—before—"

"There's enough and to spare for idle hands to do, I dare say. Haven't you seen today's paper nor heard of what's happened again at Manassas that you can sit there like that!"

She knew better than to explain that for her, Jessie Dick died again with the news of each fresh battle.

She became curiously silent for so young a girl. During those four years, she did her share with the rest of them; scraped lint, tore and rolled bandages, made hospital garments, tied comforters, knitted stockings and mittens, put up fruit and jellies and pickles for the soldiers. Chicago was a construction camp. Regiments came marching in from all the states north. Camp Douglas, south of Thirty-First Street, was at first thick with tents, afterward with wooden barracks. Charlotte even helped in the great Sanitary Fairs that lasted a week or more. You would have noticed no difference between this girl and the dozens of others who chirped about the flag-decked booths. But there was a difference. That which had gone from her was an impalpable something difficult to name. Only if you could have looked from her face to that of the girl of the old photograph—that girl in the sweeping habit, with the plume, and the rose held carelessly in one hand—you might have known. The glow, the bloom, the radiance—gone.

People forget, gradually. After all, there was so little to remember. Four years of war change many things, including perspective. Occasionally, someone said, "Wasn't there something about that older Thrift girl? Charlotte, isn't it? Yes. Wasn't she mixed up with a queer person or something?"

"Charlotte Thrift! Why, no! There hasn't been a more self-sacrificing worker in the whole—wait a minute. Now that you speak of it, I do believe there was—let's see—in love with a boy her folks didn't approve and made some kind of public scene, but just what it was—"

But Isaac and Hetty Thrift did not forget. Nor Charlotte. Sometimes, in their treatment of her, you would have thought her still the eighteen-year-old innocent of the photograph. When Black Crook came to the new Crosby Opera House in 1870, scandalizing the community and providing endless food for feminine (and masculine) gossip, Charlotte still was sent from the room to spare her maidenly blushes, just as though the past ten years had never been.

"I hear they wear tights, mind you, without skirts!"

"Not all the way!"

"Not an inch of skirt. Just—ah—trunks I believe they call them. A horrid word in itself."

"Well, really, I don't know what the world's coming to. Shouldn't you think that after the suffering and privation of this dreadful war we would all turn to higher things?"

But Mrs. Thrift's caller shook her head so emphatically that her long gold filigree earrings pranced. "Ah, but they do say a wave of immorality always follows a war. The reaction it's called. That is the word dear Dr. Swift used in his sermon last Sunday."

"Reactions are all very well and good," retorted Mrs. Thrift, tartly, "but they don't excuse tights, I hope."

Her visitor's face lighted up eagerly and unbeautifully. She leaned still closer. "I hear that this Eliza Weathersby, as she's called, plays the part of Stalacta in a pale blue bodice all glittering with silver passamenterie; pale blue satin trunks, mind you! And pale blue tights with a double row of tiny buttons all down the side of the l—"

Again, as ten years before, Mrs. Thrift raised signaling eyebrows. She emitted an artificial and absurd, "Ahem!" Then—"Charlotte, run upstairs and help poor Carrie with her English exercise."

"She's doing sums, Mother. I saw her at them not ten minutes ago."

"Then tell her to put her sums aside. Do you know, dear Mrs. Strapp, Carrie is quite amazing at sums, but I tell her she is not sent to Miss Tait's finishing school under heavy expense to learn to do sums. But she actually likes them. Does them by way of amusement. Can add a double column in her head, just like her father. But her English exercise is always a sorry affair . . . M-m-m-m . . . There, now, you were saying tiny buttons down the side of the leg—" Charlotte had gone.

When the war ended, Charlotte was twenty-two. An unwed woman of twenty-two was palpably over-fastidious or undesirable. Twenty-five was the sere and withered leaf. And soon Charlotte was twenty-five—twenty-eight—thirty. Done for.

The patchwork silk quilt, laid aside unfinished in '61, was taken up again in '65. It became quite famous; a renowned work of art. Visitors who came to the house asked after it. "And how is the quilt getting on, dear Charlotte?" as a novelist is sounded about an opus with which he is struggling, or a painter his canvas. Mrs. Hannan, the Lake Street milliner, saved all her pieces for Charlotte. Often there was a peck of them at a time. The quilt was patterned in blocks. Charlotte, very serious, would explain to the caller the plan of the block upon which she was at the moment engaged.

"This one has a purple satin center, you see. I always think purple is so rich, don't you? Then the next row will be white uncut velvet. Doesn't it have a sumptuous sound! Next blue velvet and the last row orange-colored silk." (No; not the same piece. Carrie had never relinquished her booty.) "Now, this next block is to be quite gay. It is almost my favorite. Cherry satin center—next, white velvet again—next, green velvet—and last, pink satin. Don't you think it will be sweet! I can scarcely wait until I begin that block."

The winged sweep of the fine black brows was ruffled by a frown of earnest concentration as she bent intently over the rags and scraps of shimmering stuffs. Her cheated fingers smoothed and caressed the satin surfaces as tenderly as though they lingered on a baby's cheek.

When, finally, it was finished—lined with turkey red and bound with red ribbon—Charlotte exhibited it at the fair, following much persuasion by her friends. It took first prize among twenty-five silk quilts. A day of great triumph for Charlotte Thrift. The prize was a basket worth fully eight dollars.

Chapter IV

When Charlotte was thirty, Carrie—twenty—married. After all, the innocent little indiscretion which had so thoroughly poisoned Charlotte's life was not to corrupt Carrie's matrimonial future, in spite of Mrs. Thrift's mournful prediction. Carrie, whose philosophy of life was based on that same finding's-keeping plan with which she had filched the bit of orange silk from her sister so many years before, married Samuel Payson, junior member of the firm of Thrift and Payson, Real Estate, Bonds, and Mortgages. Charlotte, it may be remembered, had disdained to pick up the scrap of orange silk on which Carrie had swooped. Just so with Samuel Payson.

Samuel Payson was destined to be a junior partner. Everything about him was deferential, subservient. The very folds of his clothes slanted away from you. He was as oblique and evasive as Isaac Thrift was upright and forthright. In conversation with you he pronounced your name at frequent intervals. Charlotte came to dread it: "Yes, Miss Charlotte . . . Do you think so, Miss Charlotte? . . . Sit here, Miss Charlotte . . ." It was like a too-intimate hand on your shrinking arm.

The fashion for men of parting the hair in the middle had just come in. Samuel Payson parted his from forehead to nape of neck. In some mysterious way it gave to the back of his head an alert facial expression very annoying to the beholder. He reminded Charlotte of someone she had recently met and whom she despised; but for a long time, she could not think who this could be. She found herself staring at him, fascinated, trying to trace the resemblance. Samuel Payson misinterpreted her gaze.

Isaac and Hetty Thrift had too late relaxed their vigilant watch over Charlotte. It had taken them all these years to realize that they were guarding a prisoner who hugged her chains. Wretched as she was (in a quiet and unobtrusive way), there is the possibility that she would have been equally wretched married to a Hardscrabble Dick. Charlotte's submission was all the more touching because she had nothing against which to rebel. Once, in the very beginning, Mrs. Thrift, haunted by something in Charlotte's eyes, had said in a burst of mingled spleen and self-defense:

"And why do you look at me like that, I should like to know! I'm sure I didn't kill your young man at Donelson. You're only moping like that to aggravate me; for something that never could have been, anyway—thank goodness!"

"He wouldn't have been killed," Charlotte said, unreasonably, and with conviction.

Had they been as wise and understanding as they were well-meaning, these two Calvinistic parents might have cured Charlotte by one visit to the Dicks' Hardscrabble kitchen, with a mangy cur nosing her skirts; a red-faced hostess at the washtub; and a ruined, battered travesty of the slim young rhyme-making Jesse Dick there in the person of old Pete Dick squatting, sodden, in the doorway.

As the years went on, they had, tardily, a vague and sneaking hope that something might happen among the GAR widowers of Chicago's better families. During the reunions of Company I and Company E, Charlotte generally assisted with the dinner or the musical program. She had a sweet, if small, contralto with notes in it that matched the fine dark eyebrows. She sang a group of old-fashioned songs: "When You and I Were Young Maggie"; "The Belle of Mohawk Vale"; and "Sleeping I Dream, Love." Charlotte never suspected her parents' careful scheming behind these public appearances of hers. Her deft capable hands at the GAR dinners, her voice lifted in song, were her offerings to Jesse Dick's memory. Him she served. To him she sang. And gradually, even Isaac and Hetty Thrift realized that the GAR widowers were looking for younger game; and that Charlotte, surrounded by blue-uniformed figures, still was gazing through them, past them, into space. Her last public appearance was when she played the organ and acted as director for *Queen Esther*, a cantata, which marked rather an epoch in the amateur musical history of the town. After that, she began to devote herself to her sister's family and to her mother.

But all this was later. Charlotte, at thirty, still had a look of vigor, and of fragrant (if slightly faded) bloom, together with a little atmosphere of mystery of which she was entirely unconscious; born, doubtless, of years of living with a ghost. Attractive qualities, all three; and all three quite lacking in her tart-tongued and acidulous younger sister, despite that miss's ten-year advantage. Carrie was plain, spare, and sallow. Her mind marched with her father's. The two would discuss real estate and holdings like two men. Hers was the mathematical and legal-thinking type of brain rarely found in a woman. She rather despised her mother. Samuel Payson used to listen to her with an air of respectful admiration and attention. But it was her older sister to whom he turned at last with, "I thought perhaps you might enjoy a drive to Cleaversville, since the evening's so fine, Miss Charlotte. What do you say, Miss Charlotte?"

"Oh, thank you—I'm not properly dressed for driving—perhaps Carrie—"

"Nonsense!" Mrs. Thrift would interpose tartly.

"But Miss Charlotte, you are quite perfectly dressed. If I may be so bold, that is a style which suits you to a marvel."

There he was right. It did. Hoops were history. The formfitting basque, the flattering neck frill, the hip sash, and the smart (though grotesque) bustle revealed, and even emphasized, lines of the feminine figure—the swell of the bust, the curve of the throat—that the crinoline had for years concealed. This romantic, if somewhat lumpy, costume well became Charlotte's slender figure and stern, sad, young face. In it Carrie, on the other hand, resembled a shingle in a flower's sheath.

This obstacle having been battered down, Charlotte raised another. "They say the Cleaversville road is a sea of mud and no bottom to it in places. The rains."

"Then," said Samuel Payson, agreeably, "we shall leave that for another time"—Charlotte brightened—"and go boating in the lagoon instead. Eh, Miss Charlotte?"

Charlotte, born fifty years later, would have looked her persistent and unwelcome suitor in the eye and said, "I don't want to go." Charlotte, with the parental eyes upon her, went dutifully upstairs for bonnet and mantle.

The lagoon of Samuel Payson's naming was a basin of water between the narrow strip of park on Michigan Avenue and the railway that ran along the lake. It was much used for boating of a polite and restricted nature.

It was a warm Sunday evening in the early summer. The better to get the breeze, the family was sociably seated out on what was known as the platform. On fine evenings, all Chicago sat out on its front steps—"the stoop" it was called. The platform was even more informal than the stoop. It was made of wooden planks built across the ditches that ran along each side of the street. Across it, carriages drove up to the sidewalk when visitors contemplated alighting. All down Wabash Avenue you saw families comfortably seated in rockers on these platforms, enjoying the evening breeze and watching the world go by. Here the Thrifts—Isaac, Hetty, and their daughter Carrie—were seated when the triumphant Samuel left with the smoldering Charlotte. Here they were seated when the two returned.

The basin reached, they had hired a boat, and Samuel had paddled about in a splashy and desultory way, not being in the least an oarsman. He talked, Miss-Charlotteing her so insistently that in ten minutes she felt thumbed all over. She looked out across the lake. He spoke of his loneliness living at the Tremont House. Before being raised to junior partner, he had been a clerk in Isaac Thrift's office. It was thus that Charlotte still regarded him—when she regarded him at all. She looked at him now, bent to the oars, his flat chest concave, his lean arms stringy; panting a little with the unaccustomed exercise.

"It must be lonely," murmured Charlotte, absentmindedly if sympathetically.

"Your father and mother have been very kind"—he bent a melting look on her—"far kinder than you have been, Miss Charlotte."

"It's chilly, now that the sun's gone," said Charlotte. "Shall we row in? This mantle is very light."

It cannot be said that he flushed then, but a little flood of dark color came into his pallid face. He rowed for the boathouse. He maneuvered the boat alongside the landing. Twilight had come on. The shedlike place was too dim for safety, lighted at the far end with one cobwebby lantern. He hallooed to the absent boatman, shipped his oars, and stepped out none too expertly. Charlotte stood up, smiling. She was glad to be in. Sitting opposite him thus, in the boat, it had been impossible to evade his red-rimmed eyes. Still smiling a little, with relief she took his proffered hand as he stood on the landing, stepped up stumbled a little because he had pulled with unexpected (and unnecessary) strength, and was horrified suddenly to see him thrust his head forward like a particularly nasty species of bird and press moist clammy lips to the hollow of her throat. Her reaction was as unfortunate as it was unstudied. "Uriah Heep!" she cried (at last! the resemblance that had been haunting her all these days), "Heep! Heep!"

and pushed him violently from her. The sacred memories of the past twelve years, violated now, were behind that outraged push. It sent him reeling over the edge of the platform, clutching at a post that was not there, and into the shallow water on the other side. The boatmen, running tardily toward them, fished him out and restored him to a curiously unagitated young lady. He was wet but uninjured. Thus dripping, he still insisted on accompanying her home. She had not murmured so much as, "I'm sorry." They walked home in hurried silence, his boots squashing at every step. The Thrifts—father, mother, and daughter—still were seated on the platform before the house, probably discussing real estate values—two of them, at least. Followed exclamations, explanations, sympathy, flurry.

"I fell in. A bad landing place. No light. A wretched hole."

Charlotte turned abruptly and walked up the front steps and into the house. "She's upset," said Mrs. Thrift, automatically voicing the proper thing, flustered though she was. "Usually it's Charlotte that falls into things. You must get that coat off at once. And the . . . Isaac, your pepper-and-salt suit. A little large but . . . Come in . . . Dear, dear! . . . I'll have a hot toddy ready . . . Carrie . . ."

It was soon after the second Chicago fire that Isaac Thrift and his son-in-law built the three-story-and-basement house on Prairie Avenue, near Twenty-Ninth Street. The old man recalled the boast made almost forty years before, that some day he would build as far south as Thirtieth Street; though it was not, as he had then predicted, a country home.

"I was a little wrong there," he admitted, "but only because I was too conservative. They laughed at me. Well, you can't deny the truth of it now. It'll be as good a hundred years from now as it is today. Only the finest houses because of the cost of the ground. No chance of business ever coming up this way. From Sixteenth to Thirtieth it's a residential paradise. Yes sir! A res-i-den-tial paradise!"

A good thing that he did not live the twenty-five years, or less, that transformed the paradise into a smoke-blackened and disreputable inferno, with dusky faces, surmounted by chemically unkinked though woolly heads, peering from every decayed mansion and tumbledown rooming house. Sixteenth Street became a sore that would not heal—scrofulous, filthy. Thirty-First Street was the center of the Black Belt. Of all that region, Prairie Avenue alone resisted wave after wave of the black flood that engulfed the streets south, east, and west. There, in Isaac Thrift's day, lived much of Chicago's aristocracy; millionaire if mercantile; plutocratic though porcine. And there its great stone and brick mansions with their mushroom-topped conservatories, their porte-cochères, their high wrought-iron fences, and their careful lawns still defied the years, though ruin, dirt, and decay waited just outside to destroy them. The window-hangings of any street are its character index. The lace and silk draperies before the windows of these old mansions still were immaculate, though the Illinois Central trains, as they screeched derisively by, spat huge mouthful of smoke and cinders into their very faces.

Isaac Thrift had fallen far behind his neighbours in the race for wealth. They had started as he had, with only courage, ambition, and foresight as capital. But they—merchants, pork-packers—had dealt in food and clothing on an increasingly greater scale, while Isaac Thrift had early given up his store to devote all his time to real estate. There had been his mistake. Bread and pork, hardware and clothing—these were fundamental needs, changing little with the years. Millions came to the man who, starting as a purveyor of these, stayed with them. At best, real estate was a gamble. And Isaac Thrift lost.

His own occasional shortsightedness was not to blame for his most devastating loss, however. This was dealt him, cruelly and criminally, by his business partner and son-in-law, the plausible Payson.

The two families dwelt comfortably enough together in the new house on Prairie. There was room to spare, even after two children—Belle, and then Lottie—were born to the Paysons. The house was thought a grand affair, with its tin bathtub and boxed-in washbowl on the second floor, besides an extra washroom on the first, off the hall; a red and yellow stained glass window in the dining room; a butler's pantry (understand, no butler; Chicago boasted no more than half a dozen of these); a fine furnace in the lower hall just under the stairway; oilcloth on the first flight of stairs; Brussels on the second; ingrain on the third; a liver-colored marble mantel in the front parlor, with anemic replicas in the back parlor and the more important bedrooms. It was an age when every possible article of household furniture was disguised to represent something it was not. A miniature Gothic cathedral was really a work basket; a fauteuil was, like as not, a music box. The Thrifts' parlor carpet was green, woven to represent a river flowing along from the back parlor folding doors to the street windows, with a pattern of full-sailed ships on it, and, by way of variety, occasional bunches of flowers strewn carelessly here and there, between the ships. On rare and thrilling occasions, during their infancy, Belle and little Lottie were allowed to crawl down the carpet river and poke a fascinated finger into a ship's sail or a floral garland.

Carrie's two children were born in this house. Isaac and Hetty Thrift died in it. And in it, Carrie was left worse than widowed.

Samuel Payson must have been about forty-six when, having gathered together in the office of Thrift & Payson all the uninvested moneys—together with negotiable bonds, stocks, and securities—on which he could lay hands, he decamped and was never seen again. He must have been planning it for years. It was all quite simple. He had had active charge of the business. Again and again Isaac Thrift had turned over to Payson money entrusted him for investment by widows of lifelong friends; by the sons and daughters of old Chicago settlers; by lifelong friends themselves. This money Payson had taken, ostensibly for investment. He had carefully discussed its investment with his father-in-law, had reported such investments made. In reality he had invested not a penny. On it had been paid one supposed dividend, or possibly two. The bulk of it remained untouched. When his time came, Samuel Payson gathered together the practically virgin sums and vanished to live some strange life of his own of which he had been dreaming behind that truckling manner and the Heepish face, with its red-rimmed eyes.

He had been a model husband, father, and son-in-law. Chess with old Isaac, evenings; wool-windings for Mrs. Thrift; games with the two little girls; church on Sundays with Carrie. Between him and Charlotte little talk was wasted, and no pretense.

A thousand times, in those years of their dwelling together, Mrs. Thrift's eyes had seemed to say to Charlotte, "You see! This is what a husband should be. This is a son-in-law. No Dick disgracing us here."

The blow stunned the two old people almost beyond realizing its enormity. The loss was, altogether, about $150,000. Isaac Thrift set about repaying it. Real estate on Indiana, Wabash, Michigan, Prairie was sold and the money distributed to make good the default. They kept the house on Prairie; clung to it. Anything but that. After it was all over, Isaac Thrift was an old man with palsied hands. Hair and beard whose color had defied the years were suddenly white. Hetty Thrift's tongue lost its venomous bite. After Isaac Thrift's death, she turned to Charlotte. Charlotte alone could quell her querulousness. Carrie acted as an irritant, naturally. They were so much alike. It was Charlotte who made broths and jellies, or milk toast and gruel with which to tempt the mother's appetite. Carrie, the mathematical, was a notoriously poor cook. Her mind was orderly and painstaking enough when it came to figuring on a piece of property or a depreciated bond. But it lacked that peculiar patience necessary to the watching of a boiling pot or a simmering pan.

"Oh, it's done by now," she would cry, and dump a pan's contents into a dish. Oftener than not it was half-cooked or burned.

Charlotte announced, rather timidly, that she would give music lessons; sewing lessons; do fine embroidery. But her tinkling tunes were ghostly echoes of a bygone day. People were even beginning to say that perhaps, after all, this madman Wagner could be played so that one might endure listening. Hand embroidery was little appreciated at a time when imitations were the craze.

Carrie it was who became head of that manless household. It was well she had wasted her time in doing sums instead of being more elegantly occupied while at Miss Tait's Finishing School, in the old Wabash Avenue days. She now juggled interest, simple and compound, with ease; took charge of the few remaining bits of scattered property saved from the ruins; talked glibly of lots, quarter sections, subdivisions. All through their childhood, Belle and Lottie heard reiterated, "Run away. Can't you see Mother's busy! Ask Aunt Charlotte." So then, it was Aunt Charlotte who gave them their bread and butter with sugar on top. Gradually, the whole household revolved about Carrie, though it was Charlotte who kept it in motion. When Carrie went to bed, the household went to bed. She must have her rest. Meals were timed to suit Carrie's needs. She became a business woman in a day when business women were practically unheard of. She actually opened an office in one of the new big Clark Street office buildings, near Washington, and had a sign printed on the door:

MRS. CARRIE PAYSON
REAL ESTATE
BONDS   MORTGAGES
Successor to late Isaac Thrift

Later she changed this to "Carrie Thrift Payson." Change came easily to Carrie. Adaptability was one of her gifts. In 1893 (World's Fair year), she was one of the first to wear the new Eton jacket and separate skirt of blue serge (it became almost a uniform with women); and the shirtwaist, a garment that marked an innovation in women's clothes. She worked like a man, ruled the roost, was as ruthless as a man. She was neither a good housekeeper nor marketer, but something perverse in her made her insist on keeping a hand on the reins of household as well as business. It was, perhaps, due to a colossal egotism and a petty love of power. Charlotte could have marketed expertly and thriftily, but Carrie liked to do it on her way downtown in the morning, stopping at grocer's and butcher's on Thirty-First Street and prefacing her order always with, "I'm in a hurry." The meat, vegetables, and fruit she selected were never strictly first-grade. A bargain delighted her. If an orange was a little soft in one spot, she reckoned that the spot could be cut away. Such was her system of false economy.

With the World's Fair came a boom in real estate, and Carrie Payson rode on the crest of it. There still were heartbreaking debts to pay and she paid them honestly. She was too much a Thrift to do otherwise. She never became rich, but she did manage a decent livelihood. Fortunately for all of them, old Isaac Thrift had bought some low swampy land far out in what was considered the wilderness, near the lake, even beyond the section known as Cottage Grove. With the fair, this land became suddenly valuable.

There's no denying that Carrie lacked a certain feminine quality. If one of the children chanced to fall ill, their mother, bustling home from the office, had no knack of smoothing a pillow or cooling a hot little body or easing a pain. "Please, Mother, would you mind not doing that? It makes my headache worse." Her fingers were heavy, clumsy, almost rough, like a man's. Her maternal guidance of her two daughters took the form of absentminded and rather nagging admonitions:

"Belle, you're reading against the light."

"Lottie, did you change your dress when you came home from school?"

"Don't bite that thread with your teeth!" Or, as it became later, merely, "Your teeth!"

Slowly, but inevitably, the Paysons dropped out of the circle made up of Chicago's rich old families—old, that is, in a city that reckoned a twenty-year building a landmark. The dollar sign was beginning to be the open sesame, and this symbol had long been violently erased from the Thrift-Payson escutcheon. To the ladies in landaus with the little screw-jointed sun parasols held stiffly before them, Carrie Payson and Charlotte Thrift still were "Carrie" and "Charlotte dear." They—and later Belle and Lottie—were asked to the big, inclusive crushes pretty regularly once a year. But the small smart dinners that were just coming in; the intimate social gayeties; the clubby affairs, knew them not. "One of the Thrift girls" might mean anyone in the Prairie Avenue household, but it was never anything but a term of respect and meant much to anyone who was native to Chicago. Other Prairie Avenue mansions sent their daughters to local private schools, or to the Eastern finishing schools. Belle and Lottie attended the public grammar school and later Armour Institute for the high school course only. Middle-aged folk said to Lottie, "My, how much like your Aunt Charlotte you do look, child!" They never exclaimed in Belle's presence at the likeness they found in her face. Belle's family resemblance could be plainly traced to one of whom friends did not speak in public. Belle was six years her sister's senior, but Lottie, with her serious brow and her clear, steady eyes, looked almost Belle's age. Though Belle was known as the flighty one, there was more real fun in Lottie. In Lottie's bedroom there still hangs a picture of the two of them, framed in passe-partout. It was taken—arm in arm—when Lottie was finishing high school and Belle was about to marry Henry Kemp; high pompadours over enormous "rats," the whole edifice surmounted by a life-size *chou* of ribbon; shirtwaists with broad Gibson tucks that gave them shoulders of a coal-heaver; plaid circular skirts fitting snugly about the hips and flaring out in great bell-shaped width at the hem; and trailing.

"What in the world do you keep that comic valentine hanging up for!" Belle always exclaimed when she chanced into Lottie's room in later years.

Often and often, during these years, you might have heard Carrie Payson say, with bitterness, "I don't want my girls to have the life I've had. I'll see to it that they don't."

"How are you going to do it?" Charlotte would ask, with a curious smile.

"I'll stay young with them. And I'll watch for mistakes. I know the world. I ought to. For that matter, I'd as soon they never married."

Charlotte would flare into sudden and inexplicable protest. "You let them live their own lives, the way they want to, good or bad. How do you know the way it'll turn out! Nobody knows. Let them live their own lives."

"Nonsense," from Carrie, crisply. "A mother knows. One uses a little common sense in these things, that's all. Don't you think a mother knows?" a rhetorical question, plainly, but:

"No," said Charlotte.

Chapter V

Anyone who has lived in Chicago knows that you don't live on the South Side. You simply do not live on the South Side. And yet Chicago's South Side is a pleasant place of fine houses and neat lawns (and this when every foot of lawn represents a tidy fortune); of trees, and magnificent parks and boulevards; of stately (if smoke-blackened) apartment houses; of children, and motor cars; of all that makes for comfortable, middle-class American life. More than that, booming its benisons upon the whole is the astounding spectacle of Lake Michigan forming the section's eastern boundary. And yet Fashion had early turned its back upon all this as is the way of Fashion with natural beauty.

We know that the Paysons lived south; and why. We know, too, that Carrie Payson was the kind of mother who would expect her married daughter to live near her. Belle had had the courage to make an early marriage as a way of escape from the Prairie Avenue household, but it was not until much later that she had the temerity to broach the subject of moving north. She had been twenty when she married Henry Kemp, ten years her senior. A successful marriage. Even now, nearing forty, she still said, "Henry, bring me a chair," and Henry brought it. Not that Henry was a worm. He was merely the American husband before whom the foreign critic stands aghast. A rather silent, gray-haired, eye-glassed man with a slim boyish waistline, a fair mashie stroke, a keen business head, and a not altogether blind devotion to his selfish, pampered semi-intellectual wife. There is no denying his disappointment at the birth of his daughter Charlotte. He had needed a son to stand by him in this family of strong-minded women. It was not altogether from the standpoint of convenience that he had called Charlotte "Charley" from the first.

Thwarted in her secret ambition to move north, Belle moved as far south as possible from the old Prairie Avenue dwelling; which meant that the Kemps were residents of Hyde Park. Between the two families—the Kemps in Hyde Park and the Paysons in Prairie Avenue—there existed a terrible intimacy, fostered by Mrs. Carrie Payson. They telephoned each other daily. They saw one another almost daily. Mrs. Payson insisted on keeping a finger on the pulse of her married daughter's household as well as her own. During Charley's babyhood, the innermost secrets of the nursery, the infant's most personal functions, were discussed daily via the telephone. Lottie, about sixteen at that time, and just finishing at Armour, usually ate her hurried breakfast to the accompaniment of the daily morning telephone talk carried on between her mother and her married sister.

"How are they this morning? . . . Again! . . . Well then give her a little oil . . . . Certainly not! I didn't have the doctor in every time you two girls had a little something wrong. . . . Oh, you're always having that baby specialist in every time she makes a face. We never heard of baby specialists when I was a . . . Well, but the oil won't hurt her. . . . If they're not normal by tomorrow get him but . . . You won't be able to go to the luncheon, of course . . . You are! But if Charley's . . . Well, if she's sick enough to have a doctor she's sick enough to need her mother at home. . . . Oh, all right. Only, if anything happens . . . How was the chicken you bought yesterday? . . . Didn't I tell you it was a tough one! You pay twice as much over there in Hyde Park . . . What are you going to wear to the luncheon? . . ."

Throughout her school years, Lottie had always had a beau to squire her about at school parties and boy-and-girl activities. He was likely to be a rather superior beau, too. No girl as clearheaded as Lottie, and as intelligently fun-loving and merry, would tolerate a slow-witted sweetheart. The word sweetheart is used for want of a better. Of sweethearting there was little among these seventeen- and eighteen-year-olds. Viewed through the wise eyes of today's adolescents, they would have seemed as quaint and stiff as their pompadours and high collars.

In a day when organized social work was considered an original and rather daring departure for women, Lottie Payson seemed destined by temperament and character to be a successful settlement worker. But she never became one. Lottie had too much humor and humaneness for the drab routine of schoolteaching; not enough hardness and aggressiveness for business; none of the creative spark that marks the genius in art. She was sympathetic without being sentimental; just and fair without being at all stern or forbidding. Above all, she had the gift of listening. The kind of woman who is better looking at thirty-five than at twenty. The kind of woman who learns with living and who marries early or never. With circumstance and a mother like Mrs. Carrie Payson against her, Lottie's chances of marrying early were hardly worth mentioning. Lottie was the kind of girl who "is needed at home."

Don't think that she hadn't young men to walk home with her from school. She had. But they were likely to be young men whose collars were not guiltless of eraser marks; who were active in the debating societies; and whose wrists hung, a red oblong, below their too-short sleeves. The kind of young man destined for utter failure or great success. The kind of young man who tries a pecan grove in Carolina, or becomes president of a bank in New York. None of these young men ever kissed Lottie. I think that sometimes, looking at her serious pretty lips closed so firmly over the white teeth, they wanted to. I'm sure that Lottie, though she did not know it, wished they would. But they never did. Lottie absolutely lacked coquetry as does the woman who tardily develops a sense of sex power. In Lottie's junior year, these gawky and studious young men narrowed down to one. His name was Rutherford Hayes Adler and he was a Jew.

There is no describing him without the use of the word genius, and in view of his novels of today (R. H. Adler), there is no need to apologize for the early use of the word. He was a living refutation of the belief that a brilliant mathematician has no imagination. His Armour report cards would have done credit to young Euclid; and he wrote humorous light verse to Lottie and sold insurance on the side. Being swarthy, black-haired, and black-eyed, he was cursed with a taste for tan suits and red neckties. These, with the high choker collar of the period, gave him the look of an end man strayed from the minstrel troupe. Being naturally shy, he assumed a swagger. He was lovable and rather helpless, and his shoestrings were always coming untied. His humor sense was so keen, so unerring, so fastidious as to be almost a vice. Armour students who did not understand it said, "He's a funny fellow. I don't know—kind of batty, isn't he?"

This young man it was who walked home with Lottie Payson all through her junior and senior years; sat next to her at meetings of the debating society; escorted her to school festivities; went bicycling with her on Saturday afternoons. The Payson household paid little attention to him or to Lottie. Belle was busy with her love affair. Henry Kemp had just appeared on her horizon. Mrs. Payson was deep in her real estate transactions. On the few occasions when Rutherford Hayes actually entered the house and sat down to await Lottie, the two were usually on their way to some innocuous entertainment or outing. So that it was Aunt Charlotte, if anybody, who said, "How do you do, young man. Oh yes, you're Mr. Adler. Lottie'll be right down." A little silence. Then kindly, from Aunt Charlotte, "H'm! How do you like your schoolwork?" Years afterwards, Adler put Aunt Charlotte into one of his books. And Lottie. And Mrs. Carrie Payson, too. He had reason to remember Mrs. Carrie Payson.

It was at the end of Lottie's senior year that Mrs. Payson became aware of this young man whose swart face seemed always to be just appearing or disappearing around the corner with Lottie either smiling in greeting or waving a farewell. End-of-the-year school festivities were accountable for this. Then, too, Belle must have registered some objection. When next young Adler appeared at the Prairie Avenue house, it was Mrs. Payson who sailed down the rather faded green river of the parlor carpet.

"How do you do," said Mrs. Payson; her glance said, "What are you doing here, in this house?"

Rutherford Hayes Adler wanted to get up from the chair into which his lank length was doubled. He knew he should get up. But a hideous shyness kept him there—bound him with iron bands. When finally, with a desperate effort, he broke them and stumbled to his feet, it was too late. Mrs. Payson had seated herself—if being seated can describe the impermanent position which she now assumed on the extreme edge of the stiffest of the stiff parlor chairs.

The sallow, skinny little Carrie Thrift had mellowed—no, that word won't do—had developed into an erect, dignified, white-haired woman of rather imposing mien. The white hair, in particular, was misleadingly softening.

"May I ask your father's name?" she said. Just that.

The boy had heard that tone used many times in the past nineteen hundred years. "Adler," he replied.

"Yes, I know. But his first name. What is his first name, please?"

"His first name was Abraham—Abraham I. Adler. The I stands for Isaac."

"Abraham—Isaac—Adler," repeated Mrs. Payson. As she uttered the words, they were an opprobrium.

"Your father's name was Isaac too, wasn't it?" said the boy.

"His name was Isaac Thrift." An altogether different kind of Isaac, you would have thought. No relation to the gentleman in the Bible. A New England Isaac not to be confused with the Levantine of that name.

"Yes. I remember I used to hear my grandfather speak of him."

"Indeed! In what connection, may I ask?"

"Why, he came to Chicago in '39, just about the time your father came, I imagine. They were young men together. Grandfather was an old settler."

Mrs. Payson's eyebrows doubted it. "I don't remember ever having seen him mentioned in books on early Chicago."

"You wouldn't," said Adler, "he isn't."

"And why not?"

"Jew," said Rutherford Hayes, pleasantly, and laconically.

Mrs. Payson stood up. So did the boy. He had no difficulty in rising now. No self-consciousness, no awkwardness. There was about him suddenly a fluid grace, an easy muscular rhythm. "Of course, Grandfather has been dead a good many years now," he went on politely, "and Father, too."

"I'm afraid Lottie won't be able to go this evening," Mrs. Payson said. "She has been going out too much. It is bad for her schoolwork. Young girls nowadays—"

"I see. I'm sorry." There was nothing of humility in the little bow he made from the waist. Ten minutes earlier you would never have thought him capable of so finished an act as that bow. He walked to the folding doors that led to the hall. On the way, his glance fell on the portrait of old Isaac Thrift over the liver-colored marble mantel. It was a fine portrait. One of Healy's. Adler paused a moment before it. "Is that a good portrait of your father?"

"It is considered very like him."

"It must be. I can see now why my grandfather took his part to the last."

"Took his part!" But her tone was a shade less corroding. "In what, if you please?"

"Grandfather lost his fortune when a firm he trusted proved—well, when a member of it proved untrustworthy."

When he grew older, he was always ashamed of having thus taken a mean advantage of a woman. But he was so young at the time; and she had hurt him so deeply. He turned again now, for the door. And there stood Lottie, brave, but not quite brave enough. She was not wearing her white dress—her party dress, for the evening. Her mother had forbidden her to come down. And yet here she was. Braver—not much, but still braver—than Charlotte had been before her.

"I—I can't go, Ford," she faltered.

"It's all right," he said, then. And there, before the white-haired relentless and disapproving Carrie Payson, he went up to her, put one lean, dark hand on her shoulder, drew her to him, and kissed her, a funny little boyish peck on the forehead. "Goodbye, Lottie," he said. And was gone.

Lottie's being needed at home began before the failure of Aunt Charlotte's sight. Aunt Charlotte had to go to the eye specialist's daily. Lottie took her. This was even before the day of the ramshackle electric. Lottie never begrudged Aunt Charlotte the service. Already between these two women, the one hardly more than twenty, the other already past sixty, there existed a curious and unspoken understanding. They were not voluble women, these two. Lottie never forgot those two hours in the waiting room of the famous specialist. Every chair was occupied, always. Silent, idle, waiting figures with something more crushed and apprehensive about them than ordinarily about the waiting ones in a doctor's outer room. The neat little stack of magazines on the center table remained untouched. Sometimes, if the wait was a long one, Lottie would run out for an hour's shopping; or would drop in at her mother's office. Mrs. Payson usually was busy with a client; maps, documents, sheafs of blue-bound papers. But if one of her daughters came downtown without dropping in at the office, she took it as a deliberate slight; or as a disregard of parental authority. Lottie hated the door marked:

CARRIE THRIFT PAYSON
REAL ESTATE
BONDS   MORTGAGES

"Oh, you're busy."

Mrs. Payson would glance up. There was nothing absentminded about the glance. For the moment her attention was all on Lottie. "Sit down. Wait a minute."

"I'll come back."

"Wait."

Lottie waited. Finally, "Aunt Charlotte will be wondering—"

"We're through now." She would sit back in her desk chair, her hands busy with the papers, her eyes on her client. "Now, if you'll come in again on Monday, say, at about this time, I'll have the abstract for you, and the trust deed. In the meantime I'll get in touch with Spielbauer—"

She would rise, as would her client, a man, usually. With the conclusion of the business in hand, she effected a quick change of manner; became the woman in business instead of the businesswoman. Sometimes the client happened to be an old-time acquaintance, in which case Carrie Payson would put a hand on Lottie's shoulder. "This is my baby."

The client would laugh genially, "Quite a baby!" This before the word had taken on its slang significance.

"I wouldn't know what to do without her," Mrs. Payson would say. "I have to be here all day."

"Yes, they're a great help. Great help. Well—see you Monday, Mrs. Payson. Same time. If you'll just see Spielbauer—"

The door closed, Mrs. Payson would turn again to Lottie. "What was the girl doing when you left?"

"Why—she was still ironing."

"How far had she got?"

"All the fancy things. She was beginning on the sheets."

"Well, I should think so! At that hour."

Lottie turned toward the door. "Aunt Charlotte'll be waiting."

Mrs. Payson must have a final thumb on the clay. "Be very careful crossing the streets." And yet there was pride and real affection in her eyes as she looked after the sturdy vigorous figure speeding down the corridor toward the elevator.

Once, when Lottie returned to the oculist's after a longer absence than usual, Aunt Charlotte had gone. "How long?" The attendant thought it must be fifteen minutes. Chicago's downtown streets, even to the young and the keen-sighted, were a maelstrom dotted at intervals by blue-uniformed figures who held up a magic arm and blew a shrill blast just when a swirl and torrent of drays, cabs, streetcars, and trucks with plunging horses threatened completely to engulf them. Added to this was the thunderous roar of the Wabash Avenue L trains. Even when the crossing was comparatively safe and clear, the deafening onrush of a passing L train above always caused Aunt Charlotte to scuttle back to the curb from which she was about to venture forth. The roar seemed to be associated in her mind with danger; it added to her confusion. Leading a horse out of a burning barn was play compared with ushering Aunt Charlotte across a busy downtown street.

"Just let me take my time," she would say, tremulously, but stubbornly immovable.

"But Aunt Charlotte, if we don't go now, we'll be here forever. Now's the time."

Aunt Charlotte would not budge. Then, at the wrong moment, she would dart suddenly across to the accompaniment of the startled whoop or curse of a driver, chauffeur, or car conductor obliged to draw a quick rein or jam on an emergency brake to avoid running her down.

Lottie, knowing all this, sped toward Wabash Avenue with fear in her heart, and a sort of anger born of fear. "Oh, dear! It does seem to me she might have waited. Mother didn't want a thing. Not a thing. I told her—"

She came to the corner of Wabash and Madison where they always took the Indiana Avenue car. She saw a little group of people near the curb, and her heart contracted as she sped on, but when she came up to them, it was only a balky automobile engine that had drawn their attention. She looked across at the corner which was their car stop. There stood Aunt Charlotte. At once cowering, brave; terrified, courageous. At sight of that timorous, peering, black-garbed figure, Lottie gave a little sob. The blood rushed back to her heart as though it had lain suspended in her veins.

"Aunt Charlotte, why did you do it?"

"I got across alone."

"But why didn't you wait for me? You knew—"

"I got across alone. But the streetcar—the wagons never stopping so a body can get out to the streetcar. And no way of telling whether it was an Indiana or a Cottage Grove. But I got across alone." She had her five-cent piece in her black-gloved, trembling hand.

Safely in the car, Lottie waxed stern again. "Why didn't you wait, Aunt Charlotte? You knew I'd be back as soon as I could. I didn't mean to be late. That was awfully naughty of you, Charlotte Thrift."

Aunt Charlotte was looking out of the car window. What she saw must have been little more than a blur to her. But something told Lottie that in the dim eyes turned away from her was still another blur—a blur of hot mist. Lottie leaned forward, covering with her own firm, cool, young grasp the hand that lay so inertly in the black silk lap. "What is it? Why—"

Aunt Charlotte turned and Lottie saw that what she had sensed was true. "It isn't right!" said Aunt Charlotte almost fiercely, and yet in a half-whisper, for the car was crowded and she had a horror of attracting public notice.

"What isn't?"

"Your calling for me, and bringing me back. Every day. Every day."

"Now! You're just a little blue today; but the doctor said you'd only have to come down for treatment a week or two more."

"It isn't me. It's you. Your life! Your life!"

A little flush crept into Lottie's face. "It's all right, dear."

"It isn't all right. Don't you think I know!" Aunt Charlotte's voice suddenly took on a deep and resonant note—the note of exhortation. "Lottie, you're going to be eaten alive by two old cannibal women. I know. I know. Don't you let 'em! You've got your whole life before you. Live it the way you want to. Then you'll have only yourself to blame. Don't you let somebody else live it for you. Don't you."

"How about Mother, slaving down in that office all day, when all the other women of her age are taking it easy—a nap at noon, and afternoon parties, and a husband to work for them?"

"Slaving fiddlesticks! She likes it. Your mother'd rather read the real estate transfers than a novel. Besides, she doesn't need to. We could live," on the rents. Nothing very grand, maybe. But we could live. And why not let you do something? That's what I'd like to know! Why not—"

"Oh, I'd love it. All the girls—that is, all the girls I like—are doing some kind of work. But Mother says—"

Aunt Charlotte sniffed. It was almost a snort. "I know what your mother says. 'No daughter of mine is going to work for her living.' Hmph!" (Which is not expressing it, but nearly.) "Calls herself modern. She's your grandfather over again and he thought he was a whole generation ahead of his generation. Wasn't, though. Little behind, if anything."

Sometimes Aunt Charlotte, the subdued, the vaguely wistful, had a sparkling pugnacity, a sudden lift of spirits that showed for a brief moment a glimpse of the girl of fifty years ago. A tiff with Carrie Payson (in which Charlotte, strangely enough, usually came *off* victorious) often brought about this brief phenomenon. At such times she had even been known to sing, in a high off-key falsetto, such ghostly, but rakish, echoes as: "Champagne Charley Was His Name," or, "Captain Jinks of the Horse Marines," or even, "Up in a Balloon Boys." Strangely enough, as she grew older, this mood became more and more familiar. It was a sort of rebirth. At times she assumed an almost jaunty air. It was as though life, having done its worst, was no longer feared by her.

In spite of objections, Lottie made sporadic attempts to mingle in the stream of life that was flowing so swiftly past her—this new life of service and self-expression into which women were entering. Settlement work; folk dancing, pageantry, juvenile and girls' court work; social service; departmental newspaper work. Lottie was attracted by all of these, and to any one of them she might have given valuable service. A woman, Emma Barton, not yet fifty, had been appointed assistant judge of the new girls' court. No woman had held a position such as that. Lottie had met her. The two had become friends—close friends in spite of the disparity in their ages.

"I need you so badly up here," Emma Barton often told Lottie. "You've got a way with girls; and you're not schoolteachery or judicial with them. That's the trouble with the regular court worker. And they talk to you, don't they? Why, I wonder?"

"Maybe it's because I listen," Lottie replied. "And they think I'm sort of simple. Maybe I am. But not so simple as they think." She laughed. A visit to Judge Barton's court always stimulated her, even while it saddened.

Chicagoans, for the most part, read in the papers of Judge Barton and pictured in their minds a stout and pink-jowled judiciary in a black coat, imposing black-ribboned eyeglasses, and careful linen. These people, if they chanced to be brought face to face with Judge Barton, were generally seen to smile uncertainly as though a joke were being played on them without success. They saw a small, mild-faced woman with graying hair and bright brown eyes—piercing eyes that yet had a certain liquid quality. She was like a wise little wren who has seen much of life and understands more than she has seen, and forgives more than she understands. A blue cloth dress with, probably, some bright embroidery worked on it. A modern workaday dress on a modern woman. Underneath, characteristically enough, a black sateen petticoat with a pocket in it, like a market woman. A morning spent in Judge Barton's court was life with the cover off. It was a sight vouchsafed to few. Emma Barton discouraged the curious and ousted the morbidly prying. Besides, there was no space in her tiny room for more than the persons concerned. It was less like a courtroom then your own office, perhaps.

Then there was Winnie Steppler, who wrote for Chicago's most lurid newspaper under the nom de plume of "Alice Yorke." A pink-cheeked, white-haired, Falstaffian woman with the look and air of a picture-book duchess and the wit and drollery of a gamin. Twice married, twice widowed; wise with a terrible wisdom; seeing life so plainly that she could not write of what she saw. There were no words. Or perhaps the gift of words had kindly been denied her. Her "feature stuff" was likely to be just that. Her conversation was razor-keen and as Irish as she cared to make it. People were always saying to her, "Why don't you write the way you talk?"

"It's lucky for my friends I don't talk the way I write."

Perhaps these two women, more than anything or anyone else, had influenced Lottie to intolerance of aimless diversion. Not that Lottie had much time for her own aimless diversion even if she had fancied it. Rheumatism of a painful and crippling kind had laid its iron fingers upon Carrie Payson. Arthritis, the doctors called it. It affected only the fingers of the left hand—but because of it the downtown real estate office was closed. The three women were home together now in the big old house on Prairie, and Mrs. Payson was talking of selling it and moving into an apartment out south. It was about this time, too, that she bought the electric—one of the thousands that now began to skim Chicago's boulevards—and to which Lottie became a galley slave. She sometimes thought humorously of the shiny black levers as oars and the miles of boulevard as an endless sea to which she was condemned. Don't think that Lottie Payson was sorry for herself. If she had been perhaps it would have been better for her. For ten years or more she had been so fully occupied in doing her duty—or what she considered her obvious duty—that she had scarcely thought of her obligations toward herself. If you had disturbing thoughts you put them out of your mind. And slammed the door on them. When she was twenty-nine, or thereabouts, she had read a story that stuck in her memory. It was Balzac's short story of the old maid who threw herself into the well. She went to Aunt Charlotte with it.

"Now that's a morbid, unnatural kind of story, isn't it?" she said.

Aunt Charlotte's forefinger made circles, round and round, on her black-silk knee. Lottie had read the story aloud to her. "No. It's true.

And it's natural."

"I don't see how you can say so. Now, when you were about forty—"

"When I was thirty-five or forty I had you and Belle. To tend to, I mean, and look after. If I hadn't had you I don't say that I would have gone off with the butcher boy, but I don't say that I wouldn't. Every time I wiped your noses or buttoned you up or spatted your hands when you were naughty it was a—well—a—"

"A sort of safety valve, you mean?" Lottie supplied the figure for her.

"Yes. Between thirty-five and forty—that's the time to look out for. You can fool nature just so long, and then she turns around and hits back."

"But look at all the girls I know—women of my age, and older— who are happy and busy and contented."

There came a soft look into the dark eyes beneath the heavy black brows. From the vantage point of her years and experience, she pronounced upon her sex. "Women are wonderful, Lottie," she said. "Just wonderful. A good thing for the race that men aren't like 'em. In self-control, I mean, and that. Wouldn't *be* any race, reckon."

Chapter VI

Lottie Payson was striding home through the early evening mist, the zany March wind buffeting her skirts—no: skirt; it is 1916 and women are knickerbockered underneath instead of petticoated. She had come from what is known on the South Side as "spending the afternoon."

Of late years Lottie had given up this spending of afternoons. Choice and circumstances had combined to bring this about. Her interests had grown away from these women who had been her schoolgirl friends. The two women with whom she lived made her the staff on which they leaned more and more heavily. Lottie Payson was head of the household in everything but authority. Mrs. Carrie Payson still held the reins.

The afternoons had started as a Reading Club when Lottie was about twenty-five and the others a year or two older or younger. Serious reading. Yes, indeed. Effie Case had said, "We ought to improve our minds; not just read anything. I think it would be fine to start with the German poets; Gerty and those."

So they had started with Goethe and those but found the going rather rough. This guttural year had been followed by one of French conversation led by a catarrhal person who turned out to be Vermontese instead of Parisian, which accounted for their having learned to pronounce *le* as "ler." After this they had turned to Modern American Literature; thence, by a process of degeneration, to Current Topics. They had a leader for the Current Topics Class, a retired Madam Chairman. She grafted the front-page headlines onto the *Literary Digest* and produced a brackish fruit tasting slightly of politics, invention, scandal, dress, labor, society, disease, crime, and royalty. One day, at the last minute, when she had failed to appear for the regular meeting—grippe, or a heavy cold—someone suggested, "How about two tables of bridge?" After that the Reading Class alternated between bridge and sewing. The sewing was quite individual and might range all the way from satin camisoles to huckabuck towels; from bead bags to bedspreads. The talk, strangely enough, differed little from that of the personally conducted Current Topics Class days. They all attended lectures pretty regularly; and symphony concerts and civic club meetings.

In the very beginning they had made a rule about refreshments. "No elaborate serving," they had said. "Just tea or coffee, and toast. And perhaps a strawberry jam or something like that. But that's all. Nobody does it any more." The salads, cakes, and ices of an earlier period were considered vulgar for afternoons. Besides, banting had come in, and these women were nearing thirty; some of them had passed it—an age when fat creeps slyly about the hips and arms and shoulder blades and stubbornly remains, once ensconced. Still, this rule had slowly degenerated as had the club's original purpose. As they read less during these afternoons they ate more. Beck Schaefer discovered and served a new fruit salad with Hawaiian pineapple and marshmallows as its plot. When next they met at Effie Case's, she served her salad in little vivid baskets made of oranges hollowed out, with one half of the skin cut away except for a strip across the top to form the basket's handle. After that there was no more tea and toast. After that, too, the attendance of certain members of the erstwhile Reading Club became more and more irregular and finally ceased altogether. These delinquents were the more serious-minded ones of the group. One became a settlement worker. Another went into the office of an advertising agency and gave all her time and thought to emphasising the desirability of certain breakfast foods, massage creams, chewing gum, and garters. Still another had become a successful science practitioner, with an office in the Lake Building and a waiting room always full of claims. As for Lottie Payson—her youth and health, her vigor and courage all went into the service of two old women. Of these the one took selfishly; the other reluctantly, protestingly. The Reading Club had long ago ceased to exist for Lottie.

In the morning she drove her mother to market in the ramshackle old electric. Mrs. Payson seldom drove it herself. The peculiar form of rheumatism from which she suffered rendered her left hand almost useless. The electric had been a fine piece of mechanism in its day, but years of service had taken the spring from its joints and the life from its batteries. Those batteries now were as uncertain as a tired old heart that may stop its labored beating any moment. A balky starter and an unreliable starter, its two levers needed two strong hands with muscle control behind them. Besides, one had to be quick. As the Paysons rumbled about in this rheumatic coach, haughty and contemptuous gas cars were always hooting impatiently behind them, nosing them perilously out of the way in the traffic's flood, their drivers frequently calling out ribald remarks about hearses.

In this vehicle drawn up at the curb outside the market, Lottie would sit reading the *Survey* (Judge Barton's influence there) while her mother carried on a prolonged and acrimonious transaction with Gus. Thirty-First Street, then Thirty-Fifth Street, had become impossible for the family marketing. There, groceries and meat markets catered frankly to the Negro trade. Prosperous enough trade it seemed, too, with the windows piled with plump broilers and juicy cuts of ham. The Payson electric waited in Forty-Third Street now.

Gus's red, good-natured face above the enveloping white apron became redder and less good-natured as Mrs. Payson's marketing progressed. New potatoes. A piece of rump for a pot roast. A head of lettuce. A basket of peaches. Echoes floated out to Lottie waiting at the curb.

"Yeh, but looka here, Mis' Payson, I ain't makin' nothin' on that stuff as it is. Two three cents at the most. Say *I* gotta live too, you know. . . Oh, you don't want *that,* Mis' Payson. Tell you the truth, they're pretty soft. Now here's a nice fresh lot come in from Michigan this morning. I picked 'em out myself down on South Water."

Mrs. Payson's decided tones: "They'll do for stewing."

"All right. 'S for you to say. You got to eat 'em, not me. On'y don't come around tomorrow tellin' me they was no good."

Her purchases piled on the leather-upholstered front seat of the electric, Mrs. Payson would be driven home, complaining acidly. This finished Gus for her. Robber! Twenty-seven cents for lamb stew!

"But Mama, Belle paid thirty-two cents last week. I remember hearing her say that lamb stew was seven or eight cents two or three years ago and now it's thirty-two or thirty—"

"Oh, Belle! I'm surprised she ever has lamb stew. Always running short on her allowance with her sirloins and her mushrooms and her broilers. I ran a household for a whole month on what she uses in a week, when I was her age. I don't know how Henry stands it."

This ceremony of marketing took half the morning. It should have required little more than an hour. On arriving home Mrs. Payson usually complained of feeling faint. Her purchases piled on the kitchen table, she would go over them with Hulda, the maidservant. "Put that lettuce in a damp cloth." The maid was doing it. "Rub a little salt and vinegar into that pot roast." The girl had intended to. "You'll have to stew those peaches." That had been apparent after the first disdainful pressing with thumb and forefinger. By this time, Hulda's attitude was the bristling one natural to any human being whose intelligence has been insulted by being told to do that which she already had meant to do. Mrs. Payson, still wearing her hat (slightly askew now) would accept the crackers and cheese, or the bit of cold lamb and slice of bread, proffered by Lottie to fend off the "faintness." Often Mrs. Payson augmented this with a rather surprising draught of sherry in a tumbler, from the supply sent by her son-in-law, Henry Kemp.

On fine afternoons Lottie often drove her mother and Aunt Charlotte to Jackson Park, drawing up at the curb along the lake walk. A glorious sight, that panorama. It was almost like being at sea, minus the discomfort of travel. The great blue inland ocean stretched before them, away and away and away until it met the sky. For the most part, the three women did nothing. Mrs. Payson had always hated sewing. Great-Aunt Charlotte sometimes knitted. Her eyes were not needed for that. But oftenest she sat there gazing out upon the restless expanse of Lake Michigan, her hands moving as restlessly as the shifting ageless waters. Great-Aunt Charlotte's hands were seldom still. Always they moved over her lap, smoothing a bit of cloth, tracing an imaginary pattern with a wrinkled parchment forefinger; pleating a fold of her napkin when at table. Hands with brown splotches on the backs. Moving, moving, and yet curiously inactive. Sometimes Lottie read aloud, but not often. Her mother was restless at being read aloud to; besides, she liked stories with what is known as a business interest. Great-Aunt Charlotte liked romance. No villain too dastardly—no heroine too lovely and misunderstood—no hero too ardent and athletic for Aunt Charlotte's taste. She swallowed them, boots, moonlight, automobiles, papers, and all. "Such stuff!" Mrs. Carrie Payson would say.

The conversation of the three women sitting there in the little glass-enclosed box was desultory, unvital. They had little to say to one another. Yet each would have been surprised to learn what a reputation for liveliness and wit the other had in her own circle. Lottie was known among "the girls" to be mischievous and gay; Carrie Payson could keep a swift and keen pace in conversation with a group of businessmen, or after a hand at bridge with women younger than she (Mrs. Payson did not care for the company of women of her own age); Great-Aunt Charlotte's sallies and observations among her septuagenarian circle often brought forth a chorus of cackling laughter. Yet now:

"Who's that coming along past the Iowa building?" (Relic of World's Fair days.)

"I can't tell from here, Mama."

"Must be walking to reduce, with that figure, on a day like this. It's that Mrs. Deffler, isn't it, that lives near Belle's? No, it isn't. She's too dark. Yes it . . . no . . ."

Lottie said aloud, "No, it isn't." And within: "If I could only jump out of this old rattletrap and into a boat—a boat with sails all spread—and away to that place over there that's the horizon. Oh, God, how I'd . . . but I suppose I'd only land at Indiana Harbor instead of at the horizon." Then aloud again, "If you and Aunt Charlotte think you'll be comfortable here for twenty minutes or so I'll just walk up as far as the pier and back."

"That's right," from Aunt Charlotte. "Do you good. What's more"—she chuckled an almost wicked chuckle—"I'd never come back, if I were you."

Mrs. Carrie Payson eyed her sister witheringly. "Don't be childish, Charlotte."

Out on the walk, her face toward the lake, her head lifted, her hands jammed into her sweater pockets, Lottie was off.

A voice was calling her.

"What?"

"Your hat! You forgot your hat!"

"I don't want it." She turned resolutely away from the maternal voice and the hat. Her mother's head was stuck out of the car door. Lottie heard, unheeding, a last faint "Sunburn!" and "Complexion." A half mile up, a half mile back. Walking gave her a sense of freedom, of exhilaration; helped her to face the rest of the day.

In the evening they often drove round to Belle's; or about the park again on warm summer nights.

But on this particular March afternoon, the Reading Club once more claimed Lottie. One of the readers had married. This was her long-planned afternoon at home for the girls. Her newly furnished four-room apartment awaited their knowing inspection. Her wedding silver and linen shone and glittered for them. Celia Sprague was a bride at thirty-six, after a ten-years' engagement.

"Now, Lottie," she had said, over the telephone, "you've just got to come. Every one of the girls will be here. It's my first party in my new home. Oh, I notice you find time for your new highbrow friends. It won't hurt you to come slumming this once. Well, but your mother can do without you for one afternoon, can't she! Good heavens, you've *some* right to your—"

Lottie came. She came and brought her knitting as did every other member of the Reading Club. Satin camisoles, lingerie, hemstitching, and bead bags had been abandoned for hanks of wool. The Reading Club, together with the rest of North America, was swaddling all Belgium in a million pounds of gray and olive-drab sweaters, mufflers, socks, caps, mittens, helmets, stomach bands. Purl and knit, purl and knit, the Reading Club scarcely dropped a stitch as it exclaimed, and cooed and *ah'd* and *oh'd* over Celia Sprague Horner's ("Oh now, that's all right! Just call me Celia Sprague. Everybody does. I can't get used to it myself, after all the years I've been—Why just last week at Shield's, when I was giving my charge, I told the clerk—") new four-room apartment on Fifty-First Street—now more elegantly known as Hyde Park Boulevard. Curiously enough, Celia, who had been rather a haggard and faded fiancee of thirty-six, was now, by some magic process, a well-preserved and attractive young matron of thirty-six. A certain new assurance in her bearing; a blithe self-confidence in her conversation; a look in her eyes. The beloved woman.

"This is the bedroom. Weren't we lucky to get two windows! The sun just pours in all day—in fact, every room is sunny, even the kitchen." The Reading Club regarded the bedroom rather nervously. Celia Sprague had been one of them so long. And now . . . Two small French beds of dark mahogany, with a silken counterpane on each. "No, just you put your things right down on the beds, girls. It won't hurt the spreads a bit. Everything in this house is going to be used. That's what it's for." On the bed nearest the wall, a little rosy mound of lingerie pillows, all afroth with filet, and Irish, and eyelet embroidery and cut work. Celia had spent countless Reading Club afternoons on this handiwork. The rosy mound served no more practical purpose than the velvet and embroidered slippers that used to hang on the wall in her grandmother's day. Two silver-backed military brushes on the dull mahogany chest of drawers—"chiffo-robe," Celia would tell you. The Reading Club eyed them, smiling a little. Celia opened a closet door to dilate upon its roominess. A whole battalion of carefully hung trousers leaped out at them from the door rack. The Reading Club actually stepped back a little, startled. "Orville's clothes take up more room than mine, I always tell him. And everything just so. I never saw such a man!" She talked as one to whom men and their ways were an old, though amusing, story. "He's the neatest thing."

Out to the living room. "Oh, Celia this *is* sweet! I love your desk. It's so different." The room was the conventional bridal living room; a plum-colored velvet davenport, its back against a long, very retiring table whose silk-shaded lamp showed above the davenport's broad back like someone playing hide-and-seek behind a hedge. There were lamps, and lamps, and lamps—a forest of them. The bookshelves on either side of the gas log grate held a rather wistful library, the wedding gift "sets" of red and gold eked out with such schoolgirl fillers as the Pepper Books, Hans Brinker, and Louisa Alcott.

"A woman twice a week—one day to clean and one to wash and iron. Orville wants me to have a maid but I say what for? She'd have to sleep out and you never can depend—besides, it's just play. We have dinner out two or three nights—"

They were seated now, twittering, each with her knitting. A well-dressed, alert group of women, their figures trim in careful corsets, their hair, teeth, complexions showing daily care and attention. The long slim needles—ebony, amber, white—flew and flashed in the sunlight.

". . . This is my sixth sweater. I do 'em in my sleep."

". . . It's the heel that's the trick. Once I've passed that—"

". . . My brother says we'll never go in. We're a peace-loving nation, he says. We simply don't believe in war. Barbaric."

The handiwork of each was a complete character index. The bride was painstaking and bungling. Her knitting showed frequent bunches and lumps. Beck Schaefer's needles were swift, brilliant, and slovenly. Effie Case's sallow sensual face, her fragile waxen fingers, showed her distaste for the coarse fabric with which she was expertly occupied. Amy Stattler, the social service worker, knitted as though she found knitting restful. A plume of white showed startlingly in the soft black of her hair. Prim sheer white cuffs and collar finished her black gown at wrists and throat. Beck Schaefer, lolling on the other side of the room, her legs crossed to show plump gray silk calves, her feet in gray suede slippers ornamented with huge cut-steel buckles, seemed suddenly showy and even vulgar in comparison. She was, paradoxically, good-hearted and unpopular. This last because she was given to indulging in that dangerous pastime known as "being perfectly frank." Instinctively, you shrank when Beck Schaefer began a sentence with, "Now, I'm going to be perfectly frank with you." She was rarely perfectly frank with the men, however. She had a way of shaking a coquettish forefinger at the more elderly of these and saying, "Will you never grow up!" People said of Beck that she lighted up well in the evening.

Lottie Payson was knitting a sleeveless, olive-drab sweater. Row after row, inch after inch, it grew and lengthened, a flawless thing. Lottie hated knitting. As she bent over the work, her face wore a look for definition of which you were baffled. Not a sullen look nor brooding, but bound. That was it! Not free.

The talk at first was casual, uninteresting.

"Lot, is that the skirt to the suit Heller made you last winter? . . . His things are as good as the second season as they are the first. Keep their shape. And he certainly does know how to get a sleeve in. His shoulder line . . ."

". . . the minute I begin to gain I can tell by my waistbands—"

". . . if you purl three knit two—"

Beck Schaefer had ceased to knit. She was looking at the intent little group. She represented a certain thwarted type of unwed woman in whom the sensual is expressed, pitifully enough, in terms of silk and lacy lingerie; in innuendo; in a hungry roving eye; in a little droop at the corners of the mouth; in an over-generous display of plump arms, or bosom, or even knees. Beck's married friends often took her with them in the evenings as a welcome third to relieve the tedium of a wedded tête-à-tête. They found a vicarious pleasure in giving Beck a good time.

Suddenly, in the midst of the brittle chatter and laughter, was thrust the steel edge of Beck Schaefer's insolent voice, high, shrill.

"Well, Cele, tell us the truth: are you happy?"

The bride, startled, dropped a stitch, looked up, looked down, flushed. "Why yes, of course, you bad thing!"

"Ye-e-es, but I mean really happy. Come on now, give us the truth. Come on. Let's all tell the truth, for once. Are you really happy, Cele?"

The others laughed a little uncomfortably. Celia's face was red. Lottie's voice, rather deeper than most women's, and with a contralto note in it, was heard through the staccato sounds.

"Well, at least, Beck, she won't have to listen to her married friends saying, 'What's the matter with the men nowadays! What do they mean by letting a wonderful girl like you stay single, h'm?'"

They laughed at that. The atmosphere cleared a little. But Beck Schaefer's eyes were narrowed. "Now I'm looking for information. We're all friends here. We're all in the same boat—all except Celie, and she's climbed out of the boat and onto a raft. I want to know if it was worth the risk of changing. Here we all are—except Celie—failures. Any unmarried woman is a self-confessed failure."

A babel of protest. "How about Jane Addams! . . . Queen Elizabeth . . . Joan of Arc!"

"Queen Elizabeth was a hussy. Jane Addams is a saint. Joan of Arc—well—"

Lottie Payson looked up from her knitting. "Joan of Arc had the courage to live her own life, which is more than any of us have. She called it listening to the voices, but I suppose what she really wanted was to get away from home. If she had weakened and said, 'Ma, I know I oughtn't to leave you. You need me to tend the geese,' her mother might have been happier, and Joan would have lived a lot longer, but the history of France would have been different."

Beck Schaefer frankly cast aside her knitting, hugged one knee with her jewel-decked hands, and waited for the laughter to subside. "You're all afraid of the truth—*that's* the truth. I'm willing to come through—"

"Goodness, Beck, where do you pick up that low talk!"

"I'm willing to come through if the rest of you are. We're all such a lot of liars. We all know Cele there had to wait ten years for her Orville because he had to support two selfish sisters and an invalid mother; and even after the mother died, the two cats wouldn't go to live in two rooms as they should have, so that Celia and Orville could afford to be happy together. No! They wanted all the comforts he'd given them for years and so Celia—"

"Beck Schaefer I won't have—" the bride's face was scarlet. She bit her lip.

"Now I know you're going to say I'm a guest in your house and so you can't—and all that. But I'm not ashamed to say what you all know. That I'd be married today if it weren't for Sam Butler's mother who ought to have died fifteen years ago."

"Beck, you're crazy! Now stop it! If you're trying to be funny—"

"But I'm not. I'm trying to be serious. And you're all scared. Old Lady Butler—'Madame Butler' she insists on it! I could die!—is almost eighty-six, and Sam's crowding fifty. He's a smart businessman—splendid mind—a whole lot superior to mine; I know that. And yet when he's with her—which is most of his spare time—he's like a baby in her hands. She makes a slave of him. She hates any girl he looks at. She's as jealous as a maniac. She tells him all sorts of things about me. Lies. He has to go out of the house to telephone me. Once, I called him up at the house and he had to have the doctor in for her. That's the way she works it; tells him that if she dies it will be on his head, or something biblical like that. Imagine! In this day! And Sam pays every cent of the household expenses and dresses his mother like a duchess. Look at me and my mother. We're always going around to summer resorts together. Just two pals! M-m-m! 'Don't tell me you're the mother of a big girl like that! Why, you look like sisters!' Big girl—me! That ought to have five chil—not that I want 'em . . . now. But whenever I see one of those young mothers with her old daughter on a summer resort veranda, I want to go up to the tired old daughter and say, 'Listen, gal. Run away with the iceman, or join a circus, or take up bare-legged dancing—anything to express yourself before it's too late.'"

They had frankly stopped their knitting now. The bride's lip was caught nervously between her teeth. Even thus her face still wore a crooked and uncertain smile—the smile of the harassed hostess whose party had taken an unmanageable turn for the worse.

It was Amy Stattler who first took up her knitting again, her face serene. "How about those of us who are doing constructive work? I suppose we're failures too!" She straightened a white cuff primly. "I have my work."

"All right. Have it. But I notice that didn't keep you from wanting to marry that brainy little kike socialist over on the West Side; and it didn't keep your people from interfering and influencing you, and making your life so miserable that you hadn't the spirit left to—"

But Amy Stattler's face was so white and drawn and haggard—she was suddenly so old—that even Beck Schaefer's mad tongue ceased its cruel lashing for a moment; but only for a moment.

Lottie Payson rolled her work into a neat bundle and jabbed a needle through it. She sat forward, her fine dark eyebrows gathered into a frown of pain and decent disapproval.

"Beck, dear, you're causing a lot of needless discomfort. You're probably nervous today, or something—"

"I'm nothing of the kind. Makes me furious to be told I'm nervous when I'm merely trying to present some interesting truths."

"The truth isn't always helpful just because it hurts, you know."

"A little truth certainly wouldn't hurt you, Lottie Payson. I suppose it wouldn't help any, either, to acknowledge that you're a kind of unpaid nurse-companion to two old women who are eating you alive!—when your friend Judge Barton herself says that you've got a knack with delinquent girls that would make you invaluable on her staff. And now that you're well past thirty, I suppose your mother doesn't sometimes twit you with your maiden state, h'm? Don't tell *me!* As for Effie Case there—"

"Oh, my goodness Beck, spare muh! I've been hiding behind my knitting needle hoping you wouldn't see me. I know what's the matter with you. You've been sneaking up to those psychoanalysis lectures that old Beardsley's giving at Harper Hall. Shame on you! Nice young gal like you."

"Yes—and I know what's the matter with you, too, Effie. Why you're always lolling around at massage parlors and beauty specialists, sleeping away half the day in some stuffy old—"

With lightning quickness Effie Case wadded her work into a ball, lifted her arm, and hurled the tight bundle full at Beck Shaefer's head. It struck her in the face, rebounded, unrolled softly at her feet. Effie laughed her little irritating hysterical laugh. Beck Schaefer kicked the little heap of wool with a disdainful suede slipper.

"Well, I wouldn't have spilled all this if Cele had been willing to tell the truth. I said we were failures and we are because we've allowed some one or something to get the best of us—to pile up obstacles that we weren't big enough to tear down. We've all gone in for suffrage, and bleeding Belgium, and no petticoats, and uplift work, and we think we're modern. Well, we're not. We're a past generation. We're the unselfish softies. Watch the eighteen-year-olds. They've got the method. They're not afraid."

Lottie Payson laughed. Her face was all alight. "You ought to hear my niece Charley talk to me. You'd think I was eighteen and she thirty-two."

Beck Schaefer nodded vehemently. "I know those girls—the Charley kind. Scared to death of 'em. They're so sorry for me. And sort of contemptuous. Catch Charley marrying ten years too late, like Celia here, and missing all the thrill."

"I haven't!" cried the harassed Celia, in desperation. "I haven't! Orville's the grandest—"

"Of course he is. But you can't have any thrill about a man you've waited ten years for. Why won't you be honest!"

And suddenly the plump little silk-clad hostess stood up, her face working, her eyes bright with tears that would not wink away.

"All right, I'll tell you the truth."

"No, Cele—no!"

"Sit down, Celia. Beck's a little off today."

"Don't pay any attention to her. Waspish old girl, that's what—"

Beck regarded her victim between narrowed lids. "You're afraid."

"I'm not. Why should I be? Orville's the kindest man in the world. I thought so before I married him, and now I know it."

"Oh—kind!" scoffed Beck. "But what's that got to do with happiness? Happiness!"

"If you mean transports—no. Orville's fifty. He's set in his ways. I—I'm nearer thirty-seven than thirty-six. And at that I've only lied one year about my age—don't tell Orville. He's crazy about me. He just follows me around this flat like a—like a child. And I suppose that's really what he is to me now—a kind of big, wonderful child. I have to pamper him, and reason with him, and punish him, and coax, and love, and—tend him. I suppose ten years ago we'd—he'd—"

She stopped suddenly, with a little broken cry.

"Beck, you're a pig!" Lottie Payson's arms were about Celia. "In her own house, too, and her first party. Really you're too—"

A colored maid stood in the doorway—a South Side Hebe—her ebony face grotesque between the lacy cap and apron with which Celia had adorned her for the day. She made mysterious signals in Celia's direction.

"'F yo' ladies come in ev'thin's all—" She smiled; a sudden gash of white in the black. The tantalizing scent of freshly made coffee filled the little flat. They moved toward the dining room, talking, laughing, pretending.

"Oh, how pretty! . . . Cele! A real party! Candles and everything . . . What a stunning pattern—your silver. So plain and yet so rich . . . My word! Chicken salad! Bang goes another pound!"

Chicken salad indeed. Little hot flaky biscuits, too, bearing pools of golden butter within. Great black, oily, ripe olives. Salted almonds in silver dishes. Coffee with rich yellow cream. A whipped-cream covered icebox cake.

"I think we ought to spank Beck and send her from the table. She doesn't deserve this."

At five thirty, as they stood, hatted and ready for the street, chorusing their goodbyes in the little hallway, a key clicked in the lock. Orville!

They looked a little self-conscious.

"Well, well, well! I've run into a harem!"

"We haven't left a thing for your dinner. And it was so good."

"Not running away because I'm home, are you?" His round face beamed on them. He smelled of the fresh outdoors, and of strong cigars, and of a vaguely masculine something that was a blending of business office and barber's lotion and overcoat. The Reading Club scented it, sensitively. Celia came over to him swiftly, there in the little hall, and slid one arm about his great waist. A plump man, Orville, with a round, kindly, commonplace face. He patted her silken shoulder. She faced the Reading Club defiantly, triumphantly. "What have you girls been talking about, h'mm?" Orville laughed a tolerant chuckling laugh. "You girls. Settled the war yet?"

Beck Schaefer threw up her chin a little. "We've been talking about you, if you really want to know."

He reeled. "Oh, my God! Cele, did you take the old man's part?"

Celia moved away from him then a little, her face flushing. Constraint fell upon the group. Lottie Payson stepped over to him then and put one hand on his broad shoulder. "She didn't need to take your part, Orville. We were all for you."

"Except me!" shrilled Beck.

"Oh, you!" retorted Orville, heavily jocular. "You're jealous." He rubbed his chin ruefully. "Wait till I've shaved, Beck, and I'll give you a kiss to make you happy."

"Orville!" But Celia's bearing was again that of the successful matron—the fortunate beloved woman.

Beck Schaefer took the others home in her electric. Lottie, seized with a sudden distaste for the glittering enameled box elected to walk, though she knew it would mean being late.

"Figger?" Beck Schaefer asked, settling her own plump person in the driver's seat.

"Air," Lottie answered, not altogether truthfully; and drew a long breath. She turned away from the curb. The electric trundled richly off, its plate-glass windows filled with snugly tailored shoulders, furs, white gloves, vivid hats. Lottie held one hand high in farewell, palm out, as the glittering vehicle sped silently away, lurched fatly around a corner, and was gone.

Chapter VII

Lottie was late. Shockingly late. Even though, tardily conscience-stricken, she had deserted walk, sunset, and lake mist for a crowded and creeping Indiana Avenue car at Forty-Seventh Street, she was unforgivably late, according to her mother's stern standards. This was Friday night. Every Friday night, Henry, Belle, and Charley Kemp took dinner with the Paysons in the old house on Prairie Avenue. Every Friday night. No matter what else the Kemps might prefer to do on that night, they didn't do it. Each Friday morning, Belle Kemp would say to her husband, "This is Friday, Henry. We're having dinner at Mama's, remember."

"I might have to work tonight, Belle. We're taking inventory this week."

"Henry, you *know* how Mama feels about Friday dinner."

"M-hmph," Henry would grunt; and make a mental note about an extra supply of cigars for the evening. His favorite nightmare was that in which he might slap his left-hand vest pocket only to find it empty of cigars at eight thirty on a Friday evening at Mother Payson's. The weekly gathering was a tradition meaninglessly maintained. The two families saw quite enough of one another without it. Mrs. Payson was always "running over to Belle's for a minute." But these Friday dinners had started before Charley was born. Now they constituted an ironclad custom. Mrs. Payson called it "keeping up the family life."

Lottie, hospitable by nature, welcomed dinner guests; but she rather dreaded these Friday nights. There was so little of spontaneity about them, and so much of family frankness. Sometime during the evening, Belle would say, "Lottie, that dress is at least two inches too long. No wonder you never look smart. Your clothes are always so ladylike."

Lottie would look ruefully down her own length, a mischievous smile crinkling the corners of her eyes. "And I thought I looked so nice! Not chic, perhaps, but nice!" Her slim, well-shod feet, her neat silken ankles, her sensible skirt, her collars and cuffs or blouses and frills were always so admirably trim, so crisply fresh where freshness was required. Looking at her you had such confidence in the contents of her bureau drawers.

"Oh—nice! Who wants to look nice, nowadays!"

Mrs. Payson always insisted on talking business with her courteous but palpably irked son-in-law. Her views and methods were not his. When, in self-defense, he hinted this to her she resented it spiritedly with, "Well, I ran a successful business and supported a household before you had turned your first dollar, Henry Kemp. I'm not a fool."

"I should think not, Mother Payson. But things have changed since your time. Methods."

He knew his wife was tapping a meaningful foot; and that Charley's mischievous intelligent eyes held for him a message of quick understanding and sympathy. Great friends, he and Charley, though in rare moments of anger he had been known to speak of her to his wife as "your daughter."

Mrs. Payson was always ready with a suggestion whereby Henry Kemp could improve his business. Henry Kemp's business was that of importing china, glassware, and toys. Before the war he had been on the road to a more than substantial fortune. France, Italy, Bohemia, and Bavaria meant, to Henry Kemp, china from Limoges; glassware from Venice and Prague; toys from Nurnberg and Munich. But Zeppelin bombs, long-distance guns, and U-boats had shivered glass, china, and toys into fragments these two years past. The firm had turned to America for these products and found it sadly lacking. American dolls were wooden-faced; American china was heavy, blue-white; American glass-blowing was a trade, not an art. Henry Kemp hardly dared think of what another year of war would mean to him.

Lottie thought of these things as the Indiana Avenue car droned along. Her nerves were pushing it vainly. She'd be terribly late. And she had told Hulda that she'd be home in time to beat up the Roquefort dressing that Henry liked. Oh, well, dinner would be delayed a few minutes. Anyway, it was much better than dinner alone with Mother and Aunt Charlotte. Dinner alone with Mother and Aunt Charlotte had grown to be something of a horror. Lottie dreaded and feared the silence that settled down upon them. Sometimes she would realize that the three of them had sat almost through the meal without speaking. Lottie struggled to keep up the table talk. There was something sodden and deadly about these conversationless dinners. Lottie would try to chat brightly about the day's happenings. But when these happenings had just been participated in by all three, as was usually the case, the brightness of their recounting was likely to be considerably tarnished.

Silence. A sniff from Mrs. Payson. "That girl's making coffee again for herself. If she's had one cup today she's had ten. I get a pound of coffee every three days, on my word."

"They all do that, Mother—all the Swedish girls." Silence.

"The lamb's delicious, isn't it, Aunt Charlotte?"

Mrs. Payson disagreed before Aunt Charlotte could agree. "It's tough. I'm going to have a talk with that Gus tomorrow."

Silence.

The swinging door squeaking at the entrance of Hulda with a dish.

"No; not for me." Aunt Charlotte refusing another helping.

Silence again except for the sound of food being masticated. Great-Aunt Charlotte had an amazingly hearty appetite. Its revival had dated from the acquisition of the new teeth. Now, when Aunt Charlotte smiled, her withered lips drew away to disclose two flawless rows of blue-white teeth. They flashed, incongruously perfect, in contrast with the sere and wrinkled fabric of her face. There had been talk of drawing Mrs. Payson's teeth as a possible cure for her rheumatic condition, but she had fought the idea stubbornly.

"They make me tired. When they don't know what else to do they pull your teeth. They pull your teeth for everything from backache to diabetes. And when it doesn't help they say, 'Pardon me. My mistake,' and there you are without your teeth and with your aches. Fads!"

She had aired these views most freely during the distressing two weeks following Aunt Charlotte's dental operation, when soft, slippery shivery concoctions had had to be specially prepared for her in the Payson kitchen.

Lottie would scurry about in her mind for possible table talk. Anything—anything but this sodden silence.

"How would you two girls like to see a picture this evening, h'm? If we go early and get seats well toward the front, so that Aunt Charlotte can see, I'll drive you over to Forty-Third. I wonder what's at the Vista. I'll look in the paper. I hope Hulda saved the morning paper. Perhaps Belle will drive over and meet us for the first show—no, she can't either, I remember; she and Henry are having dinner north tonight. Most of Belle's friends are moving north. Do you know, I think—"

"The South Side's always been good enough for me and always will be. I don't see any sense in this fad for swarming over to the north shore. If they'd improve the acres and acres out Bryn Mawr way—"

Mrs. Payson was conversationally launched on South Side real estate. Lottie relaxed with relief.

Sometimes she fancied that she caught Great-Aunt Charlotte's misleadingly bright old eyes upon her with a look that was at once knowing and sympathetic. On one occasion, that surprising septuagenarian had startled and mystified Mrs. Payson and Lottie by the sudden and explosive utterance of the word, "Game-fish!" It was at dinner.

"What? What's that?" Mrs. Payson had exclaimed; and had looked about the table and then at her sister as though that thoughtful old lady had taken leave of her senses. "What!" They were undeniably having tongue with spinach.

"Game-fish!" repeated Aunt Charlotte Thrift, gazing straight at Lottie. Lottie waited, expectantly. "Your Grandfather Thrift had a saying: 'Only the game-fish swim upstream.'"

"Oh," said Lottie; and even colored a little, like a girl.

Mrs. Payson had regarded her elder sister pityingly. "Well, how did you happen to drag that in, Charlotte?" In a tone which meant, simply— "Childish! Senile!"

On this particular Friday night, the Kemps were indeed there as Lottie ran quickly up the front steps of the house on Prairie. The Kemp car, glossy and substantial, stood at the curb. Charley drove it with dashing expertness. At the thought of Charley, the anxious frown between Lottie Payson's fine brows smoothed itself out. Between aunt and niece existed an affection and understanding so strong, so deep, so fine as to be more than a mere blood bond. Certainly no such feeling had ever existed between Lottie and her sister Belle; and no such understanding united Belle and her daughter Charley.

The old walnut and glass front door slammed after Lottie. They were in the living room—the back parlor of Isaac Thrift's day.

"Lottie!" Mrs. Payson's voice; metallic.

"Yes."

"Well!"

Mrs. Payson was standing, facing the door as Lottie came in. She was using her cane this evening. She always walked with her cane when she was displeased with Lottie or Belle; some obscure reason existed for it. She reminded you of one of these terrifying old dowagers of the early English novels.

"Hello, Belle! Hello, Henry! Sorry I'm late."

Charley Kemp came over to Lottie in the doorway. Niece and aunt clasped hands—a strange, brief, close grip, like that between two men. No words.

"Late! I should think you are late. You knew this was Friday night."

"Now, now Mother." Henry Kemp had a man's dread of a scene. "Lottie's not a child. We've only been here a few minutes."

"She might as well be—" ignoring his second remark. "Tell Hulda we're all here. Call Aunt Charlotte."

"I'll just skip back and beat up the Roquefort dressing first. Hulda gets it so lumpy . . . Minute . . ."

"Lottie!" Mrs. Payson's voice was iron. "Lottie Payson, you change your good suit skirt first!"

Henry Kemp shouted. Mrs. Payson turned on him. "Well, what's funny about that!" He buried his face in the evening paper.

Belle's rather languid tones were heard now for the first time. "Lot, is that your winter hat you're still wearing?"

"Winter?—You don't mean to tell me I ought to be wearing a summer one! Already!" Lottie turned to go upstairs, dutifully. The suit skirt.

"Already! Why, it's March. Everybody—"

"I slipped and almost fell on the ice at the corner of Twenty-Ninth." Lottie retorted, laughingly, leaning over the balustrade.

"What early difference does that make!"

A rather grim snort here from Charley who was leaping up the stairs after her aunt, like a handsome young colt.

Lottie's room was at the rear of the second floor looking out upon the backyard. A drear enough plot of ground now, black with a winter's dregs of snow and ice. In the spring and summer, Lottie and Great-Aunt Charlotte coaxed it into a riot of color that defied even the South Side pall of factory smoke and Illinois Central cinders. A border of old-fashioned flowers ran along either side of the high board fence. There were daisies and marigolds, phlox and four-o'clocks, mignonette and verbenas, all polka-dotted with soot but defiantly lovely.

On her way up the stairs, Lottie had been unfastening coat and skirt with quick, sure fingers. She tossed the despised hat on the bed. Now, as Charley entered, her aunt stepped out of the suit skirt and stood in her knickers, a trim, well set-up figure, neatly articulated, hips flat and well back; bust low and firm; legs sturdy and serviceable, the calf high and not too prominent. She picked up the skirt, opened her closet door, snatched another skirt from the hook.

Mrs. Payson's voice from the foot of the stairway. "Lottie, put on a dress—the blue silk one. Ben Gartz is coming over. He telephoned."

"Oh *dear!*" said Lottie; hung the skirt again on its hook; took out the blue silk.

"Do you mean," demanded Charley, "that Grandma made an engagement for you without your permission?" (You ought to hear Charley on the subject of personal freedom.)

"Oh, well—Ben Gartz. He and Mother talk real estate, or business."

"But he comes to see you."

Charley had swung herself up to the footboard of the old walnut bed that Lottie herself had cream-enamelled. A slim, pliant young thing, this Charley, in her straight dark blue frock. She was so misleadingly pink and white and golden that you neglected to notice the fine brow, the chin squarish in spite of its soft curves, the rather deep-set eyes. From her perch Charley's long brown-silk legs swung friendlily. You saw that her stockings were rolled neatly and expertly just below knees as bare and hardy as a Highlander's. She eyed her aunt critically.

"Why in the world do you wear corsets, Lotta?" (This "Lotta" was a form of affectation and affection.)

"Keep the ol' turn in, of course. I'm no lithe young gazelle like you."

"Gained a little, haven't you—this winter?"

"I'm afraid I have." Lottie was stepping into the blue silk and dancing up and down as she pulled it on to keep from treading on it. "I don't get enough exercise, that's the trouble. That darned old electric!"

Charley faced her sternly from the footboard. "Well, if you will insist on being the Family Sacrifice. Making a 'bus line of yourself between here and the market—the market and the park—the park and our house. The city ought to make you pay for a franchise."

"Now—Charley—"

"Oh, you're disgusting, that's what you are, Lotta Payson! You practically never do anything you really want to do. You're so nobly self-sacrificing that it's sickening. It's a weakness. It's a vice."

"Yes ma'am," said Lotta gravely. "And if you kids don't do, say, and feel everything that comes into your heads, you go around screaming about inhibitions. If you new-generation youngsters don't yield to every impulse, you think you're being stunted."

"Well, I'd rather try things and find they're bad for me than never try them at all. Look at Aunt Charlotte!"

Lottie at the mirror was dabbing at her nose with a hasty powder-pad. She regarded Charley now, through the glass. "Aunt Charlotte's more—more understanding than Mother is."

"Yes, but it's been pretty expensive knowledge for her, I'll just bet. Some day I'm going to ask her why she never married. Great-Grandmother Thrift had a hand in it; you can tell that by looking at that picture of her in the hoops trimmed with bands of steel, or something. Gosh!"

"You wouldn't ask her, Charley!"

"I would too. She's probably dying to tell. Anybody likes to talk of their love affairs. I'm going to cultivate Aunt Charlotte, I am. Research work."

"Yes," retorted Lottie, brushing a bit of powder from the front of the blue silk, "do. And lend her your Havelock Ellis and Freud first, so that she'll at least have a chance to be shocked, poor dear. Otherwise she won't know what you're driving at."

"You're a worm," said Charley. She jumped off the footboard, took her aunt in her strong young arms and hugged her close. An unusual demonstration for Charley, a young woman who belonged to the modern school that despises sentiment and frowns upon weakly emotional display; to whom rebellion is a normal state; clear-eyed, remorseless, honest, fearless, terrifying; the first woman since Eve to tell the truth and face the consequences. Lottie, looking at her, often felt puerile and ineffectual. "You don't have half enough fun. And no self-expression. Come on and join a gymnastic dancing class. You'd make a dancer. Your legs are so nice and muscular. You'd love it. Wonderful exercise."

She sprang away suddenly and stood poised for a brief moment in what is known as first position in dancing. "Tour jeté—" she took two quick sliding steps, turned ,and leaped high and beautifully—"tour jeté"—and again, bringing up short of the wall, her breathing as regular as though she had not moved. "Try it."

Lottie eyed her enviously. Charley had had lessons in gymnastic dancing since the age of nine. Her work now was professional in finish, technique, and beauty. She could do Polish Csárdás in scarlet boots, or Psyche in wisps of pink chiffon and bare legs, or Papillons d'Amour in flesh tights, ballet skirts aflare and snug pink satin bodice, with equal ease and brilliance. She was always threatening to go on the stage and more than half meant it. Charley would no more have missed a performance of the latest Russian dancers, or of Pavlova, or the opera on special ballet nights than a student surgeon would miss an important clinic. In the earlier stages of her dancing career, her locomotion had been accomplished entirely by the use of the simpler basic forms of gymnastic dance steps. She had jeté-d and coupé-d and sauté-d and turné-d in and out of bed, on L train platforms, at school, on the street.

Lottie, regarding her niece now, said, "Looks easy, so I suppose it isn't. Let's see." She lifted her skirt tentatively. "Look out!"

"No, no! Don't touch your skirts. Arms free. Out. Like this. Hands are important in dancing. As important as feet. Now! Tour jeté! Higher! That's it. *Tou*—"

"Lot-*tie!*" Mrs. Payson's voice at the foot of the staircase.

"Oh, my goodness!" All the light, the fun, the eagerness that had radiated Lottie's face vanished now. She snatched a handkerchief from the dresser and made for the stairs, snapping a fastener at her waist as she went. "Call Aunt Charlotte for dinner," she flung over her shoulder at Charley.

"All right. Can I have a drop of your perfume on my hank?" (Not quite so grown up, after all.)

As she flew past the living room on her way to the pantry, Lottie heard her mother's decided tones a shade more decisive than usual as she administered advice to her patient son-in-law.

"Put in a sideline then, until business picks up. Importing won't improve until this war is over, that's sure. And when will it be over? Maybe years and years—"

Henry Kemp's amused, tolerant voice. "What would you suggest, Mother Payson? Collar buttons—shoestrings—suspenders. They're always needed."

"You may think you're very funny, but let me tell you, young man, if I were in your shoes today I'd—"

The pantry door swung after Lottie. As she ranged oil, vinegar, salt, pepper, paprika on the shelf before her and pressed the pungent cheese against the bottom and sides of the shallow bowl with her fork, her face had the bound look that it had worn earlier in the day at Celia's. She blended and beat the dressing into a smooth creamy consistency.

They were all at table when Great-Aunt Charlotte finally came down. She entered with a surprisingly quick light step. Tonight she looked younger than her sister in spite of ten years' seniority. Great-Aunt Charlotte was undeniably dressy—a late phase. At the age of seventy, she had announced her intention of getting no more new dresses. She had, she said, a closet full of black silks and more serviceable cloth dresses collected during the last ten or more years. "We Thrifts," she said, "aren't long livers. I'll make what I've got do."

The black silks and mohairs had stood the years bravely, but on Aunt Charlotte's seventy-fifth birthday, even the mohairs, most durable of fabrics, began to protest. The dull silks became shiny; the shiny mohairs grew dull. Cracks and splits showed in the hems and seams and folds of the taffetas. Great-Aunt Charlotte at three-score ten and five had looked them over, sniffed, and had cast them off as an embryo butterfly casts off its chrysalis. She took a new lease on life, ordered a complete set of dresses that included a figured foulard, sent her ancient and massive pieces of family jewelry to be cleaned, and went shopping with Lottie for a hat instead of the bonnet to which she had so long clung.

She looked quite the grande dame as she entered the dining room now, in one of the more frivolous black silks, her white hair crimped, a great old-fashioned cabachon gold and diamond brooch fastening the lace at her breast, a band of black velvet ribbon about her neck, her eyes brightly interested beneath the strongly marked black brows. Belle came over and dutifully kissed one withered old cheek. She and Aunt Charlotte had never been close. Henry patted her shoulder as he pulled out her chair. Charley gave her a quick hug to which Great-Aunt Charlotte said, "Ouch!"—but smiled. "Dear me, I haven't kept you waiting!"

"You know you have," retorted Mrs. Carrie Payson; and dipped her spoon in the plate of steaming golden fragrant soup before her. Whereupon Great-Aunt Charlotte winked at Henry Kemp.

The Friday night dinner was always a good meal, though what is known as "plain." Soup, roast, a vegetable, salad, dessert.

"Well," said Mrs. Carrie Payson, "and how've you all been? I suppose I'd never see you if it weren't for Friday nights."

Charley looked up quickly. "Oh, Gran, I'm sorry, but I shan't be able to come to dinner any more on Fridays."

"Why not?"

"My dancing class."

Mrs. Payson laid down her spoon and sat back, terribly composed. "Dancing class! You can change your dancing class to some other night, I suppose? You know very well this is the only night possible for the family. Hulda's out Thursdays; your father and mother play bridge on Wednesdays; Lottie—"

"Yes, I know. But there's no other night?'

"You must dance, I suppose?" This Charley took to be a purely rhetorical question. As well say to her, "You must breathe, I suppose?" Mrs. Payson turned to her daughter Belle. "This is with your permission?"

Belle nibbled celery tranquilly. "We talked it over. But Charley makes her own decisions in matters like this you know, Mother."

As with one accord, Great-Aunt Charlotte and Aunt Lottie turned and regarded Charley. A certain awe was in their faces, unknown to them.

"But why exactly Friday night?" persisted Mrs. Payson. "Lottie, ring." Lottie rang, obediently. Hulda entered.

"That was mighty good soup, Mother," said Henry Kemp. Mrs. Payson refused to be mollified. Ignored the compliment. "Why exactly Friday night, if you please?"

Charley wiggled a little with pleasure. "I hoped you'd ask me that. I'm dying to talk about it. Oo! Roast chickens! All brown and crackly! Well, you see, my actual classwork in merchandising and business efficiency will be about finished at the end of the month. After that, the university places you, you know."

"Places you!"

Mrs. Carrie Payson had always had an uneasy feeling about her granddaughter's choice of a career. That she would have a career Charley never for a moment allowed them to doubt. She never called it a career. She spoke of it as "a job." In range, her choice swung from professional dancing (for which she was technically and temperamentally fitted) to literature (for the creating of which she had no talent). Between these widely divergent points, she paused briefly to consider the fascinations of professions such as licensed aviatrix (she had never flown); private secretary to a millionaire magnate (again the influence of the matinee); woman tennis champion (she held her own in a game against the average male player but stuck her tongue between her teeth when she served); and Influence for Good or Evil (by which she meant vaguely something in the Madame de Staël and general salon line). She had never expressed a desire to be a nurse.

In the middle of her University of Chicago career, this young paradox made up of steel and velvet, of ruthlessness and charm, had announced, to the surprise of her family and friends, her intention of going in for the university's newest course—that in which young women were trained to occupy executive positions in retail mercantile establishments. Quite suddenly, western coeducational universities and eastern colleges for women—Vassar, Smith, Wellesley, Bryn Mawr—were training girl students for business executive positions. Salaries of ten—twenty—twenty-five thousand a year were predicted, together with revolutionary changes in the conduct of such business. Until now such positions had been occupied, for the most part, by women who had worked their way up painfully, hand over hand, from a cash or stock girl's job through a clerkship to department head; thence, perhaps, to the position of buyer and, later, office executive. On the way they acquired much knowledge of human nature and business finesse, but it was a matter of many years. These were, usually, shrewd, hardworking, successful women; but limited and often devoid of education other than that gained by practical experience. This new course would introduce into business the trained young woman of college education. Business was to be a profession, not a rough-and-tumble game.

Charley's grandmother looked on this choice of career with mingled gratification and disapproval. Plainly it was the Isaac Thrift in Charley asserting itself. But a Thrift—a woman Thrift—in a shop!—even though ultimately occupying a mahogany office, directing large affairs, and controlling battalions of push buttons and secretaries. Was it ladylike? Was it quite nice? What would the South Side say?

So, then—"Places you?" Mrs. Payson had echoed uneasily, at dinner.

"For beginning practical experience. We learn the business from the ground up as an engineer does, or an intern. I've just heard today they've placed me at Shield's, in the blouses. I'm to start Monday."

"You don't say!" exclaimed Henry Kemp, at once amused and pleased. He could not resist treating Charley and her job as a rare joke. "Saleswoman, I suppose, to begin with. Clerk, h'm? Say, Charley, I'm coming in and ask about—"

"Clerk?" repeated Mrs. Payson, almost feebly for her. She saw herself sliding around corners and fleeing up aisles to avoid Shield's blouse section so that her grandchild need not approach her with a softly insinuating "Is there something, Madam?"

"Saleswoman! I should say not!" Charley grinned at their ignorance. "No—no gravy, thanks—" to Hulda at her elbow. Charley ate like an athlete in training, avoiding gravies, pastries, sweets. Her skin was a rose petal. "I'm to start in Monday as stock girl—if I'm in luck."

Mrs. Payson pushed her plate aside sharply as Henry Kemp threw back his head and roared. "Belle! Henry, stop that laughing! It's no laughing matter. No grandchild of mine is going to be allowed to run up and down Shield's blouse department as a stock girl. The idea! Stock—"

"Now, now Mother Payson," interrupted Henry, soothingly, as he supposed, "you didn't expect them to start Charley in as foreign buyer did you?"

Belle raised her eyebrows together with her voice. "The thing Charley's doing is considered very smart nowadays, Mother. That Emery girl who has just finished at Vassar is in the veilings at Farson's, and if ever there was a patrician-looking girl—Henry dear, please don't take another helping of potatoes. You told me to stop you if you tried. Well, then, have some more chicken. That won't hurt your waistline."

"Why can't girls stay home?" Mrs. Payson demanded. "It's all very well if you have to go out into the world, as I did. I was unfortunate and I had the strength to meet my trial. But when there's no rhyme nor reason for it, I do declare! Surely there's enough for you at home. Look at Lottie! What would I do without her!"

Lottie smiled up at her mother then. It was not often that Mrs. Payson unbent in her public praise.

Great-Aunt Charlotte, taking no part in the discussion, had eaten every morsel on her plate down to the last crumb of sage dressing. Now she looked up, blinking brightly at Charley. She put her question.

"Suppose, after you've tried it, with your education, and the time, and money you've spent on it, and all, you find you don't like it, Charley—then what? H'm? What then?"

"If I'm quite sure I don't like it, I'll stop it and do something else," replied Charley.

Great-Aunt Charlotte leaned back in her chair with a sigh of satisfaction. It was as though she found a vicarious relaxation and a sense of ease in Charley's freedom. She beamed upon the table. "It's a great age," she announced, "this century. If I'd died at seventy, as I planned, I'd be madder'n a hornet now to think of all I'd missed." She giggled a little falsetto note. "I've a good mind to step out and get a job myself."

"Don't be childish, Charlotte!"—sister Carrie, of course.

Charley leaped to her defense. "I'd get one this minute if I were you, Aunt Charlotte, yes I would. If you feel like it. Look at Mother! Always having massages and taking gentle walks in the park, and going to concerts, when there's the whole world to wallop."

Belle was not above a certain humorous argument. "I consider that I've walloped my world, Miss Kemp. I've married; I manage a household; I've produced a—a family."

"Gussie runs your household, and you know it. Being married to Father isn't a career—it's a recreation. And as for having produced a family: one child isn't a family; it's a crime. I'm going to marry at twenty, have five children one right after the other—"

The inevitable "Charley!" from Mrs. Carrie Payson.

"—and handle my job besides. See if I don't."

"Why exactly five?" inquired Henry Kemp.

"Well, four is such a silly number; too tidy. And six is too many. That's half a dozen. Five's just nice. I like odd numbers. Three would be too risky in case anything should happen to one of them, and seven—"

"Oh, my God!" from Henry Kemp before he went off into roars again.

"I never heard such talk!" Mrs. Payson almost shouted. "When I was your age, I'd have been sent from the room for even listening to such conversation, much less—"

"That's where they were wrong," Charley went on; and she was so much in earnest that one could not call her pert. "Look at Lottie! The maternal type absolutely, or I don't know my philosophy and biology. That's what makes her so corking in the Girls' Court work that she never has time to do—" she stopped at a sudden recollection. "Oh, Lotta, Gussie's having trouble with that sister of hers again."

Gussie was the Kemps' cook, and a pearl. Even Mrs. Payson was hard put to it to find a flaw in her conduct of the household. But she interposed hastily here with her weekly question, Hulda being safely out of the room.

"Is your Gussie out tonight, Belle?"

"She was still there when we left—poor child."

"And why 'poor child!' You treat her like a princess. No washing, and a woman to clean. I don't see what she does all day long. And why can't she go home for her dinner when you're out? You're always getting her extra pork chops and things."

Henry Kemp wagged his head. "She's the best little cook we ever had, Gussie is. Neat and pleasant. Has my breakfast on the table, hot, the minute I sit down. Coffee's always hot. Bacon's always crisp without being burned. Now most girls—"

"Henry, she was crying in her room when I left the house tonight. Charley told me." A little worried frown marred the usual serenity of Mrs. Kemp's forehead.

"Crying, was she?"

"That sister of hers again," explained Charley. "And Gussie's got so much pride. Jennie—that's the sister—ran away from home. Took some money, I think. It's a terrible family. Her case comes up in Judge Barton's court tomorrow."

Lottie nodded understandingly. She and Gussie had had many unburdening talks in the Kemp kitchen. "I think Judge Barton could straighten things out for Gussie. That sister, anyway."

Belle grasped at that eagerly. "Oh, Lottie, if she could. Gussie's mind isn't on her work. And I've got that luncheon next Tuesday."

Lottie ranged it all swiftly. "I'll tell you what. I'll come over to your house tomorrow morning, early, and talk with Gussie. Tomorrow's the last day of the week and the Girls' Court doesn't convene again until Tuesday. Perhaps if I speak for this Jennie when her case comes up tomorrow—"

"Oh, dear, Tuesday wouldn't do!" from Belle.

"Yes, I know. So I'll see Gussie tomorrow, and then go right down to Judge Barton's before the session opens. Gussie can come with me, if you want her to, or—"

Mrs. Payson's voice, hard, high, interrupted. "Not tomorrow, Lottie. It's my day for collecting the rents. You know that perfectly well because I spoke of it this morning. And all my Sunday marketing to do, too. It's Saturday."

Lottie fingered her spoon nervously. An added color crept into her cheeks. "I'll be back by eleven-thirty—twelve at the latest. Judge Barton will see me first, I know. We'll drive over to collect the rents as soon as I get back and then market on the way home."

"After everything's picked over on Saturday afternoon!"

Lottie looked down at her plate. Her hands were clasped in her lap, beneath the tablecloth, but there was a telltale tenseness about her arms, a rigidity about her whole body. "I thought just this once, Mother, you wouldn't mind. Gussie—"

"Are the affairs of Belle's kitchen maid more important than your own mother's! Are they?"

Lottie looked up, slowly. It was as though some force impelled her. Her eyes met Charley's, intent on her. Her glance went from them to Aunt Charlotte—Aunt Charlotte, a spare little figure, erect in her chair—and Aunt Charlotte's eyes were on her too, intent. Those two pairs of eyes seemed to will her to utter that which she now found herself saying to her own horror:

"Why, yes, Mother, I think they are in this case. Yes."

Chapter VIII

The family rose from the table and moved into the living room, a little constraint upon them. Mrs. Payson stayed behind to give directions to Hulda. Hulda, who dined in a heap off the end of the kitchen table, was rarely allowed to consume her meal in peace. Between Hulda and Mrs. Payson there was waged the unending battle of the coffeepot. After breakfast, luncheon, dinner, the mistress of the house would go into the kitchen, take the coffeepot off the gas stove and peer into its dark depths.

"My goodness, Hulda, you've made enough coffee for a regiment! That's wasteful. It'll only have to be thrown away."

"Ay drink him."

"You can't drink all this, girl. You'll be sick. You drink altogether too much coffee. Coffee makes you nervous, don't you know that? Yellow!"

Hulda munched a piece of bread and took another long gulp of her beloved beverage, her capable red hand wrapped fondly about the steaming cup. "Naw, Mrs. Pay-son. My grandfather he was drink twenty cup a day in old country."

"Yes, but what happened to him? He'd be living today—"

"He ban living today. Ninety years and red cheeks like apples."

In the living room, Lottie took up her knitting again. The front parlor was unlighted but Charley went in and sat down at the old piano. She did not play particularly well and she had no voice. Lottie, knitting as she went, walked into the dim front room and sat down near Charley at the piano. Charley did not turn her head.

"That you, Lotta?" She went on playing.

"Yes, dear."

A little silence. "Now you stick to it!"

"I will."

In the living room, Henry Kemp leaned over and kissed his wife. Straightening, he took a cigar out of his vest pocket and eyed it lovingly. He pressed its resilient oily black sides with a tender thumb and finger. He lighted it, took a deep pull at it, exhaled with a long-drawn *pf-f-f,* and closed his eyes for a moment, a little sigh of content breathing from him. He glanced, then, at his watch. Only 7:50. Good Lord! He strolled over to Great-Aunt Charlotte who was seated near the front parlor doorway and the music. Her head was cocked. He patted her black-silk shoulder, genially.

"That cigar smells good, Henry."

"Good cigar, Aunt Charlotte." He rolled it between his lips.

Aunt Charlotte's fingers tapped the arm of her chair. She waggled her head a little in time with the music. "It's nice to have something that smells like a man in the house."

"You vamp!" shouted Henry Kemp. He came over to Belle again who was seated in the most gracious chair the room boasted, doing nothing with a really charming effect. "Say, listen, Belle, we don't have to stay so very late this evening, do we? I'm all tired out. I worked like a horse today downtown."

Before Belle could answer, Charley called in from the other room, "Oh, Mother, I'm going to be called for, you know."

Belle raised her voice slightly. "The poet?"

"Yes."

"In the flivver?" Her father's question.

"Yes. Now roar, Dad, you silly old thing. Imagine a girl like me being cursed with a father who thinks poets and flivvers are funny. If you'd ever tried to manage either of them, you'd know there's nothing comic about them."

"There is too," contended Henry Kemp. "Either one of 'em's funny; and the combination's killing. The modern—uh—what's this horse the poets are supposed to ride?"

His wife supplied the classicism, "Pegasus."

"Pegasus!" he called in to Charley.

"You stick to your importing, Henry," retorted his gay young daughter, "and leave the book larnin' to Mother and me."

Henry Kemp, suddenly serious, strolled over to his wife again. He lowered his voice. "About nine o'clock, anyway, can't we? Eh, Belle?"

"Not before nine thirty. You know how Mama—"

Henry sighed, resignedly. He stood a moment, balancing from heel to toe. "Lot's a peach, that's what she is," he confided irrelevantly to his wife. He puffed a moment in silence, his eyes squinting up through the smoke. "And it's a damn shame, that's what. Damn shame."

He picked up the discarded newspaper and seated himself in the buffalo chair. The buffalo chair was a hideous monstrosity whose arms, back, and sides were made of buffalo horns ingeniously put together. Fortunately, their tips curved away from the sitter. The chair had been presented to old Isaac Thrift by some lodge or real estate board or society. It was known to the family as Ole Bull. The women never sat in it and always warned feminine callers away from it. Its horns had a disastrous way with flounces, ruffles, plackets, frills. It was one of those household encumbrances which common sense tells you to cast off at every housecleaning and sentiment bids you retain. Thus far, sentiment had triumphed on Prairie Avenue. Once you resigned yourself to him, Ole Bull was unexpectedly comfortable. Here Henry Kemp sat reading, smoking, glancing up over the top of his paper at the women folk of his family—at his wife, his daughter, his mother-in-law, thoughtfully through the soothing haze of his cigar. He pondered on many things during these family Friday evenings, did Henry Kemp. And said little.

The conversation was the intimate, frank, often brutal talk common to families whose members see each other too often and know one another too well. Belle to Lottie, for example:

"Oh, why don't you get something a little different! You've been wearing blue for ten years."

"Yes, but it's so practical; and it always looks well."

"Cut loose and be impractical for a change. They're going to wear a lot of that fawn color this spring—sand, I think they call it . . . How did Mrs. Hines get along with that old taffeta she made over for you?"

"I don't know; it kind of draws across the front, and the sleeves—I have to remember to keep my arms down. I wish you'd look at it."

"You'd have to put it on. How can I tell?"

"Too much trouble."

"Well, then, go on looking frumpy. These home dressmakers!"

Lottie did not look frumpy, as a matter of fact. No one with a figure so vigorous and erect, a back so straight, a head so well set on its fine column of a throat, a habit of such fastidious cleanliness of person, could be frumpy. But she resorted to few feminine wiles of clothing, as of speech or manner. Lottie's laces, and silks and fine white garments, like her dear secret thoughts and fancies, were worn hidden, by the world unsuspected. All the dearer to Lottie for that.

Tonight, Belle sat dangling her slipper at the end of her toe, her knees crossed. She had a small slim foot and a trick of shooting her pump loose at the heel so that it hung half on, half off as she waggled her foot in its fine silk stocking. Henry Kemp had found it an entrancing trick when first they were married. He found it less fascinating now, after twenty years. Sometimes the slipper dropped—accidentally. "Henry, dear, my slipper." Well, even the prince must have remonstrated with Cinderella if she made a practice of the slipper-dropping business after their marriage. Twenty years after.

Belle, dangling the slipper, called in now to Lottie: "Nice party, Lot?"

"Oh, nice enough."

"Who was there?"

"The girls. You know."

"Is her flat pretty? What did she serve?"

"Chicken salad with aspic—hot biscuits—olives—a cake—"

"Really!"

"Oh, yes. A party."

"Is she happy with her Orville—now that she's waited ten years for him?"

"Yes—at least, she was until this afternoon."

"Until!—Oh, come in here, Lottie. I can't shout at you like—"

Lottie, knitting as she walked, came back into the living room. Charley followed her after a moment; came over to her father, perched herself on a slippery arm of Ole Bull and leaned back, her shoulder against his.

Lottie stood, still knitting. She smiled a little. "Beck Schaefer was on one of her reckless rampages. She teased Celia until Celia cried."

"About what? Teased her about what? Pretty kind of guest, I must say."

"Oh, marriage. Marriage and happiness and—she said every unmarried woman was a failure."

"That shouldn't have bothered Celia. She's married, safe enough. She certainly had Beck there."

"Beck intimated that Orville wasn't worth waiting ten years for."

"Most men aren't," spoke up Great-Aunt Charlotte from her corner, "and their wives don't know it until after they've been married ten years; and then it's too late. Celia had plenty of time to find it out first and she married him anyway. That's better. She'll be happy with him."

"Charlotte Thrift!" called Charley, through the laughter. "You *couldn't* be so wise just living to be seventy-four. Oh, you hoopskirted gals weren't so prunes-and-prismy. You've had a past. I'm sure of it."

"How d'you suppose I could have faced the future all these years if I hadn't had!" retorted Aunt Charlotte.

"That Schaefer girl had better go slow." Henry Kemp blew a whole flock of smoke rings for Charley's edification at which Charley, unedified, announced that she could blow better rings than any of these in size, number, and velocity with a despised gold-tipped perfumed cigarette and cold sore on the upper lip. "Some day," he predicted, "some day she'll run away with a bellhop. Just the type."

"Who's run away with a bellhop?" Mrs. Payson chose this unfortunate moment to enter the living room after her kitchen conference.

"Beck Schaefer," said Charley, mischievously.

You should have seen, then, the quick glance of terror that Mrs. Payson darted at Lottie. You might almost have thought that Lottie had been the one who had succumbed to the lure of youth in blue suit and brass buttons.

"Beck! She hasn't! She didn't! Beck Schaefer!"

"No, Mama, she hasn't. Henry just thinks she will—in time."

Mrs. Payson turned on the overhead electric lights (they had been sitting in the soothing twilight of the lamps), signified that Charley was to hand her the evening paper that lay at the side of Henry's chair, and seated herself in an ancient rocker—the only rocker the house contained. It squeaked. She rocked. Glaring lights, rustling paper, squeaking chair.

The comfort of the room, of the group, was dispelled.

"I'd like to know why!" demanded Mrs. Payson, turning to the stock market page. "A good family. Money. And Beck Schaefer's a fine-looking girl."

One thought flashed through the minds of all of them. The others looked at Lottie and left the thought unspoken. Lottie herself put it into words then. Bluntly: "She isn't a girl, Mother. She's thirty-five."

"Thirty-five's just a nice age." The paper crackled as she passed to the real estate transfers. "If this keeps on I'd like to know what they're going to do about building. Material's so high now it's prohibitive." More rustling of paper and squeaking of chair. "Beck Schaefer's got her mother to look out for her."

"That's why," said Aunt Charlotte, suddenly. Lottie looked at her, knitting needles poised a moment.

"Why what?" asked Mrs. Payson. Then, as her sister Charlotte did not answer, "You don't even know what we're talking about, Charlotte. Sit there in the corner half asleep."

"It's you who're asleep," snapped Great-Aunt Charlotte tartly. "With your eyes wide open."

When the doorbell rang then, opportunely, they all sighed a little, whether in relief or disappointment.

"I'll go," said Lottie. So it was she who opened the door to admit Ben Gartz.

You heard him as Lottie opened the door. "Hello! Well, Lottie! How's every little thing with you? . . . *That's* good! You cer'nly look it."

Ben Gartz came into the living room, rubbing his hands and smiling genially. A genial man, Ben, and yet you did not warm yourself at his geniality. A little too anxious, he was. Not quite spruce. Looking his forty-nine years. A pale and mackerel eye in a rubicund countenance, had Ben

Gartz. Combed his thinning hair in careful wisps across the top of his head to hide the spreading bald spot. The kind of man who says, "H'are you, sir!" on meeting you, and offers you a cigar at once; who sits in the smokers of Pullmans; who speaks of children always as "Kiddies." He toed in a little as he walked. A plumpish man and yet with an oddly shrunken look about him somehow. The flame had pretty well died out in him. He and his kind fought a little shy of what they called "the old girls." But he was undoubtedly attracted to Lottie. Ben Gartz had been a good son to his mother. She had regarded every unmarried woman as her possible rival. She always had said, "Ben ought to get married, I'd like to see him settled." But it was her one horror. The South Side, after her death, said as one voice, "Well, Ben, you certainly have nothing to reproach yourself with. You were a wonderful son to her." And the South Side was right.

Once Mrs. Payson said of him, "He's a good boy."

Aunt Charlotte had cocked an eye. "He's uninteresting enough to be good. But I don't know. He looks to me as if he was just waiting for a chance to be bad." She had caught in Ben Gartz's face a certain wistfulness—a something unfulfilled—that her worldly-wise sister had mistaken for mildness.

Henry Kemp brightened at the visitor's entrance, as well he might in this roomful of women. "Well, Ben, glad to see you. Come into the harem."

Ben shook hands with Mrs. Payson, with Aunt Charlotte, with Belle, with Charley. "My, my look at this kiddy! Why, she's a young lady! Better look out, Miss Lottie; you'll be letting your little niece get ahead of you." Shook hands with Henry Kemp. Out came the cigar.

"No, no!" protested Henry. "You've got to smoke one of mine." They exchanged cigars, eyed them, tucked them in vest pockets and lighted one of their own, according to the solemn and ridiculous ritual of men. Ben

Gartz settled back in a chair and crossed his chubby knees. "This is mighty nice, let me tell you, for an old batch living in a hotel room. The family circle, like this. Mighty nice." He glanced at Lottie. He admired Lottie with an admiration that had in it something of fear, so he always assumed a boisterous bluffness with her. Sometimes he felt, vaguely, that she was laughing at him. But she wasn't. She was sorry for him. He was to her as obvious as a child to its mother.

"You might have come for dinner," Lottie said, kindly, "if I'd known, earlier. The folks had dinner here."

"Oh, no!" protested Ben as though the invitation were now being tendered. "I couldn't think of troubling you. Mighty nice of you, though, to think of me. Maybe some other time—"

Mrs. Carrie Payson said nothing. She did not issue dinner invitations thus, helter-skelter. She did not look displeased, though.

"Well, how's business?"

Great-Aunt Charlotte made a little clucking sound between tongue and palate and prepared to drift from the room. She had a knack of drifting out of the room—evaporating, almost. You looked up, suddenly, and she was not there. Outside, there sounded the sharp bleat of a motor horn—a one-lung motor horn. Two short staccato blasts followed by a long one. A signal, certainly.

"The poet, Charley," said Henry Kemp; and laughed his big kind laugh.

"Ask him in," Mrs. Payson said. "Aren't you going to ask your young man to come in?" Charley was preparing to go.

"What for?" she asked now.

"To meet the family. Unless you're ashamed of him. When I was a girl—"

Great-Aunt Charlotte sat back again, waiting.

"All right," said Charley. "He'll hate it." She walked across the room, smiling; opened the door and called out to the bleat in the blackness:

"Come on in!"

"What for?"

"Meet the family."

"Oh, say, listen—"

You heard them talking and giggling a little together in the hall. Then they came down the hall and into the living room, these two young things; these two beautiful young things. And suddenly the others in the room felt old—old and fat and futile and done with life. The two stood there in the doorway a moment. The very texture of their skin; the vitality of their vigorous hair as it sprang away in a fine line from their foreheads; the liquid blue-white clearness of the eyeball; the poise of their slim bodies—was youth.

She was tall but he was taller. His hair had a warmer glint; it was almost red. In certain lights it was red. The faun type. Ears a little pointed. Contemptuous of systems, you could see that; metric or rhythmic. A good game of tennis, probably. Loathing golf. So graceful as to seem almost slouchy. Lean, composed, self-possessed. White flannel trousers for some athletic reason (indoor tennis, perhaps, at the gym); a loose greatcoat buttoned over what seemed to be no shirt at all. Certainly not a costume for a Chicago March night. He wore it with a full dress air. And yet a certain lovable shyness.

Charley waved a hand in a gesture that somehow united him with the room—the room full of eyes critical, amused, appraising, speculative, disapproving.

"Mother and Dad you know, of course. Grandmother Payson, my Aunt Lottie—Lotta for short. Mr. Ben Gartz . . . Oh, forgive me, Aunt Charlotte, I thought you'd gone. There in the corner—my Great-Aunt

Charlotte Thrift . . . This is Jesse Dick."

It is a terrible thing to see an old woman blush. The swift, dull, almost thick red surged painfully to Great-Aunt Charlotte's face now, and her eyes were suddenly wide and dark, like a young girl's, startled. Then the red faded and left her face chalky, ghastly. It was as though a relentless hand had wrapped iron fingers around her heart and squeezed it and wrenched it once—tight and hard!—and then relaxed its grip. She peered at the boy standing there in the doorway; peered at him with dim old eyes that tried to pierce the veil of years and years and years. The others were talking. Charley had got her wraps from the hall and was getting into her galoshes. This cumbersome and disfiguring footgear had this winter become the fad among university coeds and South Side flappers. They wore galoshes on stormy days and fair. The craze had started during a blizzardy week in January. It was considered chic to leave the two top clasps or the two lower clasps open and flapping. The origin of this could readily be traced to breathless coeds late for classes. All young and feminine Hyde Park now clumped along the streets, slim silken shins ending grotesquely in thick black felt and rubber.

Jesse Dick stooped now to assist in the clasping of Charley's galoshes. He was down on one knee. Charley, teetering a little, put one hand on his head to preserve her balance. He looked up at her, smiling; she looked down at him, smiling. Almost sixty years of life swept back over Great-Aunt Charlotte Thrift and left her eighteen again; eighteen, and hoopskirted in her second-best merino, with a green-velvet bonnet and a frill of blond lace, and little muddied boots and white stockings.

She could not resist the force that impelled her now. She got up from her corner and came over to them. The talk went on in the living room. They did not notice her.

"I knew your—I knew a Jesse Dick," she said, "years ago."

The boy stood up. "Yes? Did you?"

"He died in the Civil War. At Donelson. He was killed—at Donelson."

The boy spatted his hands together a little, briskly, to rid them of a bit of dried mud that had clung to the galoshes. "That must have been my grandfather's brother," he said politely. "I've heard them speak of him."

He had heard them speak of him. Charlotte Thrift, with seventy-four years of a ruined life heavy upon her, looked at him. He had heard them speak of him. "Pomroy Dick? Your grandfather? Pomroy Dick?"

"Why, yes! Yes. Did you know him, too? He wasn't—we Dicks aren't—How did you happen to know him?"

"I didn't know your grandfather, Pomroy Dick," said Great-Aunt Charlotte, and smiled so that the withered lips drew away from the blue-white, even teeth. "It was Jesse I knew." She looked up at him. "Jesse Dick."

Charley leaned over and pressed her fresh dewy young lips to the parchment cheek. "Now isn't that interesting! Goodbye dear." She stopped and flashed a mischievous glance at the boy. "Was he a poet too, Aunt Charlotte?"

"Yes."

Jesse Dick turned his head quickly at that. "He was? I didn't know that. Are you sure? No one in our family ever said—"

"I'm sure," Great-Aunt Charlotte Thrift said, quietly. "Families don't always know. About each other, I mean."

"No, indeed," both he and Charley agreed, politely. They were anxious to be off. They were off, with a goodbye to the group in the living room. Charlotte Thrift turned to go upstairs. "Jesse Dick—" she heard from the room where the others sat. "Dick—" She turned and came back swiftly, and seated herself again in the dim corner. Henry Kemp was speaking, his face all agrin.

"She's a case, that kid. We never know. Some weeks it's the son of one of the professors, with horn glasses and no hat. And then it'll be a millionaire youngster she's met at a dance, and the place will be cluttered up with his Stutz and his orchids and Plow's candy for awhile. Now it's this young Dick."

Ben Gartz waggled his head. "These youngsters!" he remarked, meaninglessly. "These youngsters!"

But Mrs. Carrie Payson spoke with meaning. "Who is he? Dick? I've never heard the name. Who're his folks?"

An uneasy rustle from Belle. "He is a poet," she said. "Quite a good one, too. Some of his stuff is really—"

"Who're his folks?" demanded Mrs. Carrie Payson. "They're not poets too, are they?"

Henry Kemp's big laugh burst out again, then, in spite of Belle's warning rustle. "His father's 'Delicatessen Dick,' over on Fifty-Third. We get all our cold cuts there, and the most wonderful pickled herring. They say they're put up in some special way from a recipe that's been in the family for years. Holland Dutch, I guess—"

But Mrs. Carrie Payson had heard enough. "Well, I must say, Belle, you're overdoing this freedom business with Charley. 'Delicatessen Dick!' I suppose the poet sells the herrings over the counter? I suppose he gives you an extra spoonful of onions when you—"

Belle spoke up tartly: "He isn't in the store, Mother. His people have loads of money. They're very thrifty and nice respectable people. Of course—everybody in Hyde Park goes to Dick's for their Sunday night supper things."

"His mother's a fine-looking woman," Henry Kemp put in. "She's the smart one. Practically runs the business, I hear. Old Dick is kind of a dreamer. I guess dreaming doesn't go in the delicatessen business."

"It'll be nice for Charley," Mrs. Payson remarked, grimly. "With her training at college. I shouldn't wonder if they'd put her in charge of all the cold meats, maybe. Or the cheese."

"Now Mother Payson, Charley's only a kid. Don't you go worrying—"

Belle spoke with some hauteur. "He does not live at home. He has a room near the university. He's fond of his parents but not in sympathy with the business. His work appears regularly in *Poetry,* and they accept only the best. He worked his way through college without a penny from his people. And," as a triumphant finish—"he has a book coming out this spring."

"Ha!" laughed Henry Kemp, jovially. Then suddenly sobering, regarded the glowing end of his cigar. "But they do say it's darned good poetry. People who know. Crazy—but good. I read one of 'em. It's all about dead horses and entrails and—" he stopped and coughed apologetically. "His new book is going to be called—" Here he went off into a silent spasm of laughter.

"Henry, you know that's just because you don't understand. It's the new verse."

"His new book," Henry Kemp went on, gravely, "is called 'White Worms.'"

He looked at Ben Gartz. The two men laughed uproariously.

Mrs. Payson sat forward stiffly in her rocking chair. "And you let Charley go about with this person!"

"Oh, Mother, please. Let's not discuss Charley's affairs. Mr. Gartz can't be interested."

"Oh, but I am! Aren't you, Miss Lottie? Young folks—"

"Besides, all the girls are quite mad about him. Charley's the envy of them all. He's the most sought-after young man in Hyde Park. He wrote a poem to Charley that appeared in *Poetry* last month." Belle dismissed the whole affair with a little impatient kick of her foot that sent the dangling slipper flying. "Oh, Henry—my slipper!" Henry retrieved it. "Besides they're only children. Charley's a baby."

Mrs. Carrie Payson began to rock in the squeaky chair, violently. "You heard what she said about the five."

"The five?"

"About the five—you know."

In the laughter that followed, Great-Aunt Charlotte slipped out of the room, vanished up the stairs.

Then the war, of course. Ben Gartz was the sort that kept a map in his office, with colored pins stuck everywhere in it. They began to talk about the war. They say it'll go on for years and years; it can't, the Germans are starving; don't you believe it, they've prepared for this for forty years; aren't the French wonderful, would you believe it to look at them so shrimpy; it's beginning to look pretty black for them just the same; we'll be in it yet, you mark my words; should have gone in a year ago, that was the time; if ever we do, zowie.

Lottie sat knitting. Ben Gartz reached over and fingered the soft springy mass of wool. There was an intimacy about the act. "If we go into it and I go off to war, will you knit me some of these, Miss Lottie? H'm?"

Lottie lifted her eyes. "If you go off to fight, I'll knit you a whole outfit, complete: socks, muffler, helmet, wristlets, sweater."

"'Death, where is thy sting!'" Ben Gartz rolled a pale blue eye.

Henry Kemp was not laughing now. His face looked a little drawn and old. He had allowed his cigar to go dead in the earnestness of the war talk. "You're safe, Lottie. It'll be over before we can ever *go* into it."

Ben Gartz flapped a hand in disagreement. "Don't you be too sure of that. I've heard it pretty straight that we'll be in by this time next year—if not before. I've had an offer to go into the men's watch bracelet business on the strength of it. And if we do, I'm going to take it. Fortune in it."

"Men's watch bracelets! Real men don't wear them. Mollycoddles!"

"Oh, don't they! No, I guess not! Only engineers, and policemen and aviators and soldiers, that's all. Mollycoddles like that. They say they aren't wearing any kind *but* wristwatches over there. Well, if we go into the war, I go into the men's watch bracelet business, that's what. Fortune in it."

"Yeh," said Henry Kemp, haggardly. "If we go into the war, I *go* into the poorhouse."

Belle stood up, decisively. "It's getting late, Henry."

Mrs. Payson bristled. "It's only a little after nine. You only come once a week. I should think you needn't run off right after dinner."

"But it isn't right after dinner, Mother. Besides, Henry has been working terribly hard. He's worn out."

Mrs. Payson, who knew the state of Henry's business, sniffed in unbelief. But they went. In the hall:

"Then you'll be in tomorrow morning, Lottie?"

"Yes." Lottie seemed a little pale.

Mrs. Payson's face hardened.

You heard a roar outside. Henry warming up the engine. Snorts and chugs, then a gigantic purr. They were off.

The three settled down again in the living room. Mrs. Payson liked to talk to men. Years of business intercourse had accustomed her to them. She liked the way their minds worked, clear and hard. When Lottie had company she almost always sat with them. Lottie had never hinted that this was not quite as it should be. She never even told herself that perhaps this might have had something to do with her being Lottie Payson still.

She was glad enough to have her mother remain in the room this evening. She sat, knitting. She was thinking of Orville Sprague, and of Ben

Gartz. Of Charley and this boy—this Jesse Dick. How slim the boy was, and how young, and how—vital! That was it, vital. His jaw made such a clean, clear line. It almost hurt you with its beauty. . . . Beck Schaefer . . . Bellhop . . . So that was what Henry had meant. Youth's appeal to women of her age. A morbid appeal . . .

She shook herself a little. Her mother and Ben Gartz were talking.

"That's a pretty good proposition you got there, Mrs. Payson, if you can swing it. I wouldn't be in any hurry, if I was you. You hang on to it."

There always was talk of "propositions" and "deals" when Mrs. Payson conversed with one of Lottie's callers.

"I think a good deal of your advice, Mr. Gartz. After all, I'm only a woman alone. I haven't got anyone to advise me."

"You don't need anybody, Mrs. Payson. You're as shrewd as that Rolfe is, any day. He's waiting to see how this war's going to go. Well, you wait too. You've got a good proposition there—"

Lottie rose. "I'll get you something to drink," she said.

He caught her arm. "Now don't you bother, Miss Lottie." He always called her "Miss Lottie" when others were there, and "Lottie" when they were alone.

But she went, and came back with ginger ale, and some cookies. Something in his face as he caught sight of these chaste viands smote her kindly and understanding heart. She knew her mother would disapprove, would oppose it. But the same boldness that had prompted her to speak at dinner now urged her to fresh flights of daring.

"What would you say to a cup of nice hot coffee and some cold chicken sandwiches!"

"Oh, say, Miss Lottie! I couldn't think—this is all right." But his eyes brightened.

"Nonsense, Lottie!" said Mrs. Payson, sharply. "Mr. Gartz doesn't want coffee."

"Yes he does. Don't you? Come on in the kitchen while I make it. We'll all have a bite at the dining room table. I'll cut the bread if you'll butter it."

Ben Gartz got up with alacrity. "No man who lives in a hotel could resist an offer like that, Miss Lottie." He frisked heavily off to the kitchen in her wake. Mrs. Payson stood a moment, tasting the unaccustomed bitter pill of opposition. Then she took her stout cane from a corner where she had placed it and followed after them to the kitchen, sniffing the delicious scent of coffee-in-the-making as though it were poison gas. Later, they played dummy bridge. Lottie did not play bridge well. She failed to take the red and black spots seriously. Mrs. Payson would overbid regularly. If you had told her that this was a form of dishonesty, she would have put you down as queer. Ben Gartz squinted through his cigar smoke, slapped the cards down hard, roared at Mrs. Payson's tactics (he had been a good son to his mother, remember) and sought Lottie's knee under the table.

". . . going to marry at twenty and have five children, one right after the other—"

"Lottie Payson, what are you thinking of!" Her mother's outraged voice.

"Why—what—"

"You trumped my ace!"

Chapter IX

Every morning between eight-thirty and nine, a boy from the Elite Garage on Twenty-Sixth Street brought the Payson electric to the door. He trundled it up to the curb with the contempt that it deserved. Your self-respecting garage mechanic is contemptuous of all electric conveyances, but this young man looked on the Payson's senile vehicle as a personal insult. He manipulated its creaking levers and balky brakes as a professional pitcher would finger a soft rubber ball—thing beneath pity. As he sprang out of it in his jersey and his tight pants and his long-visored green cap, he would slam its ancient door behind him with such force as almost to set it rocking on its four squat wheels. Then he would pass round behind it, kick one of its asphalt-gnawed rubber tires with a vindictive boot, and walk off whistling back to the Elite Garage. Lottie had watched this performance a thousand times, surely. She was always disappointed if he failed to kick the tire. It satisfied something in her to see him do it.

This morning Lottie was up, dressed, and telephoning the Elite Garage before eight o'clock. She wanted to make an early start. She meant to use the electric in order to save time. Without it, the trip between the Paysons' house on Prairie Avenue and the Kemps' on Hyde Park Boulevard near the lake was a pilgrimage marked by dreary waits on clamorous corners for dirty yellow cars that never came.

Early as she was, Lottie had heard Aunt Charlotte astir much earlier. She had not yet come down, however. Mrs. Payson had already breakfasted and read the paper. After Mrs. Payson had finished with a newspaper, its page sequence was irrevocably ruined for the next reader. Its sport sheet mingled with the want ads; its front page lay crumpled upon Music and the Drama. Lottie sometimes wondered if her own fondness for a neatly folded uncrumpled morning paper was only another indication of chronic spinsterhood. Aunt Charlotte had once said, as she smoothed the wrinkled sheets with her wavering withered fingers, "Reading a newspaper after you've finished with it, Carrie, is like getting the news three days stale. No flavor to it."

Lottie scarcely glanced at the headlines as she drank her coffee this morning. Her mother was doing something or other at the sideboard. Mrs. Payson was the sort of person who does slammy flappy things in a room where you happened to be breakfasting, or writing, or reading; things at which you could not express annoyance and yet which annoyed you to the point of frenzy. She lifted dishes and put them down. She rattled silver in the drawer. She tugged at a sideboard door that always stuck. She made notes on a piece of wrapping paper with a hard pencil and tapping sounds. All interspersed with a spasmodic conversation carried on in a high voice with Hulda in the kitchen, the swinging door of the pantry between them.

"Need any rice?"

"W'at?"

"Rice!"

"We got yet."

More tapping of the pencil accompanied by a sotto voce murmur— "Soap . . . kitchen cleanser . . . new potatoes . . . see about electric light bulbs . . . coffee—" she raised her voice again: "We've got plenty of coffee I know."

Silence from the kitchen.

"Hulda, we've got plenty of coffee! I got a pound on Wednesday."

Silence. Then—"He don't last over Sunday."

"Not—why my dear young woman—" the swinging door whiffed and whoofed with the energy of her exit as she passed into the kitchen to do battle with the coffee-toper.

Lottie was quite unconscious of the frown that her rasped nerves had etched between her eyes. She was so accustomed to these breakfast irritations that she did not know they irritated her. She was even smiling a little, grimly amused.

It was a lowering Chicago March morning, gray, foggy, sodden, with a wet blanket wind from the lake that was more chilling than a walk through water and more penetrating than severe cold. The months-old soot-grimed snow and ice lay everywhere. The front page predicted rain. Not a glint of sunlight filtered through the yellow pane of the stained-glass window in the Payson dining room. "Ugh!" thought Lottie, picturing the downtown streets a morass of mud trampled to a pudding consistency. And yet she smiled. She was to have the morning alone; the morning from eight until almost noon. There was Gussie to interview. There was Judge Barton to confer with—dear Emma Barton. There was poor Jennie to dispose of. There was work to do. Real work. Lottie rose from the table and stood in the pantry doorway, holding the swinging door open with one foot as she was getting into her coat.

"I'll be back by noon, Mother, surely. Perhaps earlier. Then we'll go right over to your buildings and collect the rents and market on the way back."

"Oh," said Mrs. Payson only. Her mouth was pursed.

"For that matter, I think it's so foolish to bother about Sunday dinner. We always get up later on Sunday, and eat more for breakfast. Let's just have lunch this once. Let's try it. Forget about the leg of lamb or the roast beef—"

Mrs. Payson raised her eyebrows in the direction of the listening Hulda. "I'll leave that kind of thing to your sister Belle—this new idea of getting up at noon on Sunday and then having no proper Sunday dinner. We've always had Sunday dinners in this house and we always will have as long as I'm head of the household."

"Well, I just thought—" Lottie released the swinging door. She came back into the dining room and glanced at herself in the sideboard mirror. Lottie was the kind of woman who looks well in the morning. A clear skin, a clear eye, hair that springs cleanly away from the temples. This morning she looked more than usually alert. A little half-smile of anticipation was on her lips. The lowering weather, her mother's dourness, Hulda's slightly burned toast—she had allowed none of these things to curdle the cream of her morning's adventure. She was wearing her suit and furs and the small velvet hat whose doom Belle had pronounced the evening before. As she drew on her gloves, her mother entered the dining room.

"I'll be back by noon, surely." Mrs. Payson did not answer. Lottie went down the long hall toward the front door. Her mother followed.

"Going to Belle's?"

"Yes. I'll have to hurry."

At the door Mrs. Payson flung a final command. "You'd better go South Park to Grand."

Lottie had meant to. It was the logical route to Belle's. She had taken it a thousand times. Yet now, urged by some imp of perversity, she was astonished to hear herself saying, "No, I'm going up Prairie to Fifty-First." The worst possible road.

She did not mind the wet gray wind as she clanked along in the little boxlike contrivance, up Prairie Avenue, over Thirty-First, past gray stone and brick mansions whose former glory of façade and stone-and-iron fence and steps showed the neglect and decay following upon Negro occupancy. It was too bad, she thought. Chicago was like a colossal and slovenly young woman who, possessing great natural beauty, is still content to slouch about in greasy wrapper and slippers run down at heel.

The Kemps lived in one of the oldest of Hyde Park's apartment houses and one as nearly aristocratic as a Chicago South Side apartment house can be. It was on Hyde Park Boulevard, near Jackson Park and the lake. When Belle had married, she had protested at an apartment. She had never lived in one, she said. She didn't think she could. She would stifle. No privacy. Everything huddled together on one floor and everybody underfoot. People upstairs; people downstairs. But houses were scarce in Hyde Park and she and Henry had compromised on an apartment much too large for them and as choice as anything for miles around. There were nine rooms. The two front rooms were a parlor and sitting room, but not many years had passed before Belle did away with this. Belle had caused all sorts of things to be done to the apartment—at Henry's expense, not the landlord's. Year after year partitions had been removed; old fixtures torn out and modern ones installed; dark woodwork had been cream-enameled; the old parlor and sitting room had been thrown into one enormous living room. They had even built a "sun parlor" without which no Chicago apartment is considered complete. As it eats, sleeps, plays bridge, reads, sews, writes, and lounges in those little many-windowed peep shows, all Chicago's family life is an open book to its neighbor.

Belle's front room was a carefully careless place—livable, inviting—with its books, and lamps, and plump low chairs mothering unexpected tables nestled at their elbows—tantalizing little tables holding the last new novel, face downward; a smart little tooled leather box primly packed with cigarettes; a squat wooden bowl, very small, whose tipped cover revealed a glimpse of vivid scrunchy fruit drops within. Splashes of scarlet and orange bittersweet in luster bowls, loot of Charley's autumn days at the dunes. A roll of watermelon-pink wool and a ball of the same shade in one corner of the deep davenport, with two long amber needles stuck through, prophesied the first rainbow note of Charley's summer wardrobe. The grand piano holding a book of Chopin and a chromo-covered song-hit labeled, incredibly enough, "Tya-da-dee." It was as unlike the Prairie Avenue living room as Charley was unlike Mrs. Carrie Payson. Belle had recently had the sun parlor done in the new Chinese furniture— green enameled wood with engaging little Chinese figures and scenes painted on it; queer gashes of black here and there and lampshades shaped like some sort of Chinese headgear; no one knew quite what. Surely no Mongolian—coolie or mandarin—would have recognized the origin of anything in the Chinese sun parlor.

Gussie answered the door. An admirable young woman, Gussie, capable, self-contained, self-respecting. Sprung from a loose-moraled slovenly household, she had, somehow, got the habit of personal cleanliness and of straight thinking. Gussie's pastry hand was a light, deft, clean one. Gussie's bedroom had none of the kennel stuffiness of the average kitchen-bedroom. Gussie's pride in her own bathroom spoke in shining tiles and gleaming porcelain.

"Oo, Miss Lottie! How you are early! Mrs. ain't up at all yet. Miss Charley, she is in bathtub."

"That's all right, Gussie. I came to see you."

Gussie's eyes were red-rimmed. "Yeh . . . Jennie . . ." She led the way back to the kitchen; a sturdy young woman facing facts squarely. Her thick-tongued speech told of her Slavic origin. She went on with her morning's work as she talked and Lottie listened. Hers was a no-good family. Her step-father she dismissed briefly as a bum. Her mother was always getting mixed up with the boarders—that menace of city tenement life. And now Jennie. Jennie wasn't bad. Only she liked a good time. The two brothers (rough, lowering fellows) were always a-jumping on Jennie. It was fierce. They wouldn't let her go out with the fellas. In the street they yelled at her and shamed Jennie for Jennie's crowd right out. They wanted she should marry one of the boarders. Well, say, he had money sure, but old like Jennie's own father. Jennie was only seventeen. All this while Gussie was slamming expertly from table to sink, from sink to stove.

"Seventeen! Why doesn't she leave home and work out as you do, Gussie? Housework."

Jennie, it appeared, was too toney for housework. "Like this Jennie is." Gussie took a smudged envelope from her pocket and opened it with damp fingers. With one blunt fingertip she pointed to the signature. It was a pencil-scrawled letter from Jennie to her sister and it was signed, flourishingly, "Jeannette."

"Oh," said Lottie. "I see."

Jennie, then, worked by factory. She paid board at home. She helped with the housework evenings and Sundays. But always they yelled at her. And then Jennie had taken one hundred dollars and had run away from home.

"Jennie is smart," Gussie said, in conclusion, "she is smart like machine. She can make in her head figgers. She finished school she wanted she should go by business college for typewriter and work in office but Ma and my brothers they won't let. They yell and they yell and so Jennie works by factory."

It was all simple enough to Lottie. She had sat in many sessions of Judge Barton's court. "You'd rather not go with me, Gussie?"

Gussie shook a vehement head. "Better you should go alone. Right away I cry and yell for scared, Jennie she begin cry and yell, Ma she begin cry and—"

"All right, Gussie . . . Whose hundred dollars was it?"

"Otto. He is big brother. He is mad like everything. He say he make Jennie go by jail—"

"Oh, no, Gussie. He can't do that without Judge Barton, and she'll never—"

Gussie vanished into her bedroom. She emerged again with a stout roll of grimy bills in her hand. These she proffered Lottie. "Here is more as fifty dollar. I save'm. You should give to judge he shouldn't send Jennie to jail." Gussie was of the class that never quite achieves one hundred dollars. Seventy—eighty—eighty-five—and then the dentist or doctor.

Lottie gave the girl's shoulder a little squeeze. "Oh, Gussie, you funny dear child. The judge is a woman. And besides it isn't right to bribe the—"

"No-o-o-o! A woman! In my life I ain't heard how a woman is judge."

"Well, this one is. And Jennie won't go by jail. I promise you."

Down the hall sped a figure in a pongee bathrobe, corded at the waist, slim and sleek as a goldfish. Charley.

"I heard you come in. Finished? Then sit and talk sociable while I dress. You can speed a bit on the way downtown and make it. Step on the ol' batteries. Please! Did you fix things with Gussie?"

"Yeh," Gussie answered, comfortably, but she wore a puzzled frown. "She fix. Judge is woman. Never in my life—"

"Gussie, ma'am, will you let me have my breakfast tray in the sun parlor? It's such a glummy morning. That's a nice girl. About five minutes."

And it wasn't more than five. Lottie, watching Charley in the act of dressing, wondered what that young woman's grandmother or great-aunt would have thought of the process. She decided that her dead-and-gone great-grandmother—that hoopskirted, iron-stayed, Victorian lady all encased in linings, buckram, wool, wire, merino, and starch—would have swooned at the sight. Charley's garments were so few and scant as to be Chinese in their simplicity. She wore, usually, three wispy garments, not counting shoes and stockings. She proceeded to don them now. First she pulled the stockings up tight and slick, then cuffed them just below the knee. This cuff she then twisted deftly round, caught the slack of it, twisted that ropelike, caught the twist neatly under a fold, rolled the fold down tight and hard three inches below the knee, and left it there, an ingenious silken bracelet. There it stayed, fast and firm, unaided by garter, stay, or elastic. Above this a pair of scant knickers of jersey silk or muslin; a straight little shirt with straps over the shoulders or, sometimes, just a brassiere that bound the young breasts. Over this slight foundation went a slim scant frock of cloth. That was all. She was a pliant wheat sheaf, a gracile blade, a supple spear (see verses "To C. K." in *Poetry Magazine* for February, signed Jesse Dick). She twisted her hair into a knot that, worn low on the neck, would have been a test for anyone but Charley. She now pursed her lips a little critically and leaned forward close to her mirror. Charley's lips were a little too full, the carping said; the kind of lips known as "bee-stung." Charley hated her mouth; said it was coarse and sensual. Others did not think so. (See poem "Your Lips" in *Century Magazine,* June.)

"There!" she said and turned away from the mirror. The five minutes were just up.

"Meaning you're dressed?"

"Dressed. Why of—"

"Sketchy, I calls it. But I suppose it's all right. You're covered, anyway. Only I hope your grandmother'll never witness the sight I've seen this morning. You make me feel like an elderly Eskimo sewed up for the winter."

Charley shrugged luxuriously. "I hate a lot of clothes."

Her tray awaited her on the table in the sun parlor—fruit, toast, steaming hot chocolate. "I've got to go," Lottie kept murmuring and leaned in the doorway, watching her. Charley attacked the food with a relish that gave you an appetite. She rolled an ecstatic eye at the first sip of chocolate. "Oo, hot! Sure you won't have some?" She demolished the whole daintily and thoroughly. As she sat there in the cruel morning light of the many-windowed little room, she was as pink-cheeked and bright-eyed and scrubbed-looking as a Briggs boy ready for supper. You could see the fine pores of her skin.

Lottie began to button her coat. Charley chased a crumb of toast around her plate. "What, if any, do you think of him?"

Lottie had seen and met shoals of Charley's young men. "Suitors" was the official South Side name for them. But Charley had never asked Lottie's opinion of one of them.

"Charming youngster. I grew quite moony, after you'd gone, thinking about him, and trumped Mother's ace. He doesn't look like a poet—that is, poet."

"They never do. Good poets, I mean. I've often thought it was all for the best that Rupert Brooke—that Byron collar of his. Fancy by the time he became forty . . . you really think he's charming?"

"So does your mother. Last night she was enthusiastic—about his work."

"M-m-m. Mother's partial to young poets."

Between Charley and her mother there existed an unwritten code. Charley commanded whole squads of devoted young men in assorted sizes, positions, and conditions. Young men who liked country hikes and wayside lunches; young men who preferred to dance at the Blackstone on Saturday afternoons; young men who took Charley to the symphony concerts; young men who read to her out of books. And Mrs. Henry Kemp, youngish, attractive, almost twenty years of married life with Henry Kemp behind her, relished a chat with these slim youngsters. A lean-flanked graceful crew they were, for the most part, with an almost feline coordination of muscle. When they shook hands with you, their grip drove the rings into your fingers. They looked you in the eye—and blushed a little. Their profiles would have put a movie star to shame. Their waists were slim as a girl's (tennis and baseball). They drove low-slung cars around Hyde Park comers with death-defying expertness. Nerveless; not talkative and yet well up on the small talk of the younger set—labor, socialism, sex, baseball, Freud, psychiatry, dancing and—just now—the war. Some were all for dashing across to join the Lafayette Escadrille. Belle Kemp would have liked to sit and talk with these young men—talk, and laugh, and dangle her slipper on the end of her toe. Charley knew this. And her mother knew she knew. No pulling the wool over Charley's eyes. No pretending to play the chummy young mother with her. "Pal stuff."

So, then, "M-m-m," said Charley, sipping the last of her chocolate. "Mother's partial to young poets."

Lottie had to be off. She cast a glance down the hall. "Do you suppose she's really asleep still? I'd like to talk to her just a minute."

"You might tap once at the door. I never disturb her in the morning. But I don't think she's sleeping."

Another code rule. These two—mother and daughter—treated one another with polite deference. Never intruded on each other's privacy. Rarely interfered with each other's engagements. Mrs. Kemp liked her breakfast in bed—a practice Charley loathed. Once a week, a strapping Swedish damsel came to the apartment to give Mrs. Kemp a body massage and what is known as a "facial." You should have heard Mrs. Carrie Payson on the subject. Belle defended the practice, claiming that it benefited some obscure digestive ailment from which she suffered.

Lottie tapped at Belle's door. A little silence. Then an unenthusiastic voice bade her enter. Belle was in bed, resting. Belle looked her age in bed in the morning. Slightly haggard and a little yellow.

"I thought it must be you."

"It is."

Belle rolled a languid eye. "I woke up feeling wretched. How about this Gussie business?"

"I'm just going downtown. It'll turn out all right, I think."

"Just arrange things so that Gussie won't be upset for Tuesday. You wouldn't think she was nervous, to look at her. Great huge creature. But when she's upset! And I do so want that luncheon to be just right. Mrs. Radcliffe Phelps—"

Lottie could not restrain a little smile. "Oh, Belle."

Belle turned her head pettishly on the pillow. "Oh, Belle!" she mimicked in an astonishingly ungrown-up manner. Indeed, she sounded amazingly like the schoolgirl of Armour Institute days. "You're more like Mother every day, Lottie." Lottie closed the door softly.

Charley was waiting for her at the end of the hall. "Don't say I didn't warn you. Here—I'll give you a chocolatey kiss. Are you lunching downtown? There's a darling new tearoom just opened in the Great Lakes Building—"

"I've promised to be home by noon, at the latest."

"What for?"

"To take Mother marketing and over to the West Side—"

"Oh, for heaven's sake!"

"You have your job, Charley. This is mine."

"Oh, is it? Do you like it?"

"N-n-no."

"Then it isn't."

Lottie flung a final word at the door. "Even a free untrammelled spirit like you will acknowledge that such a thing as duty does exist, I suppose?"

Charley leaned over the railing to combat that as Lottie flew downstairs. "There is no higher duty than that of self-expression."

"Gabble-gabble!" laughed Lottie, at the vestibule door.

"Coward!" shouted Charley over the railing.

Chapter X

When she came out, the fog was beginning to lift over the lake and there was even an impression of watery lemon-colored sunshine behind the bank of gray. Lottie's spirits soared. As she stepped into the swaying old electric, there came over her a little swooping sensation of freedom. It was good to be going about one's business thus, alone. No one to say, "Slower! Not so fast!" No one to choose the maelstrom of State and Madison streets as the spot in which to ask her opinion as to whether this sample of silk matched this bit of cloth. A licorice lane of smooth black roadway ahead. Down Hyde Park Boulevard and across to Drexel. Down the long empty stretch of that fine avenue at a spanking speed—spanking, that is, for the ancient electric whose inside protested at every revolution of the wheels. She negotiated the narrows of lower Michigan Avenue and emerged into the gracious sweep of that street as it widened at Twelfth. She always caught her breath a little at the spaciousness and magnificence of those blocks between Twelfth and Randolph. The new Field Columbian Museum, a white wraith, rose out of the lake mist at her right. Already it was smudged with the smoke of the IC engines. A pity, Lottie thought. She always felt civic when driving down Michigan. On one side, Grant Park and the lake beyond; on the other, the smart shops. You had to keep eyes ahead, but now and then, out of the corner of them, you caught tantalizing glimpses of a scarlet velvet evening wrap in the window of the Blackstone shop; a chic and trickily simple poiret twill in Vogue; the glint of silver as you flashed past a jeweler's; the sooted facade of the Art Institute. She loved it. It exhilarated her. She felt young, and free, and rather important. The somber old house on Prairie ceased to dominate her for the time. What fun it would be to stay down for lunch with Emma Barton—wise, humorous, understanding Emma Barton. Maybe they could get hold of Winnie Steppler, too. Then, later, she might prowl around looking at the new cloth dresses for spring.

Well, she couldn't. That was all there was to it.

She parked the electric and entered the grim black pile that was the City Hall and County Building, threaded her way among the cuspidors of the dingy entrance hall, stepped out of the elevator on the floor that held Judge Barton's court: the Girls' Court. The attendant at the door knew her. There was no entering Judge Barton's court as a public place of entertainment. In the anteroom, red-eyed girls and shawled mothers were watching the closed door in mingled patience and fear. Girls. Sullen girls, bold girls, frightened girls. Girls who had never heard of the Ten Commandments and who had broken most of them. Girls who had not waited for the apple of life to drop ripe into their laps but had twisted it off the tree and bitten deep into the fruit and found the taste of gall in their mouths. Tear-stained, bedraggled, wretched girls; defiant girls; silk-clad, contemptuous, staring girls. Girls who had rehearsed their roles, prepared for stern justice in uniform. Girls who bristled with resentment against life, against law, against maternal authority. They did not suspect how completely they were to be disarmed by a small woman with a misleadingly mild face, graying hair, and eyes that—well, it was hard to tell about those eyes. They looked at you—they looked at you and through you . . . What was that you had planned to say . . . what was that you had . . . Oh, for God's sakes, Ma, shut up your crying! Between the girls in their sleazy silk stockings and the mothers in their shapeless shawls lay the rotten root of the trouble. New America and the Old World, out of sympathy with each other, uncomprehending, resentful. The girls in the outer room rustled, and twisted, and jerked, and sobbed, and whispered, and shrugged, and scowled; and stared furtively at each other. But the shawled and formless older women stood or sat animallike in their patience, their eyes on the closed door.

Lottie wondered if she could pick Jennie from among them. She even thought of asking for her, but she quickly decided against that. Better to see Emma Barton first.

It lacked just five minutes of ten. Lottie nodded to the woman who guarded the door and passed through the little room in which Judge Barton held court, to the private office beyond. Never was less official-looking hall of justice than that little courtroom. It resembled a more than ordinarily pleasant business office. A long flat table on a platform four or five inches above the floor. Half a dozen chairs ranged about the wall. A vase of spring flowers—jonquils, tulips, mignonette—on the table. Not a carefully planned "woman's touch." Someone was always sending flowers to Judge Barton. She was that kind of woman. You were struck with the absence of official-looking papers, documents, files. All the paraphernalia of red tape was absent.

Judge Barton sat in the cubbyhole of an office just beyond this, a girl stenographer at her elbow. Outside the great window, the city hall pigeons strutted and purled. Bright-eyed and alert as an early robin, the judge looked up as Lottie came in. She took Lottie's hand in her own firm fingers.

"Well!" Then they smiled at each other, these two women. "You'll stay down and have lunch with me. I've the whole afternoon—Saturday."

"I can't."

"Of course you can. Why not?"

"I've got to be home by noon to take Mother to market and to—"

"It sounds like nonsense to me," Emma Barton said, gently. And, somehow, it did sound like nonsense.

Lottie flushed like a schoolgirl. "I suppose it does—" she broke off, abruptly. "I came down to talk to you about Jennie. Jennie's the sister of Belle's housemaid, Gussie, and she's in trouble. Her case comes up before you this morning."

Emma Barton's eyes traveled swiftly over the charted sheets before her. "Jennie? Jennie?—Jeannette Kromek?"

"Jeannette."

"I see," said Judge Barton, just as Lottie had before her in Belle's kitchen that morning. She glanced at the chart of Jennie's case. A common enough case in that court. She listened as Lottie talked briefly. She knew the Jennie kind; Jennie in rebellion against a treadmill of working and eating and sleeping. Jennie, the grub, vainly trying to transform herself into Jeannette the butterfly. Excitement, life, admiration, pretty clothes, "a chance." That was what the Jeannettes vaguely desired: a chance.

Judge Barton did not waste any time on sentiment. She did not walk to the window and gaze out upon the great gray city stretched below. She did not say, "Poor little broken butterfly." She had not become head of this judicature thus. She said, "The world's full of Jennie—Jeannettes. I wonder there isn't more of them." The soft bright eyes were on Lottie. They said, "You're one, you know." But she did not utter the thought aloud. She glanced at her watch then (it actually hung from an old-fashioned chatelaine pinned near her right shoulder), rose, and led the way into the larger room, followed by Lottie and the girl stenographer. She mounted the low platform, slipped into the chair at the desk.

She had placed the chart of Jennie's case uppermost on the table, was about to have the case summoned when the door flew open and Winnie Steppler entered. Doors always flew open before Winnie's entrance. White-haired, pink-cheeked as a girl, looming vast and imposing in her blue cloak and gray furs, she looked more the grande dame on an errand of mercy than a newspaper reporter on the job. She rarely got a story in Judge Barton's court because Judge Barton's girls' names were carefully kept out of the glare of publicity. The human quality in the place drew her; and her friendship and admiration for Emma Barton; and the off chance there might be a story for her. She ranged the city, did Winnie Steppler, for her stuff. Her friends were firemen and policemen, newsboys and elevator starters; movie ticket sellers, newsstand girls, hotel clerks, lunchroom waitresses, manicures, taxi drivers, street sweepers, doormen, waiters, Greek bootblacks— all that vast stratum of submerged servers over whom the flood of humanity sweeps in a careless torrent leaving no one knows what sediment of rich knowledge.

At sight of Lottie, Winnie Steppler's Irish blue eyes blazed. She affected a brogue, inimitable. "Och, but you're the grand sight and me a-sickening for ye these weeks and not a glimpse. You'll have lunch with me—you and Her Honor there."

"I can't," said Lottie.

"And why not, then!"

It really was beginning to sound a little foolish. Lottie hesitated. She fidgeted with her fingers, looked up, smiling uncertainly. "I've"—with a rush—"I've got to be home by twelve to drive Mother to market and to the West Side."

"Telephone her. Say you won't be home till two. It's no life-and-death matter, is it—the market and the West Side?"

Lottie tried to picture that driving force at home waiting complacently until she should return at two. "Oh, I can't! I can't!"

Winnie Steppler, the world-wise, stared at her a moment curiously. There had been a note resembling hysteria in Lottie's voice. "Why, look here, girl—"

"Order in the court!" said Judge Barton, with mock dignity. But she meant it. It was ten o'clock. Two probation officers came in. A bailiff opened the door and stuck his head in. Judge Barton nodded to him. He closed the door. You heard his voice in the outer room. "Jeannette Kromek! Mrs. Kromek! Otto Kromek!"

A girl in a wrinkled blue cloth dress, a black velvet tam-o'-shanter, slippers, and (significant this) black cotton stockings. At sight of those black cotton stockings, Lottie Payson knew, definitely, that beneath the top tawdriness of Jeannette was Jennie, sound enough. A sullen, lowering, rather frightened girl of seventeen. Her hair was bobbed. The style went oddly with the high-cheekboned Slavic face, the blunt-fingered factory hands. With her was a shawled woman who might have been forty or sixty. She glanced about dartingly beneath lowered lids with quick furtive looks. An animal, trapped, has the same look in its eyes. The two stood at the side of the table facing Judge Barton.

"Where is Otto Kromek?"

"He didn't show up," the bailiff reported.

No case, then. But Judge Barton did not so state. She leaned forward a little toward the girl whose face was blotched and swollen with weeping.

"What's the trouble, Jennie?"

Jennie set her jaw. She looked down, looked up again. The brown eyes were still upon her, questioningly. "I—"

The shawled woman plucked at the girl's skirt and whispered fiercely in her own tongue.

"Le' me alone," hissed the girl, and jerked away.

Judge Barton turned toward the woman. "Mrs. Kromek, just stand away from Jennie. Let her talk to me. Afterward you can talk."

The two separated, glaring.

"Now then, Jennie, how did it all happen?"

The girl begins to speak. The older woman edges closer again to catch what the low voice says.

"We went ridin' with a couple fellas."

"Did you know them? Were they boys you knew?"

"No."

"How did you happen to go riding with them, Jennie?"

"We was walkin'—"

"We?"

"Me an' my girlfriend. We was walkin'. These fellas was driving 'round slow. We seen 'em. An' they come up to the curb where we was passin' by an' asked us would we like to take a ride. Well, we didn't have nothin' else to do so—"

I-sez-to-him and he-sez-to-me. The drive. Terror. A fight in the car, the sturdy girls defending themselves fiercely. Home safe but so late that the usual tirade became abuse. They had said things at home . . . well . . . she'd show'm. She'd run away. She had taken the hundred to spite him—Otto.

"Why did you go, Jennie? You knew, didn't you?"

The girl's smoldering resentment flared into open hatred. "It's her. She's always a-yellin' at me. They're all yellin' all the time. I come home from work and right away they jump on me. Nothin' I do ain't right. I'm good and sick of it, that's what. Good and sick—" She was weeping again, wildly, unrestrainedly. The older woman broke into a torrent of talk in her own thick tongue. She grasped the girl's arm. Jennie wrenched herself free. "Yeh, you!" She turned again to Judge Barton, the tears streaming down her cheeks. She made no attempt to wipe them away. The Jennies of Judge Barton's court, so prone to tears, were usually poorly equipped for the disposal of them.

Emma Barton did not say, "Don't cry, Jennie." Without taking her eyes from the girl, she opened the upper right-hand drawer of her desk, and from a neatly stacked pile of plain white handkerchiefs, she took the topmost one, shook it out of its folds and handed it wordlessly to Jennie. As wordlessly, Jennie took it and wiped her streaming eyes and blew her nose and mopped her face. Emma Barton had won a thousand Jennies with a thousand neat white handkerchiefs extracted in the nick of time from that upper right-hand drawer.

"Now then, Mrs. Kromek. What's the trouble between you and Jennie? Why don't you get along, you two?"

Mrs. Kromek, no longer furtive, squared herself to state her grievance. Hers was a polyglot but pungent tongue. She made plain her meaning. Jennie was a bum, a no-good, a stuck-up. The house wasn't clean enough for Jennie. Always she was washing. Evenings she was washing herself always with hot water it was enough to make you sick. And Jennie was sassy on the boarders.

And, "I see," said Judge Barton encouragingly, at intervals, as the vituperative flood rolled on. "I see." Jennie's eyes, round with hostility, glared at her accuser over the top of the handkerchief. Finally, when the poison stream grew thinner, trickled, showed signs of stopping altogether, Judge Barton beamed understandingly upon the vixenish Mrs. Kromek. "I understand perfectly now. Just wait here, Mrs. Kromek. Jennie, come with me." She beckoned to Lottie. The three disappeared into the inner office. Judge Barton laid a hand lightly on the girl's shoulder. "Now then, Jennie, what would you like to do, h'm? Just talk to me. Tell me, what would you like to do?"

Jennie's hands writhed in the folds of her skirt. She twisted her fingers. She sobbed final dry, racking sobs. And then she rolled the judicial handkerchief into a tight, damp, hard little ball and began to talk. She talked as she had never talked to Ma Kromek. Translated, it ran thus:

At home there was no privacy. The house was full of hulking men; pipe-smoke; the smell of food eternally stewing on the stove; shrill or guttural voices; rough jests. Book-reading, bathing, reticence on Jennie's part were all shouted down as attempts at being "toney." When she came home from the factory at night, tired, nerve-worn, jaded, the house was as cluttered and dirty as it had been when she left it in the morning. The mother went with the boarders (this Jennie told as evenly and dispassionately as the rest). She had run away from home after the last hideous family fracas. She had taken the money in a spirit of hatred and revenge. She'd do it again. If they had let her go to school, as she had wanted to—she used to talk English all right, like the teacher—but you heard the other kind of talk around the house and at the factory and pretty soon you couldn't talk the right way. They made fun of you if you did. A business college course. That was what she wanted. She could spell. At school she could spell better than anyone in the room. Only they had taken her out in the sixth grade.

What to do with Jennie?

The two older women looked at each other over Jennie's head. The course in stenography could be managed simply enough. Judge Barton met such problems hourly. But what to do with Jennie in the meantime? She shrank from consigning to a detention home or a Girls' Refuge this fundamentally sound and decent young creature.

Suddenly, "I'll take her," said Lottie.

"How do you mean?"

"I'll take her home with me. We've got rooms and rooms in that barracks of ours. The whole third floor. She can stay for awhile. Anyway, she can't go back to that house."

The girl sat looking from one to the other, uncomprehending. Her hands were clutching each other tightly. Emma Barton turned to her. "What do you say, Jennie? Would you like to go home with Miss Payson here? Just for awhile, until we think of something else? I think we can manage the business college course."

The girl seemed hardly to comprehend. Lottie leaned toward her. "Would you like to come to my house, Jeannette?" And at that, the first stab of misgiving darted through Lottie. "My house?" She thought of her mother.

"Yes," answered Jennie with the ready acquiescence of her class. "Yes."

And so it was settled, simply. Ma Kromek accepted the decision with dumb passiveness. One of the brothers would bring Jennie's clothes to the Prairie Avenue house. Jennie had only spent half of the stolen hundred. The unspent half she had returned to him. The rest she would pay back, bit by bit, out of her earnings. Winnie Steppler bemoaned her inability to make a feature story of Jennie—Jeannette. Lottie smiled at Jennie, and propelled her down the corridor and into the elevator, to the street. In her well-fitting tailor suit, and her good furs and her close little velvet hat, she looked the Lady Bountiful. The girl, shabby, tear-stained, followed. Lottie was racked with horrid misgivings. Why had she suggested it! What a mad idea! Her mother! She tried to put the thought out of her mind. She couldn't face it. And all the while she was unlocking the door of the electric, settling herself in the seat, holding out a hand to help Jennie's entrance. The watery sunshine of the early morning had been a false promise. It was raining again.

Out of the welter of State Street and Wabash, and into the clear stretch of Michigan once more, she turned suddenly to look at Jennie and found Jennie looking fixedly at her. Jennie's eyes did not drop shiftily at this unexpected encounter. That was reassuring.

"Gussie works at my sister's," she told the girl, bluntly. "That's how I happened to be in court this morning when your case came up."

"Oh," said Jennie, accepting this as of a piece with all the rest of the day's happenings. Then, after a moment, "Is that why you said you'd take me? Gussie?"

"No, I didn't even think of Gussie at the time. I just thought of you. I didn't even think of myself." She smiled a little grimly. "I'm going to call you Jeannette, shall I?"

"Yeh. Jennie's so homely. What's your name?"

"Lottie."

Jeannette politely made no comment. Lottie found herself defending the name. "It's short for Charlotte, you know. My Aunt Charlotte lives with us. We'd get mixed up. My niece is named Charlotte, too. We call her Charley."

Jeannette nodded briskly. "I know. I seen her once. I was at Gussie's. Gussie told me. She's awful pretty . . . She's got it swell . . . You like my hair this way?" She whisked off the dusty velvet tan.

"I think I'd like it better the other way. Long."

"I'll let it grow. I can do it in a net so it looks like long." They rode along in silence.

What to say to her mother! She glanced at her watch. Eleven. Well, at least she wasn't late. They were turning into Prairie at Sixteenth. She was terrified at what she had done; furious that this should be so. She argued fiercely with herself, maintaining all the while her outwardly composed and dignified demeanour. "Don't be a silly fool. You're a woman of thirty-two—almost thirty-three. You ought to be at the head of your own household. If you were, this is what you'd have done. Well, then!" But she was sick with apprehension, even while she despised herself because it was so.

Jeannette was speaking again. "The houses around here are swell, ain't they?"

"Yes," Lottie agreed, absently. Her own house was a block away.

Jeannette's mind grasshoppered to another topic. "I can talk good if you keep telling me. I forget. Home and in the works everybody talks bum English. I learn quick."

"Well, then," said Lottie. "I shouldn't say 'swell' nor 'ain't.'"

Jeannette thought a moment. "The—houses—around—here—are—grand—are—they—not?"

Suddenly Lottie reached over and covered the girl's hand with her own.

Jeannette smiled back at her. She thought her a fine-looking middle-aged person. Not a very swell dresser but you could see she had class.

"Here we are!" said Lottie aloud. The direct, clearheaded woman who had acted with authority and initiative only an hour before in the courtroom was now thinking, "Oh, dear! Oh, *dear*!" in anticipative agony. She stepped out of the electric. "Gussie'll be glad."

"Yeh—Gussie!" Jeannette's tone was not without venom. "She's her own boss. She's got it good. Sometimes for a whole month she didn't come home." She stared curiously at the grim old Prairie Avenue house. It was raining hard now. Lottie glanced quickly up at the parlor window. Sometimes her mother stood there, watching for her, impatient of any waiting. She was not there now. She opened the front door, the two entered—Jeannette the braver of the two.

"Yoo-hoo!" called Lottie with an airy assumption of cheeriness. Jeannette stood looking up and down the long dim hallway with wide ambient eyes. There was no answer to Lottie's call. She sped back to the kitchen.

"Where's Mother?"

"She ban gone out."

"Out! Where? It's raining. Pouring!"

"She ban gone out."

Even in her horror at the thought of her rheumatism-stricken mother in the downpour, she was conscious of a feeling of relief. It was the relief a condemned murderer feels whose hanging is postponed from today until tomorrow.

She came back to Jeannette. Oh, *dear*! "Come upstairs with me, Jeannette." Lottie ran up the stairs quickly, Jeannette at her heels. She went straight to Aunt Charlotte's room. Aunt Charlotte was asleep in her old plush armchair by the window. She often napped like that in the morning. She dropped off to sleep easily, sometimes dozing almost immediately after breakfast. It was light, fitful sleep. She started up, wide awake, as Lottie came in.

"Where's Mother?"

Aunt Charlotte smiled grimly. "She bounced out the minute you left."

"But where?"

"Her rents and the marketing."

"But it's raining. She can't be out in the rain. Way over there!"

"She said she was going to take the streetcar . . . What time is it, Lottie? I must have . . . Who's that in the hall?" She stopped in the middle of a yawn.

"Jeannette, come here. This is Jeannette, Aunt Charlotte. Gussie's sister. You know—Gussie, who works for Belle. I've brought Jeannette home with me."

"That's nice," said Aunt Charlotte, pleasantly.

"To live, I mean."

"Oh! Does your mother know?"

"No. I just—I just brought her home." Lottie put a hand on Aunt Charlotte's withered cheek. She was terribly near to tears. "Dear Aunt Charlotte, won't you take care of Jeannette; I'm going out after Mother. Show her her room—upstairs; you know. And give her some hot lunch. On the third floor you know—the room."

Jeannette spoke up, primly. "I don't want to make nobody trouble."

"Trouble!" echoed Aunt Charlotte. She rose spryly to her feet, asked no explanation. "You come with me, Jeannette. My, my! How pretty your hair is cut short like that. So Gussie is your sister, h'm? Well, well." She actually pinched Jeannette's tear-stained cheek.

"The dear thing!" Lottie thought, harassed as she was. "The darling old thing!" And then, suddenly: "*She* should have been my mother."

Lottie ran downstairs and into the electric. She jerked its levers so that the old vehicle swayed and cavorted on the slippery pavement.

She would drive straight over to the one-story buildings on west Halsted, near Eighteenth. Her mother usually went there first. It was a Polish settlement. Mrs. Payson owned a row of six stores occupied by a tobacconist, a shoemaker, a delicatessen, a Chinese laundry, a grocer, a lunchroom. She collected the rents herself, let out bids for repairs, kept her own books. Lottie had tried to help with these last but she was not good at accounts. Unless carefully watched, she mixed things up hopelessly. Mrs. Payson juggled account books, ledgers, checkbooks, rental lists like an expert accountant. Eighteenth Street, as Lottie drove across it now, was a wallow of liquid mud, rain, drays, spattered yellow streetcars, dim, drab-looking shops. The slippery car tracks were a menace to drivers. She had to go slowly. The row of Halsted Street buildings reached at last, Lottie ran in one store and out the other.

"Is my mother here?"

"She's gone."

"Has Mrs. Payson been here?"

"Long. She left an hour ago."

There were the other buildings on Forty-Third Street. But she couldn't have gone way up there, Lottie told herself. But she decided to try them. On the way, she stopped at the house. Her mother had not yet come in. She went on up to Forty-Third, the spring rain lashing the glassed-in hood of the electric. Yes, her mother had been there and gone. Lottie was conscious of a little hot flame of anger rising, rising in her. It seemed to drum in her ears. It made her eyelids smart and sting. She set her teeth. She swung the car over to Gus's market on Forty-Third. Her hands gripped the levers so that the ungloved knuckles showed white.

"It's a damned shame, that's what it is!" she said, aloud; and sobbed a little. "It's a damned shame, that's what it is. She could have waited. It's just pure meanness. She could have waited. I wish I was dead!"

It was as though the calm, capable, resourceful woman of the ten o'clock courtroom scene had never been.

"Gus, has my mother—?"

"She's just went. You can ketch her yet. I told her to wait till it let up a little. She was wetter'n a drowned rat. But not her! You know your ma! Wait nothin'."

Lottie headed toward Indiana Avenue and the car line. Her eyes searched the passersby beneath their dripping umbrellas. Then she spied her, a draggled black-garbed figure, bundle-laden, waiting on the corner for her car. Her left arm—the bad one—was held stiffly folded in front of her, close to her body. That meant pain. Her shoulders were hunched a little. Her black hat was slightly askew. Lottie noted, with the queer faculty one has for detail at such times, that her color was slightly yellow. But as she peered up the street in vain hope of an approaching streetcar, her glance was as alert as ever. She walked forward toward the curb to scan the empty car tracks. Lottie noticed her feet. In the way she set them down; in their appearance of ankle weakness and a certain indescribable stiffness that carried with it a pathetic effort at spryness there was, somehow, a startling effect of age, of feebleness. She toed in a little with weariness. A hot blur sprang to Lottie's eyes. She drew up sharply at the curb, flung open the door, was out, had seized the bundles, and was propelling her mother toward the electric almost before Mrs. Payson had realized her presence.

"Mother dear, why didn't you wait!"

For a moment it looked as if Mrs. Payson meant to resist stubbornly. She even jerked her arm away, childishly. But strong as her will was, her aching body protested still more strongly. Lottie hoisted her almost bodily into the electric. She looked shrunken and ocherous as she huddled in a corner. But her face was set, implacable. The car sped down the rain-swept street. Lottie glanced sideways at her mother. Her eyes were closed. They seemed strangely deep-set in their sockets.

"Oh, Mama—" Lottie's voice broke; the tears, hot, hurt, repentent, coursed down her cheeks—"why did you do it! You knew—you knew—"

Mrs. Carrie Payson opened her eyes. "You said Belle's hired girl's sister was more important than I, didn't you? Well!"

"But you knew I didn't—" she stopped short. She couldn't say she hadn't meant it. She had. She couldn't explain to her mother that she had meant that her effort to help Jeannette was her protest against stifled expression. Her mother would not have understood. It sounded silly and pretentious even in her unspoken thought. But deeper than this deprecatory self-consciousness was a new and growing consciousness of self.

She remembered Jeannette; Jeannette installed in the third-floor room, a member of the household. At the thought of breaking the news of her presence to her mother, Lottie felt a wild desire to giggle. It was a task too colossal, too hopeless for seriousness. You had to tackle it smilingly or go down to defeat at once. Lottie braced herself for the effort. She told herself, dramatically, that if Jeannette went, she, too, would go.

"I brought Jeannette home with me."

"Who?"

"Jeannette—Gussie's sister. The one who's had trouble with the family."

"Home! What for!"

"She's—she's a nice little thing, and bright. There wasn't any place to send her. We've got so much room."

"You must be crazy."

"Are you going to turn her out into the storm, Mom, like the girl in the melodrama?"

Mrs. Payson was silent a moment. Then, "Does she know anything about housework? Belle's always saying her Gussie's such a treasure. I'm about sick of that Hulda. Wastes more every week than we eat. I don't see what they *do* with it—these girls. If we used a pound of butter this last week, we used five and I hardly touch—"

"Jeannette doesn't want to do housework. She wants to go to business college."

"Well, of course, if you're running a reform school."

But she made no further protest now. Lottie, peeling off her mother's wet clothing as soon as they entered the house, pleaded with her to go to bed.

She was startled when her mother agreed. Mrs. Payson had always said, "When I go to bed in the middle of the day, you can know I'm sick." Now she crept stiffly between the covers of her big old-fashioned walnut bed with a groan that she tried to turn into a cough. An hour later they sent for the doctor. An acute arthritis attack. Lottie reproached herself grimly, unsparingly.

"I'll get up around four o'clock," Mrs. Payson said. "You don't find me staying in bed. Belle does enough of that for the whole family." At four she said, "I'll get up in time for dinner . . . Where's that girl? Where's that girl that was so important, h'm? I want to see her."

She was in bed for a week. Lottie covered herself with reproaches.

Chapter XI

No one quite knew when or how Jeannette had become indispensable to the Payson household; but she had. Most of all she had become indispensable to Mrs. Carrie Payson. Between the two there existed a lion-and-mouse friendship. Jeannette's ebullient spirits had not undergone years of quenching from the acid stream of Mrs. Payson's criticism. Jeannette's perceptions and valuations were the straightforward simple peasant sort, unhampered by fine distinctions or involved reasoning. To her, Mrs. Carrie Payson was not a domineering and rather terrible person whose word was law and whose will was adamant, but a fretful, funny, and rather bossy old woman who generally was wrong. Jeannette was immensely fond of her and did not take her seriously for a moment. About the house Jeannette was as handy as a man. And this was a manless household. She could conquer a stubborn window shade; adjust a loose castor in one of the bulky old chairs or bedsteads; drive a nail; put up a shelf; set a mousetrap.

In the very beginning she and Mrs. Payson had come to grips. Mrs. Payson's usual attitude of faultfinding and intolerance had brought about the situation. Jeannette had rebelled at once.

"I guess I'll have to leave today," she had said. "I'm going back to the factory."

"Why?"

"I can't have nobody giving me board and room for nothing. I always paid for what I got." She began to pack her scant belongings in the little room on the third floor next to Hulda's. A council was summoned. It was agreed that Jeannette should help with the household tasks; assist Hulda with the dishes; flip-flop the mattresses; clean the silver, perhaps. This silver cleaning was one of Mrs. Payson's fixed ideas. It popped into her mind whenever she saw Hulda momentarily idle. Hulda did endless yards of coarse and hideous tatting and crocheting intended ultimately for guimpes, edgings, bands, and borders on nightgowns, corset covers, and pillow slips. Pressed, she admitted an Oscar in the offing. She had mounds of stout underwear, crochet-edged, in her queer old-world trunk. When, in a leisure hour, she sat in her room or in the orderly kitchen, she was always busy with a gray and grimy ball of this handiwork. Mrs. Payson would slam in and out of the kitchen. "There she sits, doing nothing. Crocheting!"

"But Mother," Lottie would say, "her work's all done. The kitchen's like a pin. She cleaned the whole front of the house today. It isn't time to start dinner."

"Let her clean the silver, then."

Jeannette ate her meals with Hulda, and before a week had passed, she had banished the grubby and haphazard feeding off one end of the kitchen table. She got hold of a rickety old table in the basement, straightened its wobbly legs, painted it white, and set it up against the kitchen wall under the window facing the backyard. In a pantry drawer she found a faded lunch cloth of the Japanese variety, with bluebirds on it. This she spread for their meals. They had proper knives, forks, and spoons. The girl was friendly, good-natured, helpful. Hulda could not resent her— even welcomed her companionship in that rather grim household. Hulda showed Jeannette her dreambook without which no Swedish houseworker can exist; told her her dreams in detail. "It vos like I vos walking and yet I didn't come nowheres. It seems like I vos in Chicago and same time it vos old country where I ban come from and all the flowers vos blooming in fields and all of sudden a old man comes walking and I look and it vos—" etc., ad lib.

Jeannette's business college hours were from nine to four. She went downtown in one of Charley's straight smart tailor suits, revamped, and a sailor with an upturned brim that gave her face a piquant look. She did not seem to care much for what she called "the fellas." Perhaps her searing experience of the automobile ride had scarred that side of her. Lottie encouraged her to bring her "boyfriends" to the house, but Jeannette had not yet taken advantage of the offer. One day, soon after her induction into the Prairie Avenue household, she had turned her attention to the electric. Lottie had just come in from an errand with Mrs. Payson. Jeannette waylaid her.

"Listen. If you would learn me to—huh? oh—teach me to run that thing you ride around in, I bet I could catch on quick—quickly. Then I could take your ma around Saturday mornings when I ain't at school; and evenings, and you wouldn't have to, see? Will you?"

With the magic adaptability of youth, she learned to drive with incredible ease. She had no nerves; a sense of the road; an eye for distances. After she had mastered the old car's idiosyncrasies, she became adept at it. She had a natural mechanical sense, and after one or two encounters with the young man from the Elite Garage, the electric's motive powers were noticeably improved. Often, now, it was Jeannette who drove Mrs. Payson to her buildings on the West Side, or to her appointments with contractors, plumbers, carpenters, and the like. Heretofore, on such errands, Mrs. Payson had always insisted that Lottie wait in the electric at the curb. Seated thus, Lottie would watch her mother with worried anxious eyes as she whisked in and out of store doors, alleys, and basements followed by a heavy-footed workman or contractor whose face grew more sullen and resentful each time it appeared around a corner. Mrs. Payson's voice came floating back to Lottie. "Now what's the best you'll do on that job. Remember, I'll have a good deal of work later in the year if you'll do this reasonably."

Now Jeannette calmly followed Mrs. Payson in her tour of inspection. Once or twice Mrs. Payson actually consulted her about this fence or that floor or partition. The girl was good at figures, too; a natural aptitude for mathematics.

Lottie found herself possessed of occasional leisure. She could spend a half-day in the country. She could lunch in the park and stroll over to the Wooded Island to watch and wonder at the budding marvel of trees and shrubs and bushes. She even thought, boldly, of getting a Saturday job of some sort—perhaps in connection with Judge Barton's court— but hesitated to appropriate Jeannette's time permanently thus. The atmosphere of the old Prairie Avenue home was less turbid, somehow. Jeannette was a dash of clear cold water in the muddy sediment of their existence. Sometimes the thought came to Lottie that she hadn't been needed in the household after all. That is, she—Lottie Payson—to the exclusion of anyone else. Anyone else would have done as well. She had merely been the person at hand. Looking back on the past ten years, she hated to believe this. If she had merely been made use of thus, then those ten years had been wasted, thrown away, useless—she put the thought out of her mind as morbid. Sometimes, too, of late, Lottie took a hasty fearful glance into the future and there saw herself a septuagenarian like Aunt Charlotte; living out her life with Belle. "No! No! No!" protested a voice within her rising to a silent shriek. "No!"

Lottie was thirty-three the last week in April. "Now Lottie!" her mother's friends said to her, wagging a chiding forefinger, "you're not going to let your little niece get ahead of you, are you!"

She rarely saw the girls now. She heard that Beck Schaefer had taken to afternoon tea dancing. She was seen daily at hotel tearooms in company with pallid and incredibly slim youths of the lizard type, their hair as glittering as their boots; lynx-eyed; exhaling a last hasty puff of cigarette smoke as they rose from the table for the next dance; inhaling a grateful lungful before they so much as sat down again after that dance was finished. They wore very tight pants and slim-waisted coats, and their hats came down over their ears as if they were too big for their heads. Beck, smelling expensively of L'Origon and wearing very palpable slippers and stockings, was said to pay the checks proffered by the waiter at the close of these afternoons. Lottie's informant further confided to her that Beck was known in tea-dance circles as the Youth's Companion.

The last week in April, Mrs. Carrie Payson went to French Lick Springs with Belle—Mrs. Payson for her rheumatism, Belle for her digestive trouble. Henry, looking more worried and distrait than ever, was to follow them at the end of the week. You rarely heard his big booming laugh now. Mrs. Payson and her daughter Belle had never before gone away together. Always it had been Lottie who had accompanied her mother. Lottie was rather apprehensive about the outcome of the proximity of the two. Belle did not appear to relish the prospect particularly; but she said she needed the cure, and Henry had finally convinced her of the utter impossibility of his going. He was rather alarmingly frank about it. "Can't afford it, Belle," he said, "and that's the God's truth. Business is—well, there isn't any, that's all. You need the rest and all and I want you to go. I'll try to come down for Saturday and Sunday but don't count on me. I may have to go to New York any day now."

He did leave for New York that week, before the French Lick trip. Lottie and Charley took them down to the station in the Kemps' big car with the expert Charley at the wheel. Mrs. Payson kept up a steady stream of admonition, reminder, direction, caution, advice. The house was to undergo the April semiannual cleaning during her absence.

"Call up Amos again about the rugs and mattresses . . . in the yard, remember; and you've got to watch him every minute . . . every inch of the woodwork with warm water—not hot! . . . a little ammonia . . . the backs of the pictures . . . a pot roast and cut it up cold for the cleaning woman's lunch and give her plenty of potatoes . . . the parlor curtains . . ."

The train was gone. Lottie and Charley stood looking at each other for a moment, wordlessly. They burst into rather wild laughter. Then they embraced. People in the station must have thought one of them a traveler just returned from afar. They clasped hands and raced for the car.

"Let's go for a drive," said Charley. It was ten-thirty at night.

"All right," agreed Lottie. Charley swung the car back into Michigan, then up Michigan headed north. The air was deliciously soft and balmy for April in Chicago. They whisked up Lake Shore Drive and into Lincoln Park. Lottie was almost ashamed of the feeling of freedom, of relaxation, of exaltation that flooded her whole being. She felt alive, and tingling and light. She was smiling unconsciously. On the way back, Charley drew up at the curb along the outside drive at the edge of Lincoln Park, facing the lake. They sat wordlessly for a brief space in the healing quiet and peace and darkness, with the waves lipping the stones at their feet.

"Nice," from Charley.

"Mm."

Silence again. An occasional motor sped past them in the darkness. To the south, the great pier, like a monster sea serpent, stretched its mile-length into the lake. A freighter, ore-laden, plying its course between some northern Michigan mine and an Indiana steel mill was transformed by the darkness and distance into a barge of beauty—mystic, silent, glittering.

"What are you going to do with your week, Lotta?"

"H'm? Oh! Well, there's the housecleaning—"

"Oh!" Charley slammed her fist down on the motor horn. It squawked in chorus with her protest. "If what the Bible promises is true, then you're the heiress of the ages, you are."

"Heiress?"

"'The meek shall inherit the earth.'"

"I'm not meek. I'm just the kind of person that things don't happen to."

"You don't let them happen. When everything has gone wrong, and you're feeling stifled and choked, and you've just been forbidden, as if you were a half-wit of sixteen, to do something that you've every right to do, what's your method! Instead of blowing up with a loud report—instead of asserting yourself like a freeborn white woman—you put on your hat and take a long walk and work it off that way. Then you come home with that high spiritual look on your face that makes me want to scream and slap you. You're exactly like Aunt Charlotte. When she and Grandma have had a tiff, she sails upstairs and starts to clean out her bureau drawers and wind old ribbons and fold things. Well, some day in a crisis, she'll find that her bureau drawers have all been tidied the day before. *Then* what'll she do!"

"Muss 'em up."

"So will you—muss things up. You mark the words of a gal that's been around."

"You kids today are so sure of yourselves. I wonder if your method is going to work out any better than ours. You haven't proved it yet. You know, always, exactly what you want to do and then you go ahead and do it. It's so simple that there must be a catch in it somewhere."

"It's full of catches. That's what makes it so fascinating. All these centuries we've been told to profit by the advice of our elders. What's living for if not to experience? How can anyone know whether you're right or wrong? Oh, I don't mean about small things. Any stranger can decide for you that blue is more becoming than black. But the big things—those things I want to decide for myself. I'm entitled to my own mistakes. I've the right to be wrong. How many middle-aged people do you know whose lives aren't a mess this minute! The thing is to be able to say, 'I planned this myself and my plans didn't work. Now I'll take my medicine.' You can't live somebody else's life without your own getting all distorted in the effort. Now I'll probably marry Jesse Dick—"

"Charley Kemp! You don't know what you're saying. You're a nineteen-year-old infant."

"I'm a lot older than you. Of course he hasn't asked me. I don't suppose he ever will. I mean they don't put a hand on the heart and say will-you-be-mine. But he hadn't kissed me twice before I knew."

A faint, "Charley!"

"And he's the only man I've ever met that I can fancy still caring for when he's forty-three and I'm forty. He'll never be snuffy and settled and taken-for-granted. He talks to children as if they were human beings and not nuisances or idiots. I've heard him. He's darling with them. Sort of solemn and answers their questions intelligently. I know that when I'm forty he'll still be able to make me laugh by calling me 'Mrs. Dick, ma'am.' We'll probably disagree, as we do now, about the big empty things like war and politics. But we're in perfect accord about the small things that make up everyday life. And they're the things that count, in marriage."

"But Charley, child, does your mother know all this?"

"Oh, no. Mother thinks she's the modern woman and that she makes up the younger generation. She doesn't realize that I'm the younger generation. She's really as old-fashioned as any of them. She is superior in a lot of ways, Mother is. But she's like all the rest in most. She's been so used all these years to having people exclaim with surprise when she said she had a daughter of sixteen—seventeen—eighteen—that now, when I'm nineteen, she still expects people to exclaim over her having a big girl. I'm not a big girl. I'm not even what the cheap novels used to call a 'child-woman.' Mother'll have to wake up to that."

Lottie laughed a little at a sudden recollection. "When I got this hat last week, Mother went with me."

"She would," sotto voce, from Charley.

"The saleswoman brought a little pile of them—four or five—and I tried them on; but they weren't the thing, quite. And then Mother, who was sitting there, watching me, said to the girl: 'Oh, no, those won't do. Show us something more girlish.'"

"There!"

"Yes, but wasn't it kind of sweet? The clerk stared, of course. I heard her giggling about it afterward to one of the other saleswomen. You see, Mother thinks I'm still a girl. When I leave the house she often asks me if I have a clean handkerchief."

"Yes, go on, be sentimental about it. That'll help. You've let Grandma dominate your life. That's all right—her wanting to, I mean. That's human nature. The older generation trying to curb the younger. But your letting her do it—that's another thing. That's a crime against your own generation and indicates a weakness in you, not in her. The younger generation has got to rule. Those of us who recognize that and act on it, win. Those who don't, go under."

"You're a dreadful child!" exclaimed Lottie. She more than half meant it. "It's horrible to hear you. Where did you learn all this—this ruthlessness?"

"I learned it at school—and out of school. Those are the things we talk about. What did you suppose boys and girls talk about these days!"

"I don't know," Lottie replied, weakly. She thought of the girl of the old Armour Institute days—the girl who used to go bicycling on Saturdays with the boy in the jersey sweater. They had talked about school, and books, and games, and dreams, and even hopes—very diffidently and shyly—but never once about reality or life. If they had, perhaps things would have been different for Lottie Payson, she thought now. "Let's go home, Chas."

On the drive home, Charley talked of her new work. She was full of shop stories. Nightly she brought home some fresh account of the happenings in her department; a tale of a buyer, or customer, or clerk, or department head. Henry Kemp called these her stock of stock girl stories. Following her first week at Shield's, she had said grimly: "Remember that girl O. Henry used to write about, the one who kept thinking about her feet all the time? That's me. I'm that little shopgirl, I am."

Her father encouraged her dinner table conversation and roared at her rather caustic comment:

"Our buyer came back from New York today. Her name's Healy. She has her hair marcelled regularly and wears the loveliest black crepe de chine frocks with collars and cuffs that are simply priceless, and I wish you could hear her pronounce 'voile.' Like this—'vwawl.' It isn't a mouthful; it's a meal. Don't glare, Mother. I know I'm vulgar. When a North Shore customer comes in you say, 'Do let me show you a little import that came in yesterday. It's too sweet.' All high-priced blouses are 'little imports.' They're as precious as jewels since the war, of course. Healy used to be a stock girl. They say her hair is gray but she dyes it the most fetching raspberry shade. Her salary is twelve thousand a year and she could get eighteen at any one of the other big stores. She stays at Shield's because she thinks it has distinction. 'Class,' she calls it, unless she's talking to a customer or someone else she's trying to impress. Then she says 'atmosphere.' She supports her mother and a good-for-nothing brother. I like her. Her nails glitter something grand. She calls me girlie. I wonder if her pearls are real."

Lottie listened now, fascinated, amused, and yet wondering, as Charley gave an account of the meeting of the Ever Upward Club. Charley was driving with one hand on the steering wheel. She was slumped low down on her spine. Lottie thought how relaxed she looked and almost babyish, and yet how vital and how knowing. The Ever Upward Club, she explained, was made up of the women workers in Shield's. There had been a meeting of the club this morning, before the store opened at nine. It was the club's twenty-fifth anniversary. Charley, on the subject, was vitriol.

"There they sat, in their black dresses and white collars. Some of the collars weren't so white. I suppose, after a few years, washing out white collars at night when you get home from work loses its appeal. First Kiesing made a speech about the meaning of Shield's, and the loftiness of its aim. I don't know where he got his information but I gathered that to have the privilege of clerking there makes you one of the anointed. Kiesing's general manager, you know. Then he brought forward Mrs. Hough. She's pretty old and her teeth sort of stick out and her voice is high and what they call querulous, I suppose. Anyway it never drops at the end of a sentence. She told how she had started the Ever Upward Club with a membership of only fifteen, and now look at it. Considering that you have to belong to it, and pay your dues automatically when you enter the store, I don't see why she feels so set up about it. But anyway, she does. You'd think she had gone around converting the heathen to Christianity. She told us in that nasal rasping voice that it was the spirit of cheer and goodwill that made tasks light. Yes, indeed. And when we got home at night we were to help our mothers with the dishes in a spirit of cheer and with a right goodwill. Then she read one of those terrible vim-and-vigour poems. You know. Something like this:

If you think you are beaten, you are.
If you think you dare not, you don't.
If you like to win and don't think you can
It's almost a cinch you won't.

There was a lot more to it, about life's battles and the man who wins. Most of the girls looked half-dead in their chairs. They had been working overtime for the spring opening. Then a girl sprang to the platform—she's the club athletic director, a college girl, big, husky, good-looking brute, too. 'Three rousing cheers for Mrs. Hough! Hip hip—' We all piped up. And I couldn't think of anything but Oliver Twist and the beadle—what was his name?—Bumble. Then this girl told us about the value of games and the spirit of play, and how we should leap and run about—after you've done the dinner dishes with a right good will, I suppose, having previously walked eleven thousand miles in your department showing little imports and trying to convince a woman with a forty-two bust that a thirty-eight blouse is a little snug . . . 'The romance of business.' Ha!"

"But you like it, don't you, Charley?"

"Yes. Goodness knows why. Certainly I don't want to turn out a Healy, or a Hough—or even a female Kiesing. Jesse did a poem about it all."

"A good one?"

"Good—yes. And terrible. One of his sledgehammer things. He calls it 'Merchandise.' The girls, of course."

They stopped at a corner drugstore and had ice cream sodas. Charley was to spend the night at the Prairie Avenue house. She had a brilliant thought. "Let's bring a chocolate soda home to Aunt Charlotte." They ordered two in pressed paper cartons and presented them at midnight to Aunt Charlotte and Jeannette. Jeannette, looking like a rose baby, ate hers in a semi-trance, her lids weighted with sleep. But Great-Aunt Charlotte was wide awake immediately, as though a midnight chocolate ice cream soda were her prescribed nightcap. She sipped and blinked and scraped the bottom of the container with her spoon. Then, with an appreciative sigh, she lay back on her pillow.

"What time is it, Lottie?"

"After midnight. 12:20."

"That's nice," said Aunt Charlotte. "Let's have waffles for breakfast."

The mice were playing.

It was Lottie's idea that they accomplish the spring house cleaning in three volcanic days instead of devoting a week or more to it, as was Mrs. Payson's habit. "Let's all pitch in," she said, "and get it over with. Then we'll have a week to play in." Mrs. Payson was to remain ten days at French Lick.

There followed such an orgy of beating, pounding, flapping, brushing, swashing, and scrubbing as no corps of able-bodied men could have survived. The women emerged from it with shriveled fingers, broken nails, and aching spines, but the Prairie Avenue house was clean, even to the backs of the pictures. After it was over, Lottie had a Turkish bath, a manicure, and a shampoo and proclaimed herself socially accessible.

Hulda drank coffee happily, all day. Great-Aunt Charlotte announced that she thought she'd have some of the girls in for the afternoon. She invited a group of ancients whose names sounded like the topmost row of Chicago's social register. Their sons or grandsons were world powers in banking, packing, grain distribution. Some of them Aunt Charlotte had not seen in years. They rolled up in great, fat, black limousines and rustled in black silks as modish as Aunt Charlotte's own. Lottie saw to the tea and left them absolutely alone. She heard them snickering and gossiping in their high plangent voices. They bragged in a well-bred way about their sons or grandsons or sons-in-law. They gossiped. They reminisced.

"And do you remember when the Palmer House barbershop floor was paved at intervals with silver dollars and the farmers used to come from miles around to see it?"

"There hasn't been a real social leader in Chicago since Mrs. Potter Palmer died."

"Yes, I know. She's tried. But charm—that's the thing she hasn't got. No. She thinks her money will do it. Never."

"Well, it seems—"

What a good time they were having, Lottie thought. She had set the table in the dining room. There were spring flowers and candles. She saw that they were properly served but effaced herself. She sensed that her presence would, somehow, mar Aunt Charlotte's complete sense of freedom, of hospitality, of hostess-ship.

They did not leave until six. After they were gone, Aunt Charlotte stepped about the sitting room putting the furniture to rights. She was tired, but too stimulated to rest. Her cheeks were flushed.

"Minnie Parnell is beginning to show her age, don't you think? Did you see the hat Henrietta Grismore wore? Well, I should think, with all her money! But then, she always was a funny girl. No style."

When, two days later, Lottie had Emma Barton and Winnie Steppler to dinner, Aunt Charlotte kept her room. She said she felt a little tired— the spring weather perhaps. She'd have just a bite on a tray if Jeannette would bring it up to her; and then she'd go to bed. Do her good. Lottie, understanding, kissed her.

Lottie and her two friends had one of those long animated talks. Lottie had lighted a fire in the sitting room fireplace. There were flowers in the room—jonquils, tulips. The old house was quiet, peaceful. Lottie made a charming hostess. They laughed a good deal from the very start when Winnie Steppler had come up the stairs panting apologies for her new headgear.

"Don't say it's too youthful. I know it. I bought it on that fine day last week—the kind of spring day that makes you go into a shop and buy a hat that's too young for you." Her cheeks were rosy. When she laughed, she opened her mouth wide and stuck her tongue out so that she reminded you of the talcum baby picture so familiar to everyone. A woman of tremendous energy—magnetic, witty, zestful.

"Fifty's the age!" she announced with gusto, as dinner progressed. "At fifty you haven't a figger any more than you have legs—except, of course, for purposes of locomotion. At fifty you can eat and drink what you like. Chocolate with whipped cream at four in the afternoon. Who cares! A second helping of dessert. It's a grand time of life. At fifty you don't wait for the telephone to ring. Will he call me! Won't he call me! A telephone's just a telephone at fifty—a convenience without a thrill to it. Many's the time that bell has stabbed me. But not now. Nothing more can happen to you at fifty—if you've lived your life as you should. Here I sit, stays loosened, savoring life. I wouldn't change places with any young sprat I know."

Emma Barton smiled, calm-eyed. Winnie Steppler had been twice married, once widowed, once divorced. Emma Barton had never married. Yet both knew peace at fifty.

"Well," said Lottie, as they rose from the table, "perhaps, by the time I'm fifty—but just now I've such a frightened feeling as though everything were passing me by; all the things that matter. I want to grab at life and say, 'Heh, wait a minute! Aren't you forgetting me?'"

Winnie Steppler glanced at her sharply. "Look out, my girl, that it doesn't rush back at your call and drop the wrong trick into your lap."

A little flash of defiance came into Lottie's eyes. "The wrong trick's better than no trick at all."

Emma Barton looked at Lottie curiously, with much the same glance that she bestowed upon the girls who came before her each morning. "What do you need to keep you happy, Lottie?"

Lottie did not hesitate a moment. "Work that's congenial; books; music occasionally; a picnic in the woods; a five-mile hike, a well-fitting suit, a thirteen-dollar corset, Charley—I didn't mean to place her last. She should be up at the beginning somewhere."

"How about this superstition they call love?" inquired Winnie Steppler. Lottie shrugged her shoulders. Winnie persisted. "There must have been somebody, some time."

"Well, when I was seventeen or eighteen—but there never was anything serious about it, really. Since then—you wouldn't believe how rarely women of my type meet men—interesting men. You have to make a point of meeting them, I suppose. And I've been here at home. I'm thirty-three. Not bad looking. I've kept my figure, and hair, and skin. Walking, I suppose. The men I know are snuffy bachelors nearing fifty, or widowers with three children. They'd rather go to a musical show than a symphony concert; they'll tell you they do enough walking in their business. I don't mind their being bald—though why should they be?—but I do mind their being snuffy. I suppose there are men of about my own age who like the things I like; whose viewpoint is mine. But attractive men of thirty-five marry girls of twenty. I don't want to marry a boy of twenty; but neither can I work up any enthusiasm for a man of fifty who tells me that what he wants is a home, and who would no more take a tramp in the country for enjoyment than he would contemplate a trip to Mars."

Emma Barton interposed. "What were you doing at twenty-five?"

Lottie glanced around the room. Her hand came out in a little gesture that included the house and its occupants. "Just what I'm doing now. But not even thinking about it—as I do now! I think I had an idea I was important. Now that I look back on it, it seems to me I've just been running errands for the last ten years or more. Running errands up and down, while the world has gone by."

Two days before her mother's return, Lottie prevailed upon Jeannette to invite a half dozen or more of her business college acquaintances to spend the evening at the house. Jeannette demurred at first, but it was plain the idea fascinated her. Seven of them arrived at the time appointed. Their ages ranged between seventeen and twenty-two. The girls were amazingly well dressed in georgettes and taffetas and smart slippers and silk stockings. The boys were, for the most part, of the shipping clerk type. They were all palpably impressed with the big old house on Prairie, its massive furniture and pictures, its occupants. Lottie met them all, as did Aunt Charlotte who had donned her second-best black silk and her jewelry and had crimped her hair for the occasion. She sensed that what Jeannette needed was background. Aunt Charlotte vanished before nine and Lottie did likewise, to appear again only for the serving of the ice cream and cake. They danced, sang, seemed really to enjoy the evening. After they had gone, Jeannette turned to Lottie and, catching up one of her hands, pressed it against her own glowing cheek. Her eyes were very bright. They—and the gesture—supplied the meaning that her inarticulate speech lacked. "It was grand!"

It was typical of Charley and indicative of the freedom with which she lived, that her existence during the ten days of her mother's absence did not vary at all from the usual. She would have been torn between laughter and fury could she have realized the sense of boldness and freedom with which Lottie, her aunt, and Charlotte, her great-aunt, set about planning their innocent maidenly revels.

Mrs. Payson and Belle returned from French Lick the first week in May. Mrs. Payson, divesting herself of her wraps, ran a quick and comprehensive eye over the room, over Lottie, over Aunt Charlotte, Jeannette, Hulda. It was as though she read Coffee! Tea Party! Dinner! Dance! in their faces. Her first question seemed to carry with it a hidden meaning. "Well, what have you been doing while I've been gone? Did Brosch call up about the plastering? Did you have Henry and Charley to dinner? Any letters? How many days did you have Mrs. Schlagel for the cleaning? Lottie, get me a cup of tea, I feel kind of faint—not hungry, but a faint feeling. Oh—Ben Gartz was in French Lick. Did I write you? He was very attentive. Very. Every inch the gentleman. I don't know what Belle and I would have done without him."

Chapter XII

For fifteen years Mrs. Carrie Payson's bitterness at the outcome of her own unfortunate marriage had been unconsciously expressed in her attitude toward the possible marriage of her daughter Lottie. Confronted with this accusation, she would have denied it, and her daughter Lottie would have defended her in the denial. Nevertheless, it was true. During the years when all Mrs. Payson's energy, thought, and time were devoted to the success of the real estate and bond business, her influence had been less markedly felt than later. In some indefinable way, the few men who came within Lottie's ken were startled and repelled by the grim white-haired woman who regarded them with eyes of cold hostility. One or two of them had said, uncomfortably, in one of Mrs. Payson's brief absences, "Your mother doesn't like me."

"What nonsense! Why shouldn't she?"

"I don't know. She looks at me as if she had something on me." Then as Lottie stiffened perceptibly, "Oh, I didn't mean that exactly. No offence, I hope. I just meant—"

"Mother's like I am. She isn't demonstrative but her likes and dislikes are very definite." Lottie, remember, was only twenty-three or thereabouts at this time. Still, she should have known better.

"You don't say!" the young man would exclaim, thoughtfully.

Now, suddenly, Mrs. Payson had about-faced. Perhaps this in turn was as unconscious as her previous attitude had been. Perhaps the thought of a spinster daughter of thirty-three pricked her vanity. Perhaps she, like Lottie, had got a sudden glimpse into the future in which she saw Lottie a second Aunt Charlotte, tremulous and withered, telling out her days in her sister Belle's household. It was slowly borne in on Lottie that her mother regarded Ben Gartz favorably as a possible son-in-law. Her first sensation on making this discovery was one of amusement. Her mother in the role of matchmaker wore a humorous aspect, certainly. As the weeks went on this amusement gave way to something resembling terror. Mrs. Payson usually achieved her own ends. Lottie had never defined the relationship that existed between her mother and herself. She did not suspect that they were united by a strong bond of affection and hate so complexly interwoven that it was almost impossible to tell which strand was this and which that. Mrs. Payson did not dream that she had blocked her daughter's chances for a career or for marital happiness. Neither did she know that she looked down upon that daughter for having failed to marry. But both were true in some nightmarish and indefinable way. Mrs. Carrie Payson, the coarser metal, had beat upon Lottie, the finer, and had molded and shaped her as iron beats upon gold.

Lottie was still in the amused stage when Mrs. Payson remarked:

"I understand that Ben Gartz is going into that business he spoke of last spring. Men's wristwatches. We all thought he was making a mistake but it seems he's right. He's going in with Beck and Diblee this fall. I shouldn't wonder if Ben Gartz should turn out to be a very rich man some day. A ve-ry rich man. Especially if this war—"

"That'll be nice," said Lottie.

"I wish Henry had some of his push and enterprise."

Lottie looked up quickly at that, prompt in defense of Henry. "Henry isn't to blame for the war. His business was successful enough until two years ago—more than successful. It just happens to be the kind that has been hardest hit."

"Why doesn't he take up a new business, then! Ben Gartz is going into something new."

"Ben's mother left him a little money when she died. I suppose he's putting that into the new business. Besides, he hasn't a family to think of. He can take a chance. If it doesn't turn out he'll be the only one to suffer."

"Ben Gartz is an unusual boy." (Boy!) "He was a wonderful son to his mother . . . I'd like to know what you have against him."

"Against him! Why, not a thing, Mama. Only—"

Lottie hesitated. Then, regrettably, she giggled. "Only he has never heard of *Alice in Wonderland,* and he thinks the Japs are a wonderful little people but look out for 'em!, and he speaks of summer as the heated term, and he says, 'not an iota.'"

"Not an iota!" echoed Mrs. Payson almost feebly.

"Yes. You know—'not an iota of truth in it'; 'not an iota of difference.'"

"Lottie Payson, sometimes I think you're downright idiotic! *Alice in Wonderland!* The idea! Woman your age! Ben Gartz is a businessman."

"Indeed he is—strictly."

"I suppose you'd prefer going around with some young fool like this poet Charley has picked up from behind the delicatessen counter. I don't know what your sister Belle can be thinking of."

Sister Belle was thinking of a number of things, none of them pleasant; and none of them connected with Charley or Charley's poet. Henry Kemp had sold the car—the big, luxurious, swift-moving car. He had hinted that the nine-room apartment on Hyde Park Boulevard might soon be beyond his means.

"If this keeps up much longer," he had said one day to Charley, "your old dad will be asking you for a job as bundle boy at Shield's." His laugh, as he said it, had been none too robust.

Charley had been promoted from stockgirl to saleswoman. She said she supposed now she'd have to save up for black satin slippers, a French frock, a string of pearls, and filet collars and cuffs—the working girl's costume. She announced, further, that her education had reached a point where any blouse not handmade and bearing a thirty-nine-dollar price tag was a mere rag in her opinion.

Charley's Saturday afternoons and Sundays were spent in the country about Chicago—at the Indiana sand dunes; at Palos Park when May transformed its trees into puffballs of apple blossoms; in the woods about Beverly; along the far North Shore. Both she and Lottie were hardened trampers. Lottie was expert at what she called "cooking out." She could build a three-section fire with incredibly little fuel and only one match. Just as you were becoming properly ravenous, she had the coffee steaming in one section, the bacon sizzling in another, the sausages boiling in another. Now that the Kemp car was gone, these country excursions became fewer for Lottie. She missed them. The electric was impossible for country travel. It often expired even on the boulevards and had to be towed back to the garage. Charley said that Jesse Dick's flivver saved her life and youth these spring days. Together they ranged the countryside in it, a slim volume of poetry (not his own) in Jesse Dick's pocket and a plump packet of sandwiches and fruit in a corner of the seat. You were beginning to see reviews of Jesse Dicks's poems in the *Dial,* in the *New Republic,* in the weekly literary supplements of the newspapers. They spoke of his work as being "virile and American." They said it had a "warm human quality." He sang everyday life—the grain pit, the stockyards, the steel mill, the street corner, the movies. Some of the reviews said, "But this isn't poetry!" Perhaps they had just been reading the thing he called "Halsted Street." You know it:

Halsted Street. All the nations of the world.
Mill end sales; *shlag* stores; Polack women gossiping.
Look at the picture of the bride in her borrowed
wedding dress

Outside the Italian photograph gallery—
Perhaps they were right.

Still, while he did not write spring poetry of the May Day variety, it is certain that not a peach-pink petal on a wild-crab tree blossoming by the roadway bloomed in vain as Jesse and Charley passed by. Not that they were rhapsodic about it. These two belonged to the new order to whom lyricism was loathsome, abjective anathema. Fine and moving things were received with a trite or even an uncouth word or phrase. After a Brahms symphony you said, "Gee!" It was considered "hickey" or ostentatious to speak of a thing as being exquisite or wonderful. They even revived that humorously vulgar and practically obsolete word, "swell." A green and gold and pink May Day landscape was "elegant." Struck by the beauty of a scene, the majesty of a written passage, the magnificence of the lake in a storm, the glory of an orchard in full bloom, they used the crude and rustic "Gosh!" This only when deeply stirred.

Late in May, Ben Gartz bought a car of unimpressive make but florid complexion. He referred to it always as "the bus." As soon as he had mastered it, he drove round to the Paysons' and proposed a Sunday morning ride to Lottie.

"Go on, Lottie," Mrs. Payson said, "it'll do you good."

The devil of perversity seized Lottie. "I hate driving in town. I've trundled that electric of ours over these fifty miles—or is it one hundred?—of boulevards until I could follow the route blindfolded. Jackson Park to the Midway—the Midway to Washington Park—Washington to Garfield—Garfield—"

"Well, then, how about a drive in the country? Anywhere you say, Miss Lottie. The little old bus is yours to command."

"All right," said Lottie. "Let's take Charley."

"Fine!" Ben's tone was sufficiently hearty, if somewhat hollow. "Great little kid, Charley. What do you say to having lunch at one of those roadhouses along the way? Chicken dinner."

"Oh, no! Let's cook out." Ben, looking dubious, regarded the end of his cigar. But Lottie was already on her way to the kitchen. He clapped on his derby hat and went out to look over the bus. Aside from keeping it supplied with oil and gasoline, its insides were as complete a mystery to him as the workings of the solar system. Lottie, flushed and animated, was slicing bacon, cutting sandwiches, measuring out coffee. She loved a day in the country, Ben or no Ben. They telephoned Charley. She said, "Can I take Jesse? His fliv's got something the matter with its insides. We had planned to go to Thornton."

"Sure," Ben agreed again when Lottie put this to him. On the way to the Kemp apartment they stopped at a delicatessen and bought cream, fruit, wieners, cheese, salad. As she stepped out of the car Lottie saw that the fat gold letters on the window spelled "DICK'S DELICATESSEN— AND BAKERY." She was conscious of a little shock. Immediately she was ashamed that this should be so. Dick's Delicatessen was white-tiled, immaculate, smelling of things spiced and fruity and pickled. A chubby florid man with a shock of curly rust-red hair waited on her. He was affable, good-natured.

"Going on a picnic, h'm?" he said. He gave her good measure—too good for his own profit, Lottie thought. She glanced about for the wife. She must be the businessman of this concern. Mrs. Dick was not there.

"Are you Mr. Dick?" Lottie asked.

"Yes *ma'am!* I sure am." He began to total the sales, using the white marble counter as a tablet for his pencil. "Cheese—wieners—tongue— pickles—cream—that'll be one dollar and forty-three cents. If you bring back the cream bottle with this ticket you get five cents refund."

She thought of the slim and exquisite Charley; of Belle, the fastidious. "Oh, pooh!" she said to herself as she went out to the car with Ben, bundle-laden, "she's only a kid. A temporary case on a near-poet, that's all."

When they reached the Hyde Park apartment, Charley and the poet were seated on the outer steps in the sun. The poet wore becoming shabby gray tweeds, a soft shirt, and no hat. Lottie admitted to herself that he looked charming—even distinguished.

"Don't you own one?" she asked. He quirked one eyebrow. "A hat, I mean."

"Oh." He glanced at Ben's derby. Then he took from one capacious pocket a soft cloth cap and put it on. He glanced then at his hands, affecting great embarrassment. "My gloves!—stick!" He glanced frantically up and down the street. "My spats!"

The three laughed. Ben joined in a little late, and evidently bewildered. Charley presented her contribution to the picnic lunch. Gussie had baked a caramel cake the day before. Sweaters, boxes, coats, baskets, bundles—they were off.

They headed for Palos Park. Hideous as is the countryside about Chicago in most directions, this spot to the southwest is a thing of loveliness in May and in October. Gently sloping hills relieve the flat monotony of the Illinois prairie landscape. The green of the fields and trees was so tender as to carry with it a suggestion of gold. Jesse and Charley occupied the back seat. Lottie sat in front with Ben Gartz. He drove badly, especially on the hills. The two in the back seat politely refrained from comment or criticism. But on the last steep hill, the protesting knock of the tortured engine wrung interference from Charley. To her an engine was a precious thing. She could no more have mistreated it than she could have kicked a baby. "Shift to second!" she cried now, in actual pain. "Can't you hear her knocking!"

They struck camp on a wooded knoll a little ways back from the road and with a view of the countryside for miles around. Ben Gartz presented that most pathetic and incongruous of human spectacles—a fat man, in a derby, at a picnic.

He made himself useful, gathered wood, produced matches, carried water, arranged seats made up of cushions and robes from the car and was not at all offended when the others expressed a preference for the ground.

"Say, this is great!" he exclaimed, again and again, "Yessir! Nothing like getting away from the city, let me tell you, into God's big outdoors." The three smiled at what they took to be an unexpected burst of humor and were startled to see that he was quite serious. Ben tucked a napkin under his vest and played the waiter. He praised the wieners, the coffee, the bacon, the salad. He ate prodigiously, and smiled genially on Lottie and winked an eye in her direction, at the same time nodding toward Charley and Jesse to indicate that he was a party to some very special secret that Lottie shared with him. He sat cross-legged on the ground and suffered. When the luncheon was finished, he fell upon his cigar with almost a groan of relief.

"Have a cigar, sir?" He proffered a plump brown cylinder to Jesse Dick.

"No thanks," Jesse replied; and took from his own pocket a paper packet.

"A cigarette boy, eh? Well, let me tell you something, youngster. A hundred of those'll do you more harm than a barrel of these. Yessir! You take a fella smokes a mild cigar after his meal, why, when he's through with that cigar he's through—for awhile, anyway. He don't light another right away. But start to smoke a cigarette and first thing you know where's the package!"

Jesse appeared to consider this gravely. Ben Gartz leaned back, supported by one hand, palm down, on the ground. His left was hooked in the armhole of his vest. One leg was extended stiffly in front of him, the other drawn up. He puffed at his cigar.

Lottie rose abruptly. "I'll clear these things away." She smiled at Jesse and Charley. "You two children go for a walk. I know you're dying to. I'll have everything slicked up in a jiffy."

"Oh, I think not," the two answered. They knew what was sporting and rigidly followed certain forms of conduct. Having eaten, they expected to pay. They scraped, cleared, folded, packed with the deftness of practiced picnickers. Jesse Dick's eye was caught by the name on the cover of a discarded pasteboard box.

"Oh, say! You got this stuff at Father's."

"Yes; we stopped on the way—"

The boy tapped the cover of the box and grinned. "Best delicatessen in Chicago, Illinois, ladies and gents, if I say it as shouldn't. Dad certainly pickles a mean herring." His face sobered. "He's an artist in his line—Father. Did you ever see one of his Saturday night windows? He'll have a great rugged mountain of Swiss cheese in the background, with foothills of Roquefort and Edam. Then there'll be a plateau of brown crackly roasted turkeys and chickens, and below this, like flowers in the valley, all the pimento and mayonnaise things, the salads, and lettuces and deviled eggs and stuffed tomatoes. (His poem "Delicatessen Window" is now included in the volume called *Roughneck*.)

"I understand you're a poet," Ben Gartz (remarked, quizzically. For him there was humor in the very word).

"Yes."

"Now that's funny, ain't it—with your father in the delicatessen business and all?"

Again Jesse Dick seemed to ponder seriously. "Maybe it is. But I know of quite a good poet who was apprenticed to a butcher."

"Butcher! No!" Ben roared genially. "What poet was that?"

Jesse Dick glanced at Charley then. He looked a little shamefaced; and yet, having begun, he went through with it. "Shakespeare, his name was. Will Shakespeare."

"Oh, say, what's this you're giving me!" But the faces of the three were serious. "Say, is that right?" He appealed to Lottie.

"It's supposed to be true," she said gently, "though it has been doubted." Lottie had brought along the olive-drab knitting in a little flowered cretonne bag. She sat on the ground now, in the sunlight, her back against a tree, knitting.

Jesse and Charley rose, wordlessly, as though with one thought, and glanced across the little meadow beyond. It was a Persian carpet of spring flowers—little pink, and mauve, and yellow chalices. Charley gazed at it a moment, her head thrown back. She began to walk toward it, through the wood. Jesse stopped to light a cigarette. His eyes were on Charley. He called out to her. "See your whole leg through that dress of yours, Charley."

She glanced down carelessly. "Yes? That's because I'm standing in the sun, I suppose." It was a slim, little wool jersey frock. "I never wear a petticoat with this." They strolled off together across the meadow.

"Well!" exploded Ben Gartz, "that young fella certainly is a free talker." He looked after them, his face red. "Young folks now days—"

"Young folks now days are wonderful," Lottie said. She remembered an expression she had heard somewhere. "They're sitting on top of the world."

Out on the flower-strewn carpet of meadow grass, Charley was doing a dance in the sunlight all alone—a dance that looked like an inspired improvisation and that probably represented hours of careful technical training. If a wood nymph had ever worn a wool jersey frock, she would have looked as Charley looked now. Ben, almost grudgingly, admitted something like this. "Gosh, that kid certainly can dance! Where'd she pick it up?"

"She's had years of training—lessons. Boys and girls do now days, you know. They have everything. We never used to. I wish we had. If their teeth aren't perfect they're straightened. Everything's made perfect that's imperfect. And they're taught about music, and they know books, and they look the world in the eye. They're free!"

Ben dug in the soft ground with a bit of wood. "How d'you mean—free?"

"Why I mean—free," she said again, lamely. "Honest. Not afraid."

"Afraid of what?"

She shook her head then and went on with her knitting. Lottie looked very peaceful and pleasant there in the little sun-dappled wood, with the light shining on her hair, her firm strong shoulders resting against the black trunk of the tree, her slim black-silk ankles crossed primly. Ben regarded her appreciatively.

"Well, you're perfect enough to suit me," he blurted.

"Oh, Mr. Gartz, sir! You're a-flattering of me, so you are!" Inside she was thinking, "Oh, my goodness, stop him!"

But Ben himself was a little terrified at what he had said. After all, the men's watch bracelet business was still in the venturesome stage.

"Well, I'm not a man to flatter. I mean we're not so bad off, older folks like us. I'm not envying those kids anything. I guess I'm a kind of a funny fella, anyway. Different from most."

"Do you think so?" Lottie encouraged him, knitting. ("You're exactly like a million others—a million billion others.")

"I think so—yes. I've been around a good deal. I've had my ups and downs. I know this little old world from the cellar to the attic, and I don't envy anybody anything."

Lottie smiled a little, and looked at him, and wondered. How smug he was, and oily, and plausible. What seepage was there beneath the placid surface of his dull conversation. Adventure! No, not adventure. Yet this kindly, paunchy bachelor knew phases of life that she had never even approached.

"What do you mean when you say you've been around? Around where?"

"Oh, around. You know what I mean. Men—well, a nice girl like you wouldn't just understand how it is with a man, but I mean I been—uh—now—subject to the same temptations other men have. But I know there's nothing in it. Give me a nice little place of my own, my own household, a little bus to run around in and I wouldn't change places with a king. No sir. Nor a poet either." He laughed largely at that, and glanced across the meadow. "I don't know. I guess I'm a funny fella. Different. That's me. Different."

Barren as Lottie's experience with men had been, she still knew, as does any woman, that there are certain invariable reactions to certain given statements. These were scientific in their chemical precision. In conversation with the average man you said certain things and immediately got certain results. It was like fishing in a lively trout stream. This dialogue, for example, she or any other woman could have written before it had been spoken. She felt that she could see what was going on inside his head as plainly as though its working were charted. She thought. "He has his mind made up to propose to me but caution tells him to wait. He isn't quite sure of his business yet. He'd really prefer a younger woman but he has told himself that that's foolishness. The thing to do is to settle down. He thinks I'm not bad looking. He isn't crazy about me at all, but he thinks he could work himself up to a pretty good state of enthusiasm. He didn't have what they call his 'fling' in his youth; and he secretly regrets it. If I wanted to I could make him forget his caution and ask me to marry him right now."

He was talking. "I haven't said much about this new business I'm going into. I'm not a fella that talks much. Go ahead and do it, I always say, and then you don't have to talk. What you've done'll talk for you. Yessir!" Lottie looked at him—at his blunt square hands and the big spatulate thumbs—the little pouches under his eyes—at the thinning hair that he allowed to grow long at the sides so that he could plaster it over the crown, deceiving no one. And she thought, "This is a kind man. What they call a good provider. Generous. Decent, as men go. On the way to fairly certain business success. He'll make what is known as a good husband. You're not so much, Lottie. You're an old girl, with no money; nothing much to look at. Who are you to turn up your nose at him! You're probably a fool to do it—"

"—not an iota of difference to me what other people say or do. I do what I think's right and that's all anybody can do, isn't that true?" He was laboriously following some dull thought of his own.

Lottie jumped up quickly—leapt up, almost, so that the knitting bounded toward him, startled him, as did her sudden movement. "I'm going to get the infants," she said, hurriedly. "It's time we were starting back." Even as he stared up at her she was off. She ran through the little wood, down the knoll full pelt, across the field, her sturdy legs flashing beneath her short skirt, her arms outstretched. Halfway across the flower-strewn meadow, she called to Jesse and Charley. They stood up. Something of her feeling communicated itself to them. They sensed her protest. They ran to meet her, laughing; laughing, they met, joined hands, circled round and round, straining away from each other at arm's length like three mad things there in the May meadow until, with a final shout and whoop and high-flung step, they dropped panting to the ground.

Lottie, still breathing fast, was the first to rise. "I had to," she explained, "or bust."

"Sure," said the poet and Charley, together. Charley continued. "Lotta, I'll sit in the front seat going home. You and Jesse can get chummy in the back—"

"Oh, no—" But when they were ready to go it had, somehow, arranged itself in that way. Charley invariably gained her own end thus. "Will you let me drive part of the way, Mr. Gartz? Please!"

He shook a worried head. "Why, say, I'd like to, Miss Charley, but I'm afraid you don't understand this little ol' bus of mine. I'm afraid I'd be nervous with anybody else running it. You'd better just let me—"

But in the end it was Charley's slim strong hands that guided the wheel. Ben Gartz sat beside her, tense, watchful, working brakes that were not there. Under the girl's expert guidance the car took the hills like a hawk, swooped, flew, purred. "Say, you better slow down a little," Ben cautioned her again and again. Then, grudgingly, glancing sideways at her lovely young profile, vivid, electric, laughing, "You're *some* driver, kid!"

Lottie, in the back seat, was being charmed by Jesse Dick. She felt as if she had known him for years. He talked little—that is, he would express himself with tremendous enthusiasm on a topic so that you caught the spark of his warmth. Then he would fall silent and his silence was a glowing thing. He sat slumped down on the middle of his spine in a corner of the seat. He rarely glanced at Charley. His eyes flattered Lottie. She found herself being witty and a little hard. She thought now: "Here's one that's different enough. And I haven't an idea of what's going on in *his* handsome head. Not an idea. Not—" she giggled a little and Jesse Dick was so companionable that he did not even ask her what she was laughing at—"not an iota of an idea."

In August Lottie accompanied her mother and Aunt Charlotte up to one of the Michigan lake resorts. They went there every summer. The food was good, the air superb, the people typical of any Michigan first-class resort. Jeannette had gone to spend ten days in a girls' camp in Wisconsin. She had a job promised for September. The Paysons had a three-room cottage near the hotel and under the hotel's management; took their meals in the hotel dining room. The cottage boasted a vine-covered porch and a tiny garden. The days were not half bad. Mrs. Payson played bridge occasionally. Aunt Charlotte rocked and knitted and watched the young girls in their gay sweaters and flat-heeled white shoes and smart loud skirts. Lottie even played golf occasionally, when her mother and Aunt Charlotte were napping or resting, or safely disposed of on their own cottage porch or hotel veranda. There were few men during the week. On Fridays husbands and fiances swarmed down on train and boat for the weekend. On Saturday night there was a dance. Lottie, sitting on the porch of their little cottage, could hear the music. Her mother and Aunt Charlotte were always in bed by ten-thirty at the latest. Often it was an hour earlier than that. The evenings were terrible beyond words. Long, black, velvety nights during which she sat alone on the little porch guarding the two sleeping occupants of the cottage; staring out into the darkness. The crickets cheeped and chirped. A young girl's laugh rang out from the hotel veranda beyond. A man's voice sounded, low, resonant, as two quiet figures wound their way along one of the little paths that led down to the water. A blundering moth bumped its head against the screen door. A little group of hotel kitchen girls and dishwashers skirted the back of the cottage on their way to their quarters, talking gutturally. The evenings were terrible beyond words.

Chapter XIII

It was Lottie Payson's last August of that sort. When next August came round there she was folding gauze, rolling bandages, stitching pneumonia jackets with the rest of them at the Michigan Avenue Red Cross shop and thinking to herself that the conversation of the women busy about the long tables or at the machines was startlingly like that of the old Reading Club. The Reading Club was, in fact, there almost in its entirety. The girls' faces, framed in the white linen folds of their Red Cross coifs, looked strangely purified and aloof. Beck Schaefer alone wore her cap with a certain diablerie. She was captain of her section and her official coif was scarlet. She looked like Carmen strayed into a nunnery. A strange new spirit had come upon Chicago that summer. People talked high, and worked hard, prayed a good deal, gave their money away liberally and did not go to northern Michigan to escape the heat. Lottie sewed at the Red Cross shop three days every week. Even Mrs. Carrie Payson seemed to realize that driving about the parks and boulevards on summer afternoons was not quite the thing. When autumn came she was selling Liberty Bonds in the surefire manner of a professional. As for Great-Aunt Charlotte—the hand that had sewed and folded and stitched during the four years of the '60s and that had fashioned the prizewinning patchwork silk quilt in the '70s had not lost its cunning. She knitted with a speed and perfection nothing short of miraculous, turning out a sweater in three days, a pair of socks in two. The dip, bite, and recovery of her needles was machinelike in its regularity. She folded and rolled bandages as well, having enrolled in a Red Cross shop established in the parlors of a nearby hotel. Even Jeannette had been caught by the spirit of the new order. Her wage as stenographer was a queenly sum these days; and while she could not resist silk stockings, new hats, expensive blouses and gloves, and talked of a fur coat for the coming winter (every self-respecting stenographer boasted one by December) she still had enough left to contribute freely to every drive, fund, association, and relief committee connected with the war. She had long ago paid back the hundred dollars to that Otto, who had been whisked away in the first draft. Even Hulda in the kitchen had deserted her yards of crochet for a hank of wool. Henry Kemp worked nights as a member of the district draft board. Charley danced in benefits all the way from Lake Forest to South Chicago, and enrolled as emergency driver for Sunday work. Alone, of all the family, Belle remained aloof. True, she knitted now and then, languidly. But the Red Cross sewing gave her a headache, she said; the excitement affected her digestive disorder. She was anti-war, anti-draft, anti-Wilson.

And Ben Gartz thrived. If anyone had ever doubted Ben Gartz's business foresight, that person was forever silenced now. On every martial male left arm—rookie or general, gob or admiral—reposed a wristwatch. And now when Ben Gartz offered Henry a plump brown cylinder with the customary "Have a cigar!" Henry took it reluctantly, if reverently, eyed its scarlet and gold bellyband with appreciation, and knew better than to proffer one of his own inferior brand in return. "I'll smoke it after dinner," he would say, and tuck it away in his vest pocket. Henry Kemp had aged in the last year. His business was keeping its head barely above water with the makeshift of American manufactured products.

It had been during the winter before the war—February 1917—that Charley Kemp had announced one evening to her father and mother that she intended to marry Jesse Dick when she was twenty. That would be in June. He had got a job as feature writer with the Chicago News Bureau and he was acting as motion picture critic for one of the afternoon papers. His comment was caustic but highly readable. His writing in this new field was characterised by the same crude force that made his poetry a living thing.

"Well, was I right or wasn't I?" demanded Mrs. Payson of her daughter Belle. "Talking about her five children like a—like a hussy!"

"Hussies don't have five children," Belle retorted, meaninglessly.

Mrs. Payson endeavoured to arouse her daughter to the necessity for immediate action against this proposed madness of Charley's. "You've got to stop it, that's all."

"Stop it how?"

"How! By forbidding it, that's how."

Belle could even smile at that. "Oh, Mother, aren't you quaint! Nowadays parents don't forbid girls marrying this man or that, any more than they lock them up in a high tower like the princess What's-her-name in the fairy tale."

"You let me talk to her," said Mrs. Carrie Payson. "I'll do a little plain speaking."

Her plain speaking consisted in calling Jesse Dick a butcher's boy and a good-for-nothing scribbler who couldn't earn a living. Charley heard her out, a steely light in her eyes.

She spoke quietly and with deadly effect. "You're my grandmother, but that doesn't entitle you to talk to me with the disrespect you've just shown."

"Disrespect! To you! Well, upon my word!"

"Yes, I know it strikes you as extraordinary. If it had been written, 'Honor thy sons and thy daughters' along with 'Honor thy father and thy mother,' there'd have been a lot less trouble in the world. You never did respect your own people—your own family. You've never shown respect to Lottie or to Mother, or to father or to Aunt Charlotte, for that matter. So why should I expect you to respect me. I'm marrying Jesse Dick because he's the man I want to marry. I may be making a mistake but if I am, I'm willing to pay for it. At least I'll have only myself to reproach."

"You children today think you know everything, but you don't. You wait. You'll see. I know."

"No you don't. You didn't know when you married. You thought you were making a good match and your husband turned out to be a good-for-nothing rogue. I'm sorry to hurt you but you make me do it. If I'm wrong I'll have the satisfaction of knowing I went into it with my eyes open. I know all Jesse Dick's weaknesses and I love them. Five years from now he'll be a famous American poet—if not the most famous. I know just what he needs. He needs me, for one thing. In time he may go off with other women—"

"Charley Kemp, how can you sit there and talk like that!"

"—but he'll come back to me. I know. I'll keep on with my job at Shield's. In two or three years I'll be making a very respectable number of thousands a year."

"And in the meantime you'll live where, may I ask? Your father's in no position, goodness knows, to have a poet son-in-law dumped on his hands. Unless you're planning to live in the rear of the delicatessen, perhaps."

"We've got a three-room cottage in Hubbard Woods. Some time, when you're feeling stronger, I'd like to have you see it. It belongs to Dorn, the landscape painter. He built it when Hubbard Woods was a wilderness. It's got a fireplace that doesn't draw and a sink that doesn't drain and windows that don't fit. It's right on the edge of the big ravine and the very thought of it makes me happy all over. And now I'm going to kiss you, Grandma, which I think is awfully sweet of me, all things considered, you dear mistaken old-fashioned darling." Which she did, on the tip of Mrs. Payson's nose.

At the word "old-fashioned" Mrs. Carrie Payson had bristled; then, inexplicably, had slumped without voicing a word in her own defense. She seemed momentarily uncertain, bewildered almost. Still, she did allow herself a last javelin. "'In five years he'll be a famous poet.' That's a sensible reason for marrying a man! Huh!"

"But that's not my reason," Charley explained with charming good humor, "any more than because his hair is sort of red in lights, or his ears a little pointed, or his hands slim and brown or his ties always terrible."

"What is your reason?" snapped Mrs. Payson. But an honest curiosity lighted her eye.

"The same thing strikes us funny at the same time. We like the same kind of book though we may disagree about it. We like to be outdoors a lot, and we understand each other's language and we're not sentimental and we don't snarl if food is delayed and we don't demand explanations, and any one of those reasons would make marriage between two people a reasonably safe bet."

Mrs. Payson forced herself to a tremendous effort. "You haven't even said you're—" she gulped—"you're " with a rush—"in love with him."

"I haven't said anything else."

But next June, when she was twenty, Charley was saying, "But a man who won't fight—!"

"I haven't said I won't fight. I said I wouldn't enlist, and I won't. I hate war. It's against every principle I've got. If I'm drafted I'll go into the damn thing as a private and if I find that shooting a gun or jabbing a bayonet into another fellow's guts is going to stop his doing the same to me I'll shoot and jab. I don't pretend to be fired with the martial spirit simply because a European nation, grown too big for its clothes, tried to grab off a new lot and failed in the first attempt."

"I believe you're afraid."

"Of course I'm afraid. Any man who says he isn't lies. I hate living in filth and mud and lice and getting an eye shot out. But that isn't my reason for not going, and you know it. I won't voluntarily further this thing."

Charley did know it. She knew, too, that the instinct that made her want to send her man to war was a thing of low derivation yet terribly human. She did not say, definitely, "I can't marry a man who feels as you do." It was the first time in her life that she had lacked the courage to say definitely the thing she thought. But the family realized that the June wedding was no longer a thing to be combated. June came and went. The Hyde Park Boulevard apartment had not known the young poet for a month.

Jesse Dick was called in the first draft. Charley kept doggedly at her work all summer, riding back and forth in the dirt and cinders of the IC trains. It was a summer of intense heat. Daily, Charley threatened to appear at Shield's in her bathing suit or in one of the Greekest of her dancing costumes. But it was surprising to see how roselike she could look as she merged after dinner in a last year's organdie. Everyone was dancing. Sometimes Charley went to the Midway Garden at the entrance to Washington Park or over to the old Bismarck (now known as the Marigold Gardens) there to dance and dine outdoors in the moonlight. Always she was squired by a dashing blue-and-gold or white duck uniform from the Great Lakes Naval Training Station, or olive-drab and shiny tan boots from Fort Sheridan.

Jesse Dick came home just before he sailed for France. He wore an issue uniform which would have rendered grotesque a Captain Jinks or a D'Artagnan. The sleeves were too short; the collar too large; the jacket too brief. Spiral puttees wrapped his slim shanks. Army brogans—yellow—were on his feet.

Bairnsfather's drawings had already achieved a popularity in America. Charley hung between laughter and tears when Jesse struck a pose and said, "Alf."

They drove to the Marigold Gardens on the North Side. Jesse had not sold his little flivver. The place was a fairyland of lights, music, flower-banked terraces. Hundreds were dining outdoors under the moonlight, the women in pale-colored organdies and chiffons, the men in Palm Beach suits or in uniforms. No where else in America could one find just this sort of thing—nor, for that matter, in Europe even in the days before the war. In a city constantly referred to as crude, commercial, and unlovely, there flourished two garden spots unique, exquisite, and unproclaimed.

Jesse ordered a dinner that brought a look of wonder to the face of the waiter (Swiss, of course) who had gauged his prospective order after one glance at the ill-fitting issue uniform.

"Dance?" said Jesse.

"Yes." They danced, wordlessly. They danced before and after the hors d'oeuvres, the fowl, the salad, the dessert, the coffee. They talked little. The boy glanced about with cold wise young eyes. "God!"

"Yes, I know," Charley said, as if in answer to a long speech, "but after all, what good would it do if they all stayed home! They're probably all doing their share. They hate it as much as you do. Moping won't help."

"Dance?"

"Yes."

They rose and wound their way among the little green tables to the dancing platform. Charley raised her eyes to his as they danced. "Will you marry me tomorrow, Jesse? Before you go?"

"No."

"Why not?"

"That's all right for truck drivers and for sloppy emotionalists. But it's a poor plan. You're only suggesting it because of the music and my nearness and the fact that I'm leaving day after tomorrow. I'm no different than I was three months ago. I hate war as much as I ever did. If you think three months of camp training—"

"Will you marry me tomorrow, Jesse?"

"No."

"I'm afraid, Jesse."

"So am I. But not as scared as that." His cheek rested against hers. Her fingers clutched tight a fold of the bunchy cloth of his rough uniform. She could not bring herself to name the fear she felt. All the way home she pressed close to the rough sleeve—the good tangible rough cloth of the sleeve—and the muscle-hard arm within it.

Hyde Park is cut through by the Illinois Central tracks. All that summer and autumn and winter, Charley would start up in her sleep at the sound of high shrill voices like the voices of children. Lottie Payson heard them, too, at night in the old house on Prairie and could not sleep again. The Illinois Central and Michigan Central trains were bringing boys to the training camps, or from the training camps to the points of embarkation. They were boys from Illinois farms, Wisconsin towns, Minnesota, and Michigan villages. "Yee-ow!" they yelled as their trains passed through the great sleeping city. "Whoo-ee! Yip!" Keeping their courage up. Yelling defiance at a world gone mad. All that summer you heard them, and through the autumn and winter, and the next spring and summer and autumn. High young voices they were, almost like the voices of children. "Berlin or Bust" was scrawled in chalk on the outside of their cars—scrawled by some raw youth from Two Rivers, Wisconsin, who was going to camp and to war in a baseball cap and his Sunday pants and a red sweater.

Charley would pull the covers over her head and cover her ears with her hands until the last yip had died away. But Lottie would sit up in bed, her head thrown back, listening—listening as if they were calling to her.

Chapter XIV

One Saturday morning, Lottie, just returned from marketing with her mother, answered the telephone and recognized with difficulty Beck Schaefer's voice, high-pitched and hysterical as it was.

"Lot, is this you?"

"Yes."

"Lot—Lot—listen. Listen!"

"I'm listening."

"Lot, listen. You know I've always liked you better than any of the other girls, don't you? You're so sincere—so sincere and fair and everything. You know that, don't you, Lot?"

"What's the matter," parried Lottie.

"Oh, Lot darling, Sam Butler and I—Sam—you know—Sam and I, we're—"

"Not!"

"Yes! Oh, Lottie, isn't it wonderful! This afternoon. Don't breathe it. I'm scared to death. Will you be my bridesmaid? Lottie *dear.* Sam goes to Camp Funston tomorrow. He's got a captaincy you know. I'm going with him. We're to live in a shack with a tin roof and they say it's hotter than hell down there in the summer and, oh, Lottie, I'm so happy! We're to be married at the parsonage—Dr. Little. Mother doesn't know a thing about it. Neither does Sam's mother. Sam's going to tell his mother's companion after it's all over this afternoon, and then we'll go up there. I hate to think . . . Mama said she wanted to go to California again this fall because it was going to be so uncomfortable here this winter, and Lottie, when she said that something in me just went kind of crazy . . . Can you hear me? I don't want to talk any louder . . . I called up Sam and began to cry and we met downtown and we decided to get married right away . . . goodness knows I don't deserve . . . and oh, Lottie, I feel so *religious!* You'll come, won't you? Won't you!"

Lottie came.

Beck had taken a room at the Blackstone Hotel and there she had packed, written letters, dressed for her wedding. Lottie joined her there. Beck had lost her telephone hysteria and was fairly calm and markedly pale. She wore a taffeta frock and a small blue hat and none of her jewelry. "I haven't even got an engagement ring," she said almost in triumph to Lottie. "We didn't have time. Sam's going to buy it now—or after we're married. I spent the whole morning on Michigan Avenue, shopping. Look."

"How's the Camp Funston laundress going to handle that, Beck dear?"

"I don't care. I wanted it nice. I've waited so long. But I'd have been willing to go away with one shirtwaist and a knitted union suit, honestly I would. It wouldn't have made any difference to me. I got back here at twelve and had a bath and a bite of lunch and I packed and dressed, and then Lottie, I knelt down by the bed and prayed. I don't know why I knelt down by the bed, exactly. I suppose because that's the way you see them kneeling in the pictures or something. But anyway I liked doing it. Lot, do you think I'm too pale? H'm? I put on quite a lot of rouge and then I took it all off and now—"

A message from the hotel office announced Sam. They went down. With Sam was a nervous and jocular best man, Ed Morrow. They drove to the minister's study adjoining the church. It was an extremely unbridal-looking party. Lottie, in her haste, was wearing an old Georgette dress and a sailor hat recently rained on (no one was buying new clothes these days) and slightly out of shape. The best man waxed facetious. "Cheer up, Sam old boy! The worst is yet to come." He mopped his face and winked at Lottie. They were ushered into the minister's little study. He was not yet there. They laughed and talked nervously. There was a warm-looking bottle of mineral water on the window ledge; a bookcase full of well-bound books with an unread look about them; a bust of Henry Ward Beecher; a brown leather chair scuffed, dented, and shiny with much use; a little box of digestive tablets on the flat-topped desk. Sam, in his smartly tailored uniform, seemed to fill the room. Beck did not take her eyes from him. He was not at all the chubby middle-aged person that Lottie had known. He looked a magnificently martial figure. The fact that he was in the ordnance department did not detract from the fit, cut, and becomingness of his uniform.

Dr. Little came in, a businesslike figure in gray tweed. A little silence fell upon the four. The wedding service began. Dr. Little's voice was not the exhorting voice of the preacher. Its tone, Lottie thought, was blandly conversational. All of a sudden, he was saying, "pronounce you man and wife," and Lottie was kissing the bride and the groom and even the best man who, immediately afterward, looked startled and then suspicious.

Beck had a calm and matronly air. It had descended upon her, complete, like an all-enveloping robe.

And so they were married. After it was over, Lottie went back to the Red Cross shop. Three days later she had a letter from Beck. It was not one of the remote and carefully impersonal letters of the modern bride. It was packed with all the old-fashioned terms in which honeymoon brides of a less sophisticated day used to voice their ecstasy.

". . . Most wonderful man . . . happiest girl in the world ... I thought I knew him but I never dreamed he was so . . . makes me feel so humble

. . . wonder what I have ever done to deserve such a prince among . . ."

Lottie told her mother and Aunt Charlotte about it that evening at dinner. It was very hot. Lottie had been ashamed of her own waspishness and irritability before dinner. She attributed it to the weather. Sometimes, nowadays, she wondered at her own manner. Was she growing persnickety, she asked herself, and faultfinding and crabbed? It seemed to her that the two old women were calmer, more tolerant, less faultfinding than she. She was the crotchety one. It annoyed Lottie to see Aunt Charlotte munching chocolates just before dinner. "Oh, Aunt Charlotte, for heaven's sake! Can't you wait until after dinner? You won't eat a thing."

"It doesn't matter if I don't, Lottie," Aunt Charlotte returned, mildly. Aunt Charlotte, at seventy-five, and rapidly approaching seventy-six, was now magnificently free. She defied life. What could it do to her! Nothing that it had not already done. So she ate, slept, talked as she pleased. A second youth seemed to have come upon her.

Tonight, after Lottie's story of Beck Schaefer's marriage, Mrs. Carrie Payson had said, with apparent irrelevance, "I won't be here always, Lottie. Neither will Aunt Charlotte." A little pause, then, "I wish you were settled, too."

Lottie deliberately pretended to misunderstand. "Settled, Mama! My goodness, I should think I'm settled enough!" She glanced about the quiet old room. But she knew what her mother meant and resented it. Settled. Shelved. Her mother was thinking of Ben Gartz, Lottie knew.

Amazing things had happened to Ben Gartz in the last six months. He had sold the bus. In its place was a long, low, smooth-running, powerful gray car with special wheels and special tires and special boxes and flaps and rods. Ben Gartz was transformed from a wistful, fusty, and almost shabby middle-aged bachelor into a dapper beau in a tailored Palm Beach suit, saw-edge sailor, and silk hose. He carried a lemon-colored cane. He had two rooms at an expensive Hyde Park hotel near the lake. He had had the Paysons and the Kemps to dinner there. There were lamps in the sitting room, and cushions, and a phonograph with opera records. Ben put on some of these after dinner and listened, his head on one side. He said it was the only way to live—with your own things around you. "My books," he said, and waved a hand toward a small sectional bookcase, in which thirty or forty volumes leaned limply against each other. One or two had slipped down and now lay supine on the roomy shelves. Lottie strolled over to the bookcase and glanced at the titles. *The Mystery of the Purple Shroud. One Hundred Ways to Use the Chafing Dish. Eat and Grow Thin.* Ben Gartz's waistline had been one of the first things about him to register a surprising change. Though his method of living had expanded, his girth had decreased. He made no secret of his method. "A Turkish bath once a week," he said. "No sugar, no butter, no sweets or starches of any kind. And I feel better for it. Yessir! I never felt so well in my life. Sleep better. Walk better. Twenty-five pounds off already and I'll do another twenty-five before I'm through. I don't even miss the sugar in my coffee. I used to take saccharine. Not now. I don't even miss it. Take my coffee black. Got so now I think you miss the real flavor and spoil it using sugar and cream."

His face was a trifle jaundiced and haggard, one thought. The surprised muscles were showing their resentment at the suddenly withdrawn supports and cushions of fat.

Ben Gartz loved to play the host. He talked about the war, about business, about Chicago's part in the war, about his own part in it. He had bought bonds, sold bonds, given to this, that, the other. "Now take these Eyetalians, for instance. How long do you suppose they'd held out against the Austrians? Or the French, either, for that matter against the Germans? They were just about all in, now I'm here to tell you." His conversational facts were gleaned from the front-page headlines, yet he expounded them with a fervor and an assurance that gave them the effect of being inside information.

Of all his listeners Aunt Charlotte was the grimmest.

"Wasn't he interesting about the war?" Mrs. Carrie Payson had asked, after they had left.

"About as interesting as a bill of lading," Aunt Charlotte had snapped.

Henry Kemp had laughed one of his hearty laughs so rare now. "What do you know about bills of lading, Aunt Charlotte?"

"Not a thing, Henry. I don't even rightly know what a bill of lading is. But it always sounded to me like about the dullest thing in the world."

Ben Gartz had escorted them to the very elevator and had said, with a final wave of the hand, just as they were descending, "Now that you've found the way, come often."

Charley and Lottie, looking at each other, had given way completely.

Just after dinner, on the evening of Beck Schaefer's wedding day, Ben Gartz telephoned. The telephone call had followed less than a minute after Lottie's rebellious thoughts about him. "I hope my thinking of him didn't do it," she said to herself as she answered the telephone.

Would she go driving? No, she didn't feel like it. Oh come on! Do you good. We'll drop in at the Midway. There's a new revue there that's a winner. She pleaded a headache. Then it's just what you need. Won't take no for an answer. She went.

She wore her white wash-satin skirt and the pink sports coat and her big hat and looked very well indeed. They drove to the Midway Gardens in Ben's new car. Ben, parking the car, knew the auto starter. "H'are you, Eddie." He knew the uniformed doorman. "H'are you, Jo." He knew the head waiter. "H'are you, Al. Got a nice table for me?"

"Always find a table for you, Mr. Gartz. Yes, Mr. Gartz." Ben surveyed the gardens largely from the top of the terrace. They were worth surveying. Your Chicago South Side dweller bores you with details. "Look at that! Notice anything queer about this place?" he asks you.

You survey its chaste white beauty. "Queer? No, it's lovely—"

"Not a curved line in it!" announces the South Sider, largely. "Frank Lloyd Wright designed it. Not a curved line in it—roof, balcony, pillars, statues—anywhere."

Your surprised and grateful eyes confirm this boast as you glance about at the scene before you.

Ben Gartz was fussy about his table. Near one of three dancing platforms—but not too near. Near the music—but not too near. On the terrace where one could see and be seen—but not too exposed to the public gaze. At last they found it.

It was deliciously cool there in that great unroofed space. There was even a breeze, miraculously caught within the four walls of the garden. They ordered iced drinks. There was a revue, between the general dancing numbers. Ben applauded this revue vigorously. He seemed to know a good deal about the girls who took part in it. Very young girls they were, and exquisitely slim. Some of them had almost the angular lines of adolescence. In one number they were supposed to represent Light— Candlelight, Gaslight, Lamplight, Electricity, Moonlight, Sunlight, Starlight. Their costumes were bizarre, scanty to a degree that would have been startling had they been less young and reticent of flesh.

"I see you've got a couple of new ones," Ben remarked to Albert, the head waiter, as that urbane individual passed their table.

"Yes," said Albert; and again, "Yes," in order not to seem less than unctuous.

Lottie said to herself, "Oh, Lottie, don't be so magnificent. He isn't so bad. He's enjoying himself, that's all. You're just a middle-aged old gal who ought to be glad of the chance to spend a cool evening in the Midway

Garden, drinking claret lemonade. Glad of the chance."

But she wasn't.

Ben was all for dancing, of course. He had become amazingly proficient at it, as does your plump middle-aged playboy. Lottie liked to dance, too. She discovered that she didn't particularly like to dance with Ben, though he was light, expert, and skillful at avoiding collisions even on that crowded floor. Proximity proved him moist, soft, and protuberant.

Seated at their table it was cool and almost restful. A row of slim trees showed a fairy frieze above the tiled balcony that enclosed the garden. The lights of the garden fell on them and gave them an unreal quality. They seemed weird, dazzling. Lottie thought they looked like trees in a Barrie fantasy. She opened her lips to utter this thought. Then, "He won't know what I mean," she said to herself. Ben was eating an ice out of a tall silver goblet. "Take a fruit ice like this," he had explained, "there's nothing fattening in it. Now ice cream, that's different. Not for me. Ice is all right, though. Raspberry ice."

"Those trees," said Lottie, and nodded toward them. Ben turned heavily, a spoonful of raspberry ice poised halfway. "They're like fairy trees in a Barrie play. Fantastic."

"Yeh," said Ben, and carried the laden spoon to his mouth. "Light's bad for 'em, I guess, shining on 'em that way. Look how yellow the leaves are already."

"There!" shouted Lottie, not aloud, but to her inner self. "You can't expect me to marry a man who doesn't know what I'm talking about, can you?"

"What are you smiling at, you little rascal!" Ben was saying. "Tell me the joke."

"Was I smiling? I didn't know—" You little rascal! No one had ever called Lottie a little rascal. She tried, now, to think of herself as a little rascal and decided that the term was one that Ben had found useful, perhaps, in conversation with the young ladies of the Light Revue. She did not resent being called a little rascal. She resented the fact that Ben could not see the absurdity of applying the term to a staid-appearing, conventionally dressed, rather serious woman of thirty-three or -four. She thought of Beck. Beck, in the old days, would have shaken a forefinger at him and said, "Will you never grow up, you bad boy!" Suddenly Lottie felt a little sick. "Let's go," she said. "Do you mind? I'm—I've had a trying day."

On the way home Ben grew expansive. "Some fellas in my position would have a shofe but I like to drive my own bus. I come home in the evening and have my bath and my dinner and go out in the little wagon and it rests me. Yessir! Rests me . . . I'm thinking of moving north. A little flat, maybe, and a housekeeper. A fella gets pretty sick of hotels."

"That would be nice. Everyone seems to be moving to the North Side."

"It's the place to live. The South Side is getting worse all the time— dirt, and the IC smoke and all. And now that they've brought all these niggers up from the South to work over at the Yards since the war, it isn't fit to live in, that's what. Why, look at Grand Boulevard! Black way up to Forty-Third Street. All those old houses. It's a shame!"

He was driving with one hand, expertly. The other was hung negligently over the back of the seat. Lottie could feel it touching her shoulder blades. It was touching them so lightly that she could not resent the contact by moving slightly. Besides, she did not want to move. She had a little amused curiosity about the arm. She wanted to know what it would do next. She made up her mind that she would see the evening through. She smiled to herself in the warm darkness. She relaxed a little. She took off her hat and held it in her lap. The cool breeze on her brow was like a drink of water to one thirsting.

They were driving slowly through Washington Park on the way home. Lottie closed her eyes. How deliciously cool it was. Her bedroom at home would be hot, she thought. It faced east, and tonight the scant breeze was from the west. The car stopped. She opened her eyes. They were parked by the roadside near the sunken gardens. The negligent arm behind her suddenly tightened into a band of bone and muscle. The loose-hung hand grasped her shoulder tight and hard. Ben Gartz was bent over her. She was conscious of a smell of cigarettes and shaving lotion and whiskey (he had had a highball earlier in the evening). Ben Gartz was kissing Lottie with a good deal of vehemence and little restraint and no finesse. It was an unexpected and open-mouthed kiss, mucous, moist, and loathsome. She didn't enjoy it. Lottie felt besmeared, befouled. Still, she did none of those statuesque or dramatic things that ladies are supposed to do who have been unhandsomely kissed against their will. For that matter, it had not been against her will. She had not expected it, true, but she had had a mild and amused curiosity about its possibility. She was now seized with a violent and uncontrollable shudder. She had released herself with a push of her strong hand against Ben's chest. Her eyes were wide and rather staring. She wiped her mouth with the back of her hand, hard.

"I want to go home," she said.

"Oh, say, Lottie, honestly, you're not mad! I don't know what made me—say, on the square—"

Lottie put on her hat. "I'm not a bit angry, Ben. I just want to go home. I'm sleepy."

But he refused to believe her, even while he shifted gears and drove home at a sharp clip through the almost deserted park and down the boulevard. It was almost as if he felt she should be resentful. "Say, you must think I'm a bum, that's what. Why, Lottie, I didn't mean anything.

Why, I think you're one of the grandest girls I know. A fine girl. There isn't a girl I respect more."

"Do you?" She said nothing more. She had nothing more to say. She felt calm and almost happy. It was as though that kiss had cleansed her, even while it soiled. She sensed that he was thinking hard. She could almost hear his baffled mind scurrying about for words. She sensed, too, that he had almost spoken of marriage but had cautiously thought better of it in time.

They were at the curb outside the Prairie Avenue house. "Lottie, you're sore; and I don't blame you. I'm dead sorry. On the square. I'm— say, you'll prob'ly never speak to me again." He was as argumentative as though he had trod on her toe.

She smiled as she turned at the steps. "I'm glad you kissed me, Ben. I didn't like it. But I'm glad you kissed me."

She left him staring. She let herself into the house, ran quietly up the stairs to the second floor. She went into the bathroom and turned on the cold water faucet and washed her mouth inside and out with cold water. Then with listerine. Then she saw a bottle marked "Peroxide" and took a mouthful. I think that if there had been a carbolic in the house she might have taken a gargle of that, as a final cleanser, in her zeal to be rid of the taste of the wet red kiss. She spat forcefully and finally now, made a wry face, and went into her bedroom. She took off her clothes, came back and washed with soap and a rough cloth, brushed her hair, put on a fresh nightgown, and went to bed.

Lottie's middle-aged romance with Ben Gartz was over.

Chapter XV

The Paysons and the Kemps, together with the rest of the world, were to be tossed about now like straws in a storm. But Mrs. Carrie Payson, reading the paper next morning in the dining room window, after breakfast, was the dispassionately interested spectator. Though this was a manless household, it received its morning and evening paper regularly. You saw Mrs. Payson in that. She had no patience with women who did not read the newspapers. Sometimes when Belle said, "What wedding?" or "What murder?" or "What sale?" Mrs. Payson would exclaim, "For heaven's sake, don't you read the papers! How do you expect to know what's going on!"

Mrs. Payson knew what was going on. She knew the price of coal, and the whereabouts of the Sinhalese troops, and the closing steel quotations, and whether duvetyne was going to be good this winter, and how much the Claflin estate amounted to, and why the DeWitts dropped their divorce proceedings. More than this, she read aloud extracts from these items and commented thereon. She was the kind of woman who rarely breakfasts in a kimono. When she did, it was so restrained and somber in cut and color that the Nipponese would have failed to recognize its origin. Her white hair was primly dressed. Through spectacles worn at a rakish angle and set rather low down on her nose, she surveyed the antics of the world and pronounced upon them as a judge upon a day's grist of cases. To one who preferred to get the first-page news first-hand, it was a maddening practice.

"I see they predict a coal famine. I don't know what we'll do in this house. If I didn't know I'd practically have to give it away I'd sell and move into a flat out south. . . . They're going to wear those capes again next winter. I should think they'd freeze in 'em. Though I remember we used to wear them altogether—dolmans, we called them. I see your friend Winnie Steppier has gone to France for her paper. Woman of her age! I should think she'd stay home . . . H'm! Ben Gartz is captain of the Manufacturing Jewelers' Liberty Loan Committee . . . What time did you come in last night, Lottie? I didn't hear you." Aunt Charlotte, breakfasting across the table, looked up.

Lottie poured herself another cup of coffee. She was drinking a great deal of coffee lately; using it frankly as a stimulant. "About midnight."

"Did you have a nice time?"

"Interesting," Lottie said, gravely. She sensed that her mother was listening intently behind the newspaper. "Did you mean what you just said about wanting to sell the house and moving into a flat out south?"

Mrs. Payson's spectacles showed, half-moons, above the paper's horizon. "I might. Hulda's going to marry that man. He doesn't want to go to war. They say you can't get a girl now for less than fifteen dollars a week. Fifteen! Well! I see myself! And now this coal shortage—and a four-story house. Still, we'd need a pretty big apartment."

Lottie made her tone casual. "You ought to marry off Jeannette—and me."

She knew that Ben Gartz leaped from a position of doubt to one of hope in her mother's mind. She knew, too, that her mother could no more force herself to speak of this hope than she could wear a pink silk and lace negligee. She would have considered both, somehow, indecent. She turned a page of the paper, elaborately careless. "I'd move out of this barn fast enough if there was only Charlotte and me to keep it up for."

Lottie laughed a little. "You'd have to have a special room for Ole Bull, and your walnut bed and the hall hat rack. No modern flat—"

"I'd sell them. For that matter, I might even take rooms in a hotel, and give up housekeeping altogether. It's too hard these days."

"Why Mama, you talk as if you had it all planned out! You know perfectly well you couldn't get along without me."

"Oh, couldn't I! I'd like to know why not! Jeannette thinks more of my comfort this minute than you do." She folded the sheets of the paper into an untidy mass and slapped the crumpled whole down on the breakfast table.

"You oughtn't to expect Jeannette to act as a sort of unpaid companion."

"Companion! I'm not in my dotage yet. I don't need a companion, paid or unpaid. I don't need anybody for that matter. You're not so terribly important. Don't think it. I'd manage to live without you, very well."

"Do you really mean that, Mama?"

At her tone Mrs. Payson stopped, one hand outstretched toward the pantry door. "That I could get along without you? I certainly—"

"That if I hadn't been here to run the electric and take you to market and shopping when you or Aunt Charlotte needed clothes, or hats, or corsets—you wouldn't have missed me? All these years?"

"I'd have got along. So would your Aunt Charlotte. Nobody's so important that the world can't get along without them. I'd have managed."

"I suppose you would," Lottie said, dully. "I suppose you would."

Her mother passed into the kitchen. Aunt Charlotte, across the table, reached for the mangled newspaper and began to smooth it out sheet by sheet, and to fold it painstakingly into its original creasings. At the apprehensive look in her eyes, Lottie smiled reassuringly, got up, and came round to her. She patted the shriveled cheek. "Don't look so disappointed in your maiden niece, Charlotte Thrift. She isn't as desperate as that. Don't think it."

"Well, just for a minute"—there was relief in her voice—"I thought—but you've got some plan in your head?"

"Yes."

"Don't let anybody stop you then, whatever it is. Don't let anybody stop you. It's your last chance, Lottie."

The pantry door swung open. "What's her last chance?" demanded Mrs. Payson, entering. She had a way of making timely—or untimely— entrances with the precision of a character in a badly written play.

"Oh, nothing." Aunt Charlotte smiled and nodded coquettishly and her sister thought of Ben Gartz, as Aunt Charlotte had meant she should. Lottie knew this. At the knowledge, a hot little flame of wrath swept over her.

Then, for three weeks, the household went about its business. Lottie sewed at the Red Cross shop; Aunt Charlotte knitted; Mrs. Payson talked Liberty Bonds, managed her household, protested at the increased cost of living, berated Belle for what she termed her extravagance, quizzed Henry about his business at the Friday night family dinner. At the end of the month Hulda left to marry her unmartial Oscar. Though she and Mrs. Payson had carried on guerilla warfare for years, Hulda, packing her trunk, wept into the crochet-edged trousseau and declared that Mrs. Payson had been, of all mistresses, the kindest. Mrs. Payson, on her part, facing the prospect of breaking in a pert new incompetent at a weekly wage far beyond that of the departing and highly capable Hulda, forgave her everything, including her weakness for coffee. She even plied her with a farewell cup of that black brew as Hulda, dressed for departure, sat waiting red-eyed in the kitchen for the drayman.

With the advent of a new maid, Jeannette began to take her meals with the family. Somehow the kitchen was no longer the place for Jeannette. She had acquired a pretty manner, along with a certain comeliness of feature and figure. It had been a sudden blossoming. Hers were the bright-eyed assurance, the little upward quirk at the corners of the mouth, the preenings and flutterings of the duckling who is transformed miraculously into a swan. Jeannette had a "boyfriend." Jeannette had invitations for every night in the week (censored by Mrs. Payson). Jeannette went to the War Camp community dances on Saturday nights at the Soldiers' and Sailors' Club and was magically transformed from a wallflower into a rose. Jeannette, the erstwhile plain, bloomed into beauty—the beauty that comes of being told one is beautiful and desirable. She danced expertly and gracefully (private sessions with Charley had accomplished this) and she had endless patience with the wistful lads from the nearby naval training station and camps who swarmed into the city on leave, seeking diversion where they could find it. At these carefully supervised community affairs, Jeannette danced with boys from Texas and boys from Massachusetts; boys from Arizona and Kansas and Ohio and Washington. But though she danced with them all with indefatigable patience and good humor, it was Nebraska's step that perfectly matched her own after the first few weeks and it was Nebraska who took her home at a gallop in order not to overstay his shore leave. Nebraska was an embryo ensign. He talked of the sea as only a boy can who has known but the waves of the wheat rippling before the wind across miles of inland prairie. When Lottie suggested that Jeannette invite Nebraska to dinner on Sunday Mrs. Payson, surprisingly enough, agreed. They made conversation.

"And where is your home?"

"I'm from Nebraska, ma'am."

"Oh, Nebraska!"

"Yes, ma'am."

"How do you like Chicago?"

"I like it fine." A quick glance at Jeannette. "Everybody here is certainly grand."

Now that Jeannette was regularly at dinner, the silences that had tortured Lottie's nerves were banished quite. The girl chattered endlessly but engagingly, too. One of the girls at the office had gone and got married during the noon hour—did you see the parade on Michigan today?—that actress with the Liberty Loan speaker at the corner of Monroe and State had given a signed photograph with every bond purchased—there was a fur coat in Olson's window for only one hundred and fifty—all the girls were going to buy those short fur coats this winter.

"Mercy on us!" from Aunt Charlotte. Jeannette and Aunt Charlotte were great friends. Aunt Charlotte's room had, for Jeannette, something of the attraction of a museum. In it were all those treasures accumulated by a lonely woman throughout almost half a century of living in one house. Ribbons, flowers, buttons, photographs, scraps of lace, old hats, mounds of unused handkerchiefs and bottles of perfume and boxes of time-yellowed writing paper representing the birthdays and Christmases of years; old candy boxes; newspaper clippings; baby pictures of Lottie, Belle, Charley; family albums. There was always a bag of candy of the more durable sort—hard peppermints, or fruit drops. And, treasured of all, the patchwork silk quilt. When Belle and Lottie were little girls, the patchwork quilt had been the covering of convalescence during the milder periods of childhood indispositions. At very sight of its prismatic folds now, Lottie was whisked back twenty-five years to days of delicious languor on the sitting room sofa, the silk quilt across her knees, cups of broth and quivering rosy gelatines to tempt the appetite, and the button box for endless stringing and unstringing.

Today, as Lottie passed Aunt Charlotte's room just before dinner, she saw her sitting by the window with the silk quilt in her lap. Of late it had been packed away in one of the room's treasure boxes and brought out only for purposes of shaking and dusting.

Lottie entered and stood over Aunt Charlotte as she sat there in her chair by the window, looking out on the ornate old houses across the way. "I haven't seen it in years." She passed her fingers over the shining surface of the silk and satin. Frayed squares and triangles marred many of the blocks now. A glistening butterfly still shone in yellow silk in one corner; a spider wove an endless web in another. Time had mellowed the vivid orange and purple and scarlet and pink until now the whole had the vague softness and subdued gleam of an ancient Persian carpet or an old cathedral window.

Aunt Charlotte looked down at it. One tremulous finger traced the pattern of wheels and circles and blocks. "I always thought I'd give it to the first one of the family that married. But Belle—of course not, in that grand apartment. For awhile I thought Charley and that young lad—I'd have liked to tell them how I came to make it. The boy would have liked to hear it. Jesse Dick. He'd have understood. But he's gone to war again. Jesse Dick has gone to war again. Oh, dear! Why didn't Charlotte marry him before he went?"

"She's wandering a little," Lottie thought, with a pang. "After all, she's very old. We haven't realized." Aloud she said, smiling, "And how about me, Charlotte Thrift? You're forgetting your old niece entirely."

"No, I haven't forgotten you, Lottie. I think I got it out because of you today. A curious feeling. Something's going to happen. I've lived a long time, Lottie. Nearly seventy-six years. Old maids usually don't live that long. Did you know that? Short-lived, they are—unmarried women. Here I am, nearing seventy-six. And every now and then I get the feeling—that unsettled feeling as if something might still happen in my life. I don't know. It's like listening for a bell to ring. Something's going to happen."

Lottie looked at her strangely, almost fearfully. She stooped, suddenly, and gathered Aunt Charlotte and the silk quilt into her arms.

"Oh, Aunt Charlotte! Aunt Charlotte! I've done something terrible. I'm scared, I'm—"

"Lot-tie!" from the foot of the stairs. "Lottie! What's the matter with you and Aunt Charlotte! Dinner's waiting."

"You don't say!" Aunt Charlotte stood up facing Lottie, suddenly alert, vitalized. "You don't say!" Something about the commonplaceness of her expression of approval seemed to restore Lottie's balance. "Don't let her scare you. They always try and if you're weak you give in. But don't you. Don't you!" A sudden suspicion—"It isn't that pink fat man!"

"Ben? No. It's something I never thought I'd—"

"What's it matter? Only don't give in." She propelled her almost fiercely ahead of her to the stairway and down to the dining room. It was as though she feared Lottie would change her mind if they paused on the way. All through dinner Aunt Charlotte glowed and beamed upon her. Occasionally she shook her head vehemently to convey encouragement to the silent Lottie.

Jeannette was full of plans for the evening. "If we don't start early, we won't get there in time for the first show and then we'll have to stand and wait. They say it's a wonderful picture. The man who takes the part of the Kaiser looks exactly like him." Evidently she and Mrs. Payson were going Hunning among the films.

Aunt Charlotte looked up from her dessert. "I thought you wanted me to show you that new block stitch this evening." Jeannette's knitting was more ambitious than expert.

"I do. But I've got a date with my girlfriend to go to the movie first." She grinned at the stately white-haired companion of her revels and the two giggled like schoolgirls. Jeannette's rollicking peasant humor appealed to Mrs. Payson. She seemed to draw new life from the abounding health and spirits of Jeannette.

They had eaten their dessert. In another moment they would leave the table. Jeannette and Mrs. Payson would get their wraps and clank off in the old electric toward the Arcadia. Lottie sat back in her chair and gave a little indrawn gasp like a swimmer who plunges into icy water.

"I had my first inoculation today, and my vaccination."

The minds of the three other women at the table, busy with their own small projects, refused to grasp the meaning of this statement thrust so suddenly upon them. "Vaccination?" Mrs. Payson had caught this one familiar word and now held it dully, awaiting an explanation.

"I'm going to France two weeks from today," said Lottie. She braced herself, one hand clutching her napkin tight as if that would sustain her.

But there was no storm. Not yet. Mrs. Carrie Payson's will refused to accept the message that her ears had flashed to her brain.

"Don't be silly, Lottie," she said. She brushed a cookie crumb from the front of her waist.

Lottie leaned forward. "Mama, don't you understand? I'm going to France. I'm going in two weeks. I've signed. It's all arranged. I'm going. In two weeks."

"Oh golly!" cried Jeannette, "how perfectly grand!" Aunt Charlotte's hand was weaving nervous palsied circles on the tablecloth, round and round. She champed her teeth as always when she was terribly excited. But Mrs. Payson sat suddenly waxen and yellow. You saw odd lines etched in her face that had not been there a moment before. She stared at Lottie. The whites of her eyes showed below the iris.

"This is a stroke," Lottie said to herself in a moment of hideous detachment. "She's going to have a stroke, and I've done it."

The red surged up into Mrs. Payson's face. "Well, you're not going, that's all. You're not going."

"Yes I am, Mama," Lottie said then, quietly.

"And I say you won't. France! What for! What for!"

Aunt Charlotte stood up, her face working, her head shaking. She pointed a lean aspen finger at her sister. "Carrie Thrift, don't you stand in the way of her going. Don't you! Don't you!"

Even then Mrs. Payson's middle-class horror of being overheard by the servant in the kitchen triumphed over her anger. "Come on into the sitting room. I'm not going to have that girl listening." She went to the swinging door. "We're through, Liela. You can clear off." She eyed the girl sharply before the door swung back.

They marched into the sitting room in silence.

In the two weeks that followed, Mrs. Payson never once relaxed her opposition. Yet she insisted on accompanying Lottie throughout the orgy of shopping that followed—scouring the stores for such commonplace articles as woollen stockings, woollen underwear, heavy shoes, bed socks, flannel bloomers, soap, hot water bag, candles, sugar, pins, needles. Sometimes her mother barely spoke to Lottie for hours. Yet strangely enough, Lottie had twice heard her say to a sympathetic clerk when she did not know Lottie was listening: "Yes, they are for my daughter who's going to France. . . . Yes, it is hard, but we've got to do our share." There had even been a ring of pride in her voice. Lottie heard her speaking at the telephone. "We'll miss her; but they need her more than we do." One could almost call it bragging.

She had a strangely detached feeling about it all. When Henry spoke gravely of U-boats she felt immune, as when one hears of typhus in China. This person who was going to France was not Lottie Payson at all—Lottie Payson, aged thirty-three, of Prairie Avenue, Chicago, Illinois. This was some new, selfish, driven being to whom all the old familiar things and people—the house, the decrepit electric, Aunt Charlotte, her mother, Emma Barton—were remote and inconsequential.

She and Charley had had one brief honest moment together. "I wanted to go too," Charley had said. "I do still. But I'm not going. I want to see Jesse. I want him so much that sometimes I find myself doing things that I thought only women in novels did. Stretching out my arms to him in the dark. . . . The girls of my sort who are going are going for the excitement of it—for the trip, you might almost say. Oh, I know a lot of women—thousands—are moved by the finest kind of patriotism. But—well, for example, that pretty Olive Banning who's in our advertising department. She's going. She says all the men are over there."

The night before leaving, Lottie Payson suffered that agony of self-reproach and terror which unaccustomed travelers feel who are leaving all that is dear and safe and familiar. She lay there in bed in her quiet room and great waves of fear and dread swept over her—not fear of what she was going to but of what she was leaving behind.

She sat up in bed. Listened. If only she might hear some sound to break the stillness—the grinding of a Cottage Grove Avenue car—the whistle of an Illinois Central train. Suddenly she swung her legs over the side of the bed, thrust her feet into slippers and stole down the hall to her mother's room. She wanted to talk to her. She'd be awake; awake and sitting up, alone and fearful, just as she herself was. Her mother's door was open. The room was dark, quite. Lottie peered in, sure of a little breathless silence that should precede her mother's whispered, "Is that you, Lottie?" But from within the room came a sleeper's breathing, deep, full, regular. Her mother was asleep. Her mother was asleep! The knowledge hurt her, angered her. She ought to be awake—awake and fearful. Lottie leaned against the doorsill and pitied herself a little. An occasional strangled snore came from the bed. "I should have gone years ago," Lottie told herself.

She turned back to her room, not taking the trouble to tiptoe now. Past Aunt Charlotte's room.

"Lottie! Is that you?"

Lottie groped in the darkness for the bed and that shrill whisper. "Yes. I—I couldn't sleep—"

"I should think not. Come here to Auntie." That was what she had always said in the first years, long ago, when Lottie and Belle were children, afraid or hurt. "Come here to Auntie." Her hand was on Lottie's shoulder, warm and comforting. "Child alive, you haven't got a thing around you! Here, get the silk quilt. It's over the foot of the bed. I didn't put it away."

"I've got it." Lottie hunched it gratefully about her chilly shoulders. They were talking in guilty whispers. Lottie huddled at the side of the bed. "I can't go, Aunt Charlotte. I can't go."

"Fiddlesticks! That's the middle of the night talking. Wait till you've had a cup of coffee at eight tomorrow morning and see how you feel about going."

Lottie knew she was right. Yet she must justify her own terror. "It isn't fair to Jeannette. I've been thinking of her."

Great-Aunt Charlotte snickered a little. "Never you mind about Jeannette."

"But I do. I brought her here. I'm responsible—"

"Listen to me, Lottie. I went up to Jeannette's room a few nights ago to bring her that little brooch I gave her. The garnet one. She was standing in front of the mirror in her nightgown—don't say a word to your ma— you know how Jeannette always brushes her hair and leaves it loose when she goes to bed? Well, there she was, doing it different ways to see which was most becoming in bed. I saw her. And tying it with a big pink bow." She snickered again, wickedly.

"Why Aunt Charlotte Thrift?"

"Yes *ma'am!* She'll probably marry that boy before he's off for service.

And stay right on here until he comes back. So don't you worry about her being a human sacrifice, Lottie Payson. It's the Jeannettes that make the world go round. They don't stop to think. They just act."

Lottie went back to bed feeling reassured, almost lighthearted. Next morning at breakfast, her mother said, "I didn't close my eyes all night."

They made a good-sized group at the station. Her mother, Aunt Charlotte, Jeannette, Belle, Henry, Charley, of course. Then, all the girls. And Emma Barton was there. Winnie Steppler was in France for her syndicate of papers, sending back stories about the Kansas and Nebraska and Wyoming lads in Paris—the best stories of her career. And Ben Gartz was at the station. He was there in spats, and a check suit, and what is known as a trench coat, with a belt and full skirt; and a little green soft hat with a tiny scarlet feather stuck in the band, toward the back. He had regained some of his former weight, and though he was dapper and spruce, he looked plump and pink-jowled and prime. Surprisingly young, too. It was said that, quite outside the flourishing wristwatch business, he had just made a little fortune in war steel. He joked with Charley. "You little rascal!" Lottie heard him say; and Charley had laughed and looked arch. When he came over to Lottie, his admiring eyes were still on Charley's slim young figure. "That little niece of yours is a card! She's a wonder, that kid." Ben and the girls had brought books, candy, flowers, magazines. Ben had taken the name of the New York hotel at which she was to stop overnight. She saw, in anticipation, more books, flowers, candy. She wished he wouldn't. Effie Case's eyes were red. Lottie wished that the train would start. They were standing round, with nothing more to say. How old Henry looked. What a dear he was. Fine. Too fine and good.

The train gave a tremendous jerk. She stood on the car steps, looking down on them. They, on the platform, waved hands, handkerchiefs, their faces upturned to her.

"Cable the minute you land."

"Goodbye! Goodbye!"

"If you see Vernon Hatch tell him—"

"Stationed at Nancy I think—or maybe it's Soissons."

"Woollen stockings when you get—"

"Goodbye! . . . 'Bye!"

The train gathered speed. They dwindled. Ben Gartz, standing just beside Charley, took hold of her arm above the elbow and, leaning over her, looked down into her face, laughing and saying something. Dimly, Lottie saw the little group turning away. Ben's arm still grasped Charley's, proprietorially.

A wave of fear and apprehension so violent as to be almost dizzying swept over Lottie. "Wait a minute!" she cried to the astonished porter who was carrying in bags and boxes piled on the car platform. "Wait a minute!"

"Too late now, lady. Ef yo' fo'got som'hum Ah kin sen' yo' wiah at Elkhart. Elkhart's nex' stop, lady."

Chapter XVI

The family thought that Ben Gartz was being heavily attentive.
A man who paid court to a woman through her family was an
attentive man. But after the first few weeks following Lottie's
departure, it was unmistakably plain that his attentions were concentrating
on the Kemp branch of the family rather than on the Payson. The first box
of candy sent to Charley, for example, came a week after Lottie's sailing. It
was one of those large satin, brocade, lace-and-gold affairs. You have seen
them in the two-dollar-a-pound shops and have wondered who might be so
fatuous or so rich or so much in love as to buy them. Charley, coming from
work on a cool autumn day, found a great square package on the dressing
table in her bedroom. Her letters and packages and telephone calls always
were placed there, ready for homecoming.

"Any mail?" she said today. Her quick eye had seen there was none.
And yet she so wanted some—one letter in particular—that she asked,
hopefully. Mail, to Charley, meant, those days, one of those thin envelopes
with a strip pasted over one end to show where the censor had opened
it. Then she had seen the box. It was an unavoidable box holding, as it
did, five pounds of Wood's most intricate sweets. In these self-sacrificing
days, candy was one of the things you had learned to forego. Therefore,
"Wood's!" exclaimed Charley, removing the wrappers. "Who do you
suppose?—Oh, my goodness! It looks like a parlor davenport; or a dressy
coffin. Why, it's from that Ben Gartz! Well! Lotta can't say I'm not keeping
the home fires burning."

She gave the brocade box to Jeannette for her dresser and more than
half its contents to her grandmother and Aunt Charlotte, both of whom

ate sweets in appalling quantities, the flickering flame of their bodily furnaces doubtless calling for this quick form of fuel. She herself scarcely tasted it, thinking more of a clear skin than a pleased palate. She meant to write Ben a note of thanks. She even started one; addressed one of her great square stiff art-paper envelopes in her dashing hand. But something called her away and she never finished it. He called at the house a week later, after dinner—just dropped in as he was driving by—and mentioned it delicately.

"Oh, Miss Charley, I sent you a little—I wondered if you got it—"

Then she was honestly ashamed. "Oh, Mr. Gartz, what a pig you must think me! I started a note to you. Really—" She even ran back to her room and returned with the envelope and the sheet of paper on which she had written his name, and the date. He said he was going to keep the piece of paper, and tucked it into his left-hand vest pocket with a soulful look.

The box containing his second gift made the first one seem infinitesimal. Mrs. Kemp was the recipient. She had said, characteristically, that she didn't mind doing without white bread, or sugar in her coffee, or new clothes, but it was hard not being able to have flowers. She had always had flowers in the living room until now—a standing order at the florist's. The box held two dozen American Beauties whose legs stuck out through a slit in the end. It was November, and American Beauties were fifteen dollars a dozen. There weren't enough tall vases in the house to accommodate them all. Their scarlet heads glowed in the jade-green background of the sun parlor and all over the living room and even spilled back into Belle Kemp's bedroom. Charley told her father that he ought to realize the seriousness of it. "Where's your pride and manhood, Henry Kemp! Two dozen American Beauties! It's equivalent to jewelry."

Henry, eyeing them, rubbed a rueful hand over his chin, even while he grinned. "Next time I wish old Ben'd send the cash."

Things had come to a bad pass with Henry Kemp. It was no longer necessary for him to say that business was not going. Business, for him, was gone. Importing was as dead as war and U-boats could make it. His house, together with many less flourishing and important ones, had closed for lack of goods. It had been wiped out so completely that there remained of it nothing to tell the tale except the exquisite collection of Venetian glass, and Bohemian liqueur sets, and French enamel opera glasses and toilette table pieces, and Hungarian china and embroidery which Belle had acquired during the years in which her husband had dealt in these precious things. Sometimes you saw Henry looking at them—picking up a fine old piece of French china or Italian glass from the buffet or dresser and turning it over to scan its familiar stamp. He knew them as an expert knows diamonds. His eye could detect any flaw in glaze or color.

Now, at fifty, Henry Kemp, for years a successful merchant and importer, was looking about for an opening. He would get something. The young men were being drawn away by the hundreds of thousands. He had been offered a position which would require his traveling for six months in the year. He had no illusions about it. On the road, a traveling salesman, at fifty. It was a bitter pill for Henry Kemp. He could not yet force himself to swallow it.

His day stretched, empty, before him, but he made himself busy. Each morning he rose at the hour to which his business had accustomed him for years. He bathed and shaved and dressed carefully, as usual. He breakfasted and glanced at the paper, doing both with the little air of hurry that had meant the car waiting outside, or the 8:45 IC train to catch. For twenty-five years he had gone downtown daily at a certain time, his face alight with the eager alert expression which meant the anticipation of a heavy mail and a day crowded with orders. He still followed out this program. But the eager look was absent. His springy step was suddenly heavy, lagging. Belle sometimes wondered where he went—how he filled his day. He belonged to clubs—big, comfortable, prosperous clubs housed on Michigan Boulevard. But clubs, to American businessmen, meant a place for a quiet business talk at luncheon. During the day they were, for the most part, deserted. Sometimes Charley said, "Lunch with me, Father?"

"I've got to see a man at twelve. It's a conference. I can't tell how long it'll last."

Henry Kemp presented that most tragic of spectacles, the American businessman at leisure.

In fairness to Belle Kemp, it must be said that she did not nag him, or reproach him, or bewail her lot or mope. He would get something, she knew. He had a reputation for business acumen; a standing in the community; hosts of influential friends. Besides, there was money for present needs. They had lived well, the Kemps. Henry had denied his wife and daughter nothing. Still Henry Kemp sensed that his wife was thinking, "Failure." Failure at fifty. She was too much her mother's daughter to think otherwise. So he walked off, jauntily, every morning, with a haste that deceived no one, least of all himself.

Ben Gartz got into the way of sending tickets to the Kemps. Tickets for concerts, tickets for war benefits, for the theatre. "I wonder if you wouldn't like to use these? I can't go and I thought—"

He heard Charley speak of a book she had tried to get, and failed. He sent to New York for it and had it mailed to her. It was *The Bab Ballads*. He did not know that she wanted them for Jesse. She and Jesse had read them together often. Now she thought that if she could send them to him if only to amuse him for a day, or an hour even, in the trenches or back of the lines, it would be something. Ben Gartz had never heard of the book but he had written down the name, carefully, in his little leather notebook.

When Charley told him that she had sent the volume ($4.50 net) to Jesse, in France, his face wore the strangest look.

When Mrs. Payson heard of these things, as she inevitably did, she looked a little aggrieved. "He's been here once since Lottie left—just once. I can't blame him. Lottie treated him like a dog. If ever there was an attentive man. But what's he come to your house so much for?"

"Oh, he and Henry—" Belle said lamely.

Aunt Charlotte spoke up from the silence which now enveloped her more and more. "I suppose there's nothing Henry needs just now more than candy and roses and theatre tickets and one thing and another."

Following these attentions—rather, breaking into the midst of them as they came, thick and fast—the Kemps had Ben Gartz in to dinner. They had had few dinner guests of late. Belle made a very special effort and the dinner was delicious; a thing to tempt Ben's restaurant-jaded appetite. The meat sauce was smooth, rich, zestful; the dressing for the salad properly piquant but suave; the sweet just light enough to satisfy without cloying. Ben Gartz had become a connoisseur in these things as does your fleshly man who learns late in life of gastronomic delights.

After dinner he and Henry talked business. "Have a cigar, Henry."

"Thanks, but I don't smoke those heavy ones any more. They don't agree with me. Try one of these."

Ben took it, eyed it, tucked it into his vest pocket, and lighted one of his own. He rolled it between his lips. He squinted up through the smoke.

"Well now, Kemp, you hold on for awhile longer, will you? There may be something pretty big breaking for you."

"How do you mean, breaking for me?"

"I don't want to say, right now. But I mean—well, I mean in our business. We knew we had a big thing but we didn't know what we really had. Why, it's colossal. There's only me—and Beck and Diblee. Beck's getting pretty old. He's a pioneer among the jewelry manufacturers. Crowding seventy, Beck is. Diblee's all right but he doesn't do for the trade. He hasn't got the trick of mixing. He wears those eyeglasses with a black ribbon, you know, and talks about the east, where he came from, and they get sore, the wholesalers do . . . Got any capital, Henry? Not that we need capital, y'understand. Lord no! What we need is brains and business experience and a mixer. I've got all three, but say, I can't be everywhere."

As if by magic, Henry Kemp's face filled out, became firm where it had sagged, glowed where it had been sallow with the jaundice of discouragement.

"Why, say Ben—look here—you don't mean—"

"I don't mean anything, Kemp. Not yet. And perhaps I oughtn't to have said anything. Of course old Beck and Diblee've got to be considered. But I think I could swing it—if I pushed hard enough. The business is getting to be enormous, I'm telling you. Four million kids in service, every one of 'em with a watch on his wrist, y'understand, from doughboy to general; and millions and millions more to come. Why, say, before we're through with this thing—"

He gave Henry a tip on war stocks.

"No thanks," Henry said. "I can't afford to take any chances just now."

"But this isn't a chance, you chump. Where's your nerve! Can't you trust a fellow that's giving it to you straight!"

Henry was tempted, but privately decided against it. It wasn't fair to Belle and Charley to take the chance, he thought. A week later, Ben telephoned him.

"Sell out on that stuff Henry—you know—that I told you about."

"I didn't buy."

"Didn't—!"

"No."

"Why you darned fool, I just cleaned up twenty-five thousand on it, that's all. My God, why—"

Henry put it out of his mind, grimly. He told himself he had done the right thing. Sometimes Henry Kemp thought of his insurance. He carried a big insurance. When he died it would amount to a tidy fortune for Belle and Charley. But it had to be kept up. It was all clear now but it had to be kept up. . . . He put that thought out of his mind. An ugly thought.

Ben was just as good a sport about small stakes as he was about big ones. He made a bet with Charley, for example. He seemed so certainly on the losing side that Charley said, "But I won't bet on that. I'm sure of it. You haven't a sporting chance."

"Oh, haven't I! That's what everybody thinks before the other fellow wins. I'm just as sure as you are. I'm so sure that I'll bet you a pair of gloves to a set of dice. What size do you wear? Understand, I'm only asking to observe the formalities, that's all. I'm safe." He laughed a fat chuckling laugh and took Charley's slim strong young fingers in his own pulpy clasp. Charley was surprised to find herself snatching her hand away, hotly. She hadn't meant to. It was purely involuntary. The reaction against something distasteful. She won the bet. He sent her half a dozen pairs of finest French glacé gloves. Charley fingered them, thoughtfully. There was nothing pleased about her expression. She was not a fool, Charley. But she told herself that she was; poo-pood'd the idea that was growing in her mind. But now, steadily, when he called at the house, telephoned, wrote, sent flowers or candy, she was out; did not answer; ignored the gifts. He found out that she and her mother had arranged to meet at a tearoom for lunch during Charley's noon hour one day, intercepted them, carried them off almost bodily to the Blackstone. There, in the rich splendor of the rose-and-cream dining room looking out upon the boulevard and the lake beyond, he was in his element. A table by the window—the center window. Well, Maurice, what have you got out of season, h'm? Lobster? Japanese persimmons? Artichokes? Corn on the cob? He remembered that Charley had once said she adored lobster thermidor as the Blackstone chef prepared it. "But none of your little crabsized lobsters now, Maurice! This young lady may be a baby vamp but she doesn't want your little measly baby lobster, remember. A good big one. And hot. And plenty of sauce. . . . Now then, Mrs. Kemp. How about you?"

Charley ate two bites of the big succulent crustacean and left the rest disdainfully as a reproach and a punishment for him. She talked little, and then of Lottie. Her manner was frigid, remote, baffling. A baby vamp—she, Charley Kemp! who loathed cheapness, and bobbed hair, and wriggling ways, and the whole new breed of her contemporaries who were of the hard-drinking, stairway-kissing, country-club petting class. She thought of Jesse, looked out across the broad avenue to the great blue expanse of lake as though it were in reality the ocean that lay between them, and left her sweet untouched on her plate.

Mrs. Kemp did not speak to Charley of Ben Gartz's insistent attentions. Probably she did not even admit to herself the meaning of them at first. But there is no doubt that she began, perhaps unconsciously, a process of slow poisoning.

"They all say this will go on for years. There won't be a young man left in the world—nor a middle-aged man, for that matter. Nothing but old men and children. Look at France, and Poland, and Germany! I don't know what the women are going to do."

"Do?" queried Charley, maliciously; she knew perfectly well what her mother meant.

"Do for husbands. Girls must marry, you know."

"I don't see the necessity," said Charley, coolly. (Charley, who stretched out her arms in the dark.)

"Well I do. How would you like to be another Aunt Charlotte? Or a Lottie, for that matter?"

"There are worse fates, Mother dear. For that matter, I know a lot of married women who envy me my independence. I don't know any married women I envy."

"That's complimentary to your father, I must say."

"Now, don't be personal, Mother. I'd rather have Dad for a father than any father I've ever seen. Why, he's darling. I love the way he doesn't get me; and his laugh; and his sweetness with you; and his fineness and dignity; and the way he's kept his waistline; and his fondness for the country. Oh, everything about him as a father. But as the type of husband for me, Dad lacks the light touch . . . What a conversation! I'm surprised at you, Belle Kemp!"

One day, in midwinter, Henry Kemp came home looking more lined and careworn than usual. It was five o'clock. His wife was in their bedroom. He always whistled an inquiring note or two when he let himself in at the front door. It was a little conjugal call that meant, "Are you home?" In her babyhood days, Charley always used to come pattering and staggering down the long hall at the sound of it. But though he caught the child up in his arms, he always kissed his wife first. Not that Belle had always been there. She was not the kind of wife who makes a point of being home to greet her lord when he returns weary from the chase. As often as not a concert, or matinee, or late bridge delayed her beyond her husband's homecoming time. Then the little questioning whistle sounded plaintively in the empty apartment, and Henry went about his tidying up for dinner with one ear cocked for the click of the front door lock.

Tonight he whistled as usual. You almost felt the effort he made to pucker his lips for the sound that used to be so blithe. Belle answered him. "Yoo-hoo!" For the first time he found himself wishing she had been out. He came into their bedroom. A large, gracious, rose-illumined room it was. Belle was standing before the mirror doing something to her hair. Her arms were raised. She smiled at him in the mirror. "You're home early."

He came over to her, put his arm about her and kissed her rather roughly. He was still in love with his somewhat selfish wife, was Henry Kemp. And this kiss was a strange mixture of passion, of fear, and defiance and protest against the cruel circumstance that was lashing him now. Here he was, the lover, the generous provider, the kind and tolerant husband and father, suddenly transformed by a malicious force he was powerless to combat, into a mendicant; an asker instead of a giver; a failure who had grown used to the feel of success. So now he looked at this still-pretty woman who was his wife, and his arm tightened about her and he kissed her hard, as though these things held for him some tangible assurance.

"Henry!" she shrugged him away. "Now look at my hair!" He looked at it. He looked at its reflection in the mirror; at her face, unlined and rosy; at his own face near hers. He was startled at the contrast, so sallow and haggard he seemed.

He rubbed a hand over his cheek and chin. "Gosh! I look seedy."

"You need a shave," Belle said, lightly. She turned away from the mirror. He caught her arm, faced her, his face almost distorted with pain.

"Belle, we'll have to get out of here."

"Out of—how do you mean?"

"Our lease is up in May. We'd have to go then, anyway. But I was talking to a fellow today—Leach, of the David, Anderson company. They've made a pile in war contracts. His wife's looking for an apartment about this size and neighborhood. They'd take it off our hands—the lease I mean."

"Now? You mean now!"

"Yes. We could take something smaller. We—we'll have to, Belle."
She threw a terrified glance around the room. It was a glance that
encompassed everything, as though she were seeing it all for the first time. It
was the look one gives a cherished thing that is about to be snatched away. A
luxurious room with its silken bedcovers and rosy hangings. The room of a
fastidious luxury-loving woman. Its appointments were as carefully chosen
as her gowns. The beds were rich dark walnut, magnificently marked—not
at all the walnut of Mrs. Payson's great cumbersome edifice in the old Prairie
Avenue house—but exquisite pieces of bijouterie; plump, inviting; beds
such as queens have slept in. The reading lamp on the small table between
gave just the soothing subdued glow to make one's eleven o'clock printed
page a narcotic instead of a stimulant. Beside it, a little clock of finest French
enamel picked out with platinum ticked almost soundlessly.

Terror lay in her eyes as they turned from their contemplation of this to
the man who stood before her. "Oh, Henry, can't we hold out just for a while?
This war can't last much longer. Everybody says it'll be over soon—the spring,
perhaps—" She who had just spoken to Charley of its endlessness.

"It's no use, Belle. No one knows how long it'll last. I hate to give it
up. But we've got to, that's all. We might as well face it."

"How about Ben Gartz? He promised to take you into the business—
that wonderful business."

"He didn't promise. He sort of hinted. He didn't mean any harm.
He's a big talker, Ben."

"But he meant it. I know he did. I know he did." A sudden thought
came to her. "How long has it been since he talked to you about—since
he last mentioned it to you?"

"Oh, it's been three weeks anyway."

She calculated quickly. It was three weeks since the Blackstone luncheon when Charley had been so rude to him. She tucked this away in the back of her mind; fenced for time. "Couldn't we sublet? I'd even be willing to rent it furnished, to reliable people."

"Furnished? What good would that do? Where would we live?"

She had thought of that, too. "We could go to Mother's to live for awhile. There's loads of room. We could have the whole third floor, for that matter, until this blows over. Lots of families—"

But at that his jaws came together and the lower one jutted out a little in the line she had seen so seldom and yet knew so well. It meant thus far and no farther.

"No, Belle. I may be broke, but I'm not that broke—yet. I'll provide a home for my family. Maybe it won't be quite what we're used to; but it'll be of my own providing. When I let you go back to your mother's to live, you can know I'm licked, beaten, done. But not until then, understand."

She understood.

"Well, dear, we'll just have to do the best we can. When do you have to give Leach your answer?"

"Within the week, I should say. Yes."

She smiled up at him, brightly. She patted his lean cheek with her soft cool scented hand. "Well, you never can tell. Something may happen." She left him to shave and dress.

He thought, "What a child she is. Women are."

She thought. "He's like a child. All men are. . . . Well, I've got to manage this."

There were two telephone connections in that big apartment—one in the front hall, another in the dining room at the rear. She went down the hall, closed the dining room door carefully, called Ben Gartz's office number in a low tense voice. It was not yet five-thirty. He might still be there. He must be, she told herself.

He was. His tone, when he heard her name, was rather sulky. But she had ways. We haven't seen a thing of you. Forgotten your old friends since you've made all that horrid money. Talking of you only yesterday. Who? Charley. Why not come up for dinner tonight. Just a plain family meal but there was a rather special deep-dish pie.

He would come. You could hear that it was against his better judgment. But he would come. When she had hung up the receiver, she sat for a minute, breathing fast, as if she had been running a close race. Then she went into the kitchen and began feverish preparations. Halfway, she stopped suddenly, went back into the dining room, picked up the receiver and gave her own telephone number, hung up quickly, opened the door that led from the dining room to the long hall, and let the telephone bell ring three times before she answered it. The maid opened the swinging door that led to the kitchen but Belle shook her head. "Never mind. I'll answer it." She said "hello," then hung up again once the buzzing had ceased. Then, carefully, she carried on a brief conversation with someone who was not there—someone who evidently wanted to come to see them all; and wouldn't he like to run in to dinner. She went to the hall door and called. "Henry! Oh, Henry!"

A mumble from the direction of the bathroom meant that he was handicapped by shaving lather.

"I just wanted to tell you. That was Ben Gartz who just called up. He wanted to come up so I asked him to dinner. Is that all right?"

"'S all right with me."

Grapefruit. Olives. A can of mushrooms to be opened. For over half an hour she worked furiously. At six Charley came home.

"Hello, Dad. Where's Mother?" He was reading the evening paper under the amber-silk light of the living room. Charley kissed the top of his head, patted his shoulder once, and went back to her room. A little subdued these days was Charley—for Charley. "Any mail? I wonder what's the matter with Lotta. I haven't had a letter in a month."

Her bedroom was down the long hall, halfway between the living room and dining room. Her mother was already there, waiting. "Any mail? . . . How pretty you look, Mother! Your cheeks are all pink." But her eyes went past her mother to the little sheaf of envelopes that lay on her dressing table. She went toward them, quickly. But her mother stopped her.

"Listen, Charley. Ben Gartz is coming to dinner tonight." Charley's eyebrows went up ever so slightly. She said nothing. "Charley, Ben Gartz could do a great deal for your father—and for all of us—if he wanted to."

"Doesn't he want to?"

"Well, after all, why should he? It isn't as if we were related—or as if he were one of the family."

"Lottie, you mean?" She knew what her mother meant. And yet she wanted to give her a chance—a chance to save herself from this final infamy.

"N-n-no." Her voice had the rising inflection. "I don't think he cares about Lottie any more."

"Then that snatches him definitely out of the family clutches, doesn't it? Unless Aunt Charlotte—"

"Don't be funny, Charley. He's a man to be respected. He's good-looking, not old; more than well-to-do—rich, really."

Charley's eyes were cold and hard. And they were no longer mother and daughter, but two women, battle-locked. "M-m-m . . . A little old and fat though, don't you think, for most purposes? And just a wee bit common? H'm?"

"Common! Well, when it comes to being common, my dear child, I don't think there was anything fastidious about the choice you made last June. After all, Delicatessen Dick isn't exactly—"

"Just a minute, Mother. I want to get this thing straight. I'm to marry your chubby little friend in order to save the family fortunes—is that it?"

"N-no. I don't mean just that. I merely—"

"What do you mean, then? I want to hear you say it?"

"You could do a really big thing for your father. You must have seen how old he's grown in the last six months. I don't see how you can stand by and not want to help. He had a chance. Ben Gartz practically offered to take him into the business. But you were deliberately rude to him. No man with any pride—"

Charley began to laugh then; not prettily. "Oh, Mother, you quaint old thing!" Belle stiffened. "I don't want to insult you, don't you know, but I can't make a thing out of what you've said except that if I marry this chubby little ridiculous old sport he'll take Dad into the business and we'll all live happily ever after and I'll be just like the noble heroine who sells herself to the rich old banker to pay the muggidge. Oh Mother!" She was laughing again; and then, suddenly, she was crying, her face distorted. She was crying terribly.

"Sh-sh-sh! Your father'll hear you! There's nothing to make a scene about."

"No scene!" said Charley, through her tears. "If you can't cry when your mother dies when can you cry!"

She turned away from her then. Belle Kemp looked a little frightened. But at the door she said what she still had to say. "He's coming here to dinner tonight."

Charley, lifting heavy arms to take off her hat, seemed not to hear. She looked at herself in the mirror a moment—stared at the tear-stained red-eyed girl. At what she saw she began to sob again, weakly. Then she shook herself angrily, and pushed her hair back from her forehead with a hand that was closed into a fist. She went into the living room, stood before her father reading there.

"Dad."

He looked up from his paper; stiffened. "Why, Charley, what's—" Charley almost never cried. He was as disturbed as if this had been a man standing there before him, red-eyed and shaken.

"Listen, Dad. You know that thing Ben Gartz spoke to you about a little while ago? The business. Taking you into it, I mean?"

"That? Yes. What of it?"

"He hasn't said anything lately, has he?"

"Well, he—he—wasn't sure, you know. I thought at the time it was a little wild. Ben's good-hearted, but he's a gabby boy. Doesn't mean quite all he says."

"He meant it all right, Dad. But you see he—he'd like to have me marry him first."

He stared, half willing to laugh if she gave him any encouragement. But she did not. His newspaper came down with a crash, then, as his fingers crushed it and threw it to the floor. "Gartz! You marry Ben Gartz!" She was crying again, helplessly. His two hands gripped her shoulders. "Why, the damned old l—" he stopped himself, shaking a little.

"That's it," said Charley, and she was smiling as she sobbed. "That's the word . . . I knew I could count on you, Dad. I knew."

His arms were about her. Her face was pressed against the good rough cloth of his coat. "Sh-sh-sh, Charley. Don't let your mother hear you. We mustn't let her know. She'd be wild. He's coming here to dinner, the oily old fox. Gosh, Charley, are you sure you—"

"I'm sure."

"We won't say anything to Mother, will we?"

"No, Dad."

"She'd be sick, that's what. Sick. We'll fix him and his business, all right."

"Yes. Talk about Jesse. Talk about Jesse a lot. And make it plain. About Jesse. Then see what he has to say about his business."

The doorbell sounded. Charley was out of his arms and off to her room. Belle came swiftly down the hall and darted into her bedroom for a hasty dab at her flushed face with the powder pad. Henry opened the door. Ben's voice boomed. Henry answered with hollow geniality.

"Come in, come in! Here, let me have that. Belle'll be here in a minute."

Belle was there becomingly flushed, cordial. Ben was pressing her hand. "It was mighty nice of you, let me tell you, to call me—"

She was panic-stricken but Henry had not heard, apparently. He had interrupted with a foolish remark of his own.

"It's probably the last time in this place anyway, Ben. We're giving up this flat, you know. End of the month."

"How's that?"

"Can't afford it."

Ben pursed his lips, drummed with his fingers on the arm of the deep comfortable chair. "Well, now, perhaps—"

Charley came in, smiling a watery smile and palpably red-eyed. Her father caught her and hugged the slender shoulder with a paternal and yet quizzical gesture. "Nobody's supposed to notice that Charley's been crying a little. She didn't get a letter from her boy in France and she doesn't feel happy about it." She looked up at him, gratefully. He patted her shoulder, turned pride fully to Ben. "Charley and her poet are going to be married, you know, when this war's over—if it ever *is* over. Look at her blush! I guess these newfangled girls have got some old-fashioned ways left, after all, eh, Chas?"

"Yes, Dad."

Chapter XVII

They were in the midst of packing and moving when the news came of Jesse Dick's death. She had no formal warning. No official envelope prepared her. And yet she received it with a dreadful calm, as though she had expected it, and had braced herself for it. She and her father were at breakfast, surrounded by wooden packing boxes and burlap rolls. Charley, in peril of missing the 8:35 IC train, contented herself with the morning's news secondhand. Henry Kemp had the paper.

"What's the daily *schrecklichkeit,* Dad?"

He had not answered. Suddenly the weight of his silence struck her. She looked up as though he had spoken her name. The open newspaper shielded his face. Something in the way he held it. You do not hold a paper thus when you are reading, "Dad!" The paper came down slowly. She saw his face.

"Dead?"

"Yes."

He stood up. She came around to him. She wanted to see it on paper, printed.

That morning she actually caught the 8:35 as usual. She sold little imports all that morning, went out at the lunch hour, and never returned to Shield's. Outwardly, she practiced the stoicism of her kind. She cried herself to sleep night after night, indeed; beat on her pillow with an impotent fist; sat up, feverish and wakeful, to rage at life. But she was up next morning, as usual, pale and determined.

There was a curious scene with Great-Aunt Charlotte. At news of Jesse Dick's death, she had summoned Charley; had insisted that she must see her; had been so mysteriously emphatic that Charley had almost rebelled, anticipating a garrulous hour of senile sympathy and decayed advice. Still she went, ascended the stairs to Aunt Charlotte's room (she came downstairs more and more rarely now) and at Aunt Charlotte's first words, "I knew he'd never come back, Charley," would have fled incontinently if something in the grim earnestness of the black-browed old countenance had not held her. There was no soft sentimentality in Great-Aunt Charlotte's word or look. Rather she seemed eager, vitalized, as though she had an important message to convey. Charley did groan a little, inwardly, when Aunt Charlotte brought out the yellow old photograph of the girl in the full-skirted wasp-waisted riding habit, with the plume and the rose. And she said vaguely, "Oh, yes," as she took it in her hand, and wished that she had not come. And then, "Why, Aunt Charlotte! You lovely thing! You never showed me this picture before! You're the family beauty. Your face is—the look—it sort of glows—"

"Just for a little while. Jesse Dick brought that look to it."

"How do you mean—Jesse Dick?"

And quietly, masterfully, with the repression of more than fifty years swept away before the urgence of this other Charlotte's need, she told her own brief stark story. "I was eighteen, Charley, when the Civil War began. That's the picture of me, taken at the time—"

Charley listened. Sometimes her eyes dwelt on the withered old countenance before her; sometimes she looked down, mistily, at the glowing face of the girl in the picture. But her attention never wandered. For the first time she was hearing the story of the first Jesse Dick. For the first time Great-Aunt Charlotte was telling it. She was telling it, curiously enough, with the detachment of an outsider—without reproach, without regret, without bitterness. When she had finished she sat back, and glanced about the bedroom—the neat, shabby, rather close-smelling bedroom of an old, old woman—and then she opened her hands on her knees, palms out, as though in exposition. "And this is I," said the open palms and dim old eyes. "This is I, Charlotte Thrift."

As though in answer—in defense of her—Charley leaned forward, impetuously, and pressed her fresh young cheek against the sallow withered one. "You've been wonderful, Aunt Charlotte. You have! What would Grandma Payson have done without you!—or Lottie, or Mother, for that matter."

But Great-Aunt Charlotte shook her head. She seemed to be waiting for something. And then Charley said, "I'll be all right. I'm the kind that goes on. You know. I'm too curious about life to want to miss any of it. I'll keep on trying things and people and I'll probably find the combination. Not the perfect combination, like Jesse. You don't, twice. But I suppose I'll marry—sometime."

"That's it. Don't you give in. You're twenty. Don't you give in. I was scared when you left your work—"

"Oh, that. I couldn't stay. I don't know. Restless."

"That's all right," said Aunt Charlotte, satisfied. "Restless is all right. Restless is better than resigned."

Of Jesse Dick's poems, two made a little furor. The reviewers all had a line or two or three about his having been one of the most promising of the younger poets of the virile school. They said his was American poetry, full of crude power. One poem—the one called "Chemin des Dames"—they even learned in the schools, mispronouncing its title horribly, of course. They took it seriously, solemnly. Charley alone knew that it had been written in satire and derision. It was his protest against all the poems about scarlet poppies and Flanders fields. Taken seriously, it was indeed a lovely lyric thing. Taken as Charley knew he had meant it, it was scathing, terrible.

People thought the one called "Death" was a little too bitter. Good—but bitter, don't you think? That part beginning:

They said you were majestic, Death.
Majestic! You!
I know you for the foolish clown you are;
A drooling zany, mouth agape and legs asprawl,
A grotesque scarecrow on a barbed wire fence.

. . . .

When Charley read that one, as she often did, she would beat with her hard young fist on her knee and cry impotent tears of rage at the uselessness of it all.

They made a book of his poems and brought it out in the autumn, just before the armistice. A slim book of poems. There had been so few of them.

Chapter XVIII

C harley was away when Lottie came home in February, following that historic hysteric November. Charley was in Cincinnati, Ohio, dancing with the Krisiloff Russian ballet. They were playing Cincinnati all that week, and the future bookings included Columbus, Cleveland, Toledo, Akron. Charley wrote that they would be back in Chicago for two weeks at the end of March, showing one week at the Palace and one at the Majestic.

" . . . And what's all this," she wrote Lottie, "about your having brought back a French war orphan? There never was such a gal for orphans. Though I must say you did pretty well with Jeannette. Mother wrote me about her wedding. But this orphan sounds so young. And a girl, too. I'm disappointed. While you were about it, it seems to me you might have picked a gentleman orphan. We certainly need some men in our family. Send me a picture, won't you? I hope she isn't one of those awfully brune French babies that look a mixture of Italian and Yiddish and Creole. In any case I'm going to call her Coot. Are you really going to adopt her? That would be nice, but mad. Did Grandmother raise an awful row? I'm sorry she's feeling no better. Mother wrote you have a trained nurse now. . . ."

Lottie's homecoming had been a subdued affair. She had slipped back into the family life of the old house on Prairie Avenue as if those months of horror and exaltation and hardship had never been. But there was a difference. Lottie was the head of the household now.

Mrs. Carrie Payson lay upstairs in the second-floor front bedroom, a strangely flat outline beneath the covers of the great walnut bed. She made a bad patient. The eyes in the pointed sallow face were never still. The new nurse said, almost automatically now, "Don't try to talk, Mrs. Payson. You want to save your strength."

"Strength! How can I ever get my strength lying here! I never stayed in bed. I'll get up tomorrow, doctor or no doctor. Everything's going to rack and ruin. I engaged the painters for the first of March. There's repairing to do on everything in the spring. Did they send in the bill for fixing the shed?"

But when next day came, she threatened to get up tomorrow. And next day. Her will still burned, indomitable, but the heart refused to do its bidding. The thing they called rheumatism had leaped and struck deep with claws and fangs, following a series of disturbing events.

Mrs. Payson had looked upon the Kemp's removal from the Hyde Park apartment to the small Fifty-Third Street flat as a family disgrace. The Thrifts, she said, had always gone forward, never back. She tried vainly to shake Henry's determination not to take advantage of the roominess of the Prairie Avenue house. Henry had remained firm. He had a position as manager of the china and glass department in a big wholesale house whose specialty was the complete equipment of hotels, restaurants, and country clubs. His salary was less than one-fourth of what his income had been in the old days. He said it would have to do. The Hyde Park Boulevard furnishings fitted strangely into the cheap-woodwork-and-wallpaper background of the new apartment. Belle refused to part with any of them. She said that some day they would be back where they belonged. What she could not use she stored in the top floor of her mother's house. By early spring she was white-enameling almost happily, and dickering with the dour landlord as to his possible share of the expense of plain plaster in the living room. She had the gift of making a house habitable in spite of herself.

The Friday night family dinners persisted. Mrs. Payson even continued to administer business advice to the long-suffering Henry.

Things that had seemed unbearable in prospect now adjusted themselves well enough. And then Charley had horrified them all by discarding the black uniform of a Shield's employee for the chiffon and fleshings of the Krisiloff Ballet. Belle and even Henry opposed it from the first moment of surprise and disapproval, but Mrs. Carrie Payson fought it like a tigress. They had all thought she would return to Shield's. But she had announced, calmly, her decision never to return. "Go back? Why should I go back there! The thought makes me ill."

Her father and mother had received this with amazement. "But Charley, you were promoted just last week. You said you liked it. Let me tell you, three thousand a year isn't to be sneezed at by a kid of twenty. In another five—"

"Yes, I know. In another five I'll be earning five thousand. I'll be twenty-five then. And in another five I'll be earning ten, and I'll be thirty. And in another five and another five and another five!... And then I'll color my hair a beautiful raspberry shade, too, just like Healy, and wear imported black charmeuse and maybe my pearls will be real and my manicure grand and glittering, and while I shan't call the stockgirls 'girlie,' I'll have that hard finish. You get it in business—if you're in it for business."

"Well, what *were* you in it for?"

"For Jesse, I suppose."

They were at dinner at home. Belle left the table, weeping. Charley and her father went on with their meal and their discussion like two men, though Charley did become a little dramatic toward the end. Later, Belle, overcome by curiosity at the sound of their low-voiced conversation, crept back, red-eyed, to know the rest.

Henry Kemp, wise enough in the ways of womenfolk, as well he might be—the one man in that family of women—groped bewildered for a motive in Charley's sudden revolt. "But you liked it well enough, Charley. You liked it real well. You said so. You seemed to be getting a lot of fun out of it. Maybe something's happened down there. Anything wrong?"

"Not a thing, Dad. I'm not interested in it any more. It's just that— it's just that—well, you see, Jesse furnished enough color and light and poetry for both of us. When I say poetry I don't mean verses on paper. I mean rhythm and motion and joy. Does that sound silly to you?"

"Why no, Charley, it doesn't sound silly. I guess maybe I get what you mean, sort of."

"Well—" Then it was that Belle came creeping back into the room, sniffling. Charley looked up at her calm-eyed. "Mother, I'd like to have you understand this, too. I've been thinking about it quite a lot. I don't want you to imagine I'm just popping off, suddenly."

"Off!" Belle snatched at the word.

Charley nodded. "You see I've got to have color and motion and life. And beauty. You don't find them at Shield's. But before Jesse—went—I knew I could hit it off beautifully down there and that he'd furnish me with enough of the other thing. One of us had to buckle down, and I was the one. I wanted to be. We were both going to be married and free at the same time. The little house in Hubbard Woods was there to come to, every day or once a week. It was going to be every day for me. But a man like Jesse can't write—couldn't write—his kind of stuff without feeling free to come and go. So there I was going to be. And I'd have my job, and some babies in between . . . Well, there's nothing in it for me now. Plodding away. It's ridiculous. What for! Oh, it's interesting enough. It's all right if . . . I want a change. Dancing! Krisiloff's going out with his company. He's got forty-two solid weeks booked. I'm going with them. He's going to let me do the Gypsy Beggar dance alone." She pushed her plate away, got up from the table. "It'll be good to dance again." She raised her arms high above her head. "'Can I show you something in blouses, madam?' Ugh!"

Mrs. Payson, when she heard of it, was aroused to a point that alarmed them all. "A grandchild of mine—Isaac Thrift's great-granddaughter—dancing around the country on the stage! What did I tell you, Belle! Haven't I always told you! But no, she had to take dancing lessons. Esthetic dancing. Esthetic! I'd like to know what's esthetic about a lot of dirty Russians slapping about in their bare feet. I won't have it. I won't have it. Color, huh? Life and beauty! I'd show her color if I were you. A spanking—that's what she needs. That'd show her a little life and color. She shan't go. Hear me!"

When Charley refused to discuss it with her grandmother, Mrs. Payson forbade her the house. The excitement had given her tremendous energy. She stamped about the house and down the street, scorning the electric.

Charley joined the Krisiloffs in August. Her letters home omitted many details that would have justified Mrs. Payson in the stand she had taken. But Charley was only slightly disgusted and often amused at the manners and morals of the Krisiloffs. She hated the stuffy hotels and the uninviting food but loved exploring the towns. Audiences in medium-sized Middle West towns were rather startled by the fury and fire which she flung into the Gypsy Beggar dance. Her costume of satin breeches and chiffon shirt was an ingenious imitation of a street beggar's picturesque rags and tatters. As she finished her dance, and flung herself on her knees, holding out her tambourine for alms, the audiences would stare at her uncomfortably, shifting in their seats, so haggard and piteous and feverish was her appeal. But always there was a crash of applause, sharp and spontaneous. She had some unpleasant moments with other women of the company who were jealous of the favor with which her dance was received.

When the rest of the company was sleeping, or eating, or cooking messes over furtive alcohol stoves in hotel bedrooms, Charley was prowling about bookshops, or walking in the town's outskirts, or getting a quiet private enjoyment out of its main street. She missed Lottie. She often wanted to write her many of the things that the other members of the family would not have understood. In the life and color and beauty she had craved, she had found, as well, much drudgery and sordidness and hardship. But she loved the dancing. The shifting from town to town, from theatre to theatre, numbed her pain. She caught herself looking at beauty through Jesse Dick's eyes. In her Cincinnati letter to Lottie, she dismissed dancing in ten words and devoted three pages to a description of the Nürnberg quality of the turreted buildings on the hill overlooking the river, from the park. The money she earned, aside from that which she needed for her own actual wants, she sent regularly to the Red Cross. Before she had left, "I suppose I could be cutting sandwiches," she had said, "and dancing with the kids passing through Chicago; or driving an emergency car. I'd rather not. There are fifty girls to every job of that kind."

Contrary to Aunt Charlotte's prediction, Jeannette's Nebraska sailor had not become Jeannette's Nebraska husband until after the armistice. She was married at Christmas and left for the West with him. The wedding was held in the Prairie Avenue house. It turned out to be rather a grim affair, in spite of Jeannette's high spirits and her Bohemian relatives and the postwar reaction and the very good supper provided by Mrs. Payson. For Belle and Henry thought of Charley; and Mrs. Payson thought of Lottie; and Aunt Charlotte thought of both, and of the girl of sixty years ago. And Jeannette said bluntly: "You look as if it was a funeral instead of a wedding." She herself was a little terrified at the thought of this great unknown prairie land to which she was going, with her smart fur coat and her tricotine dress and her silk stockings and gray kid shoes. As well she might be.

After it was over, an unnatural quiet settled down upon the house. The two old women told each other that it was a blessed relief after the flurry and fuss of the wedding, but looked at each other rather fearfully during the long evenings and awaited Lottie's return with such passionate eagerness as neither would have admitted to the other. They expected her to pop in, somehow, the day after the armistice.

"Well, Lottie'll be home now," Mrs. Payson would say, "most any day." She took to watching for the postman, as she used to watch at the parlor window for Lottie on the rare occasions when she was late. When he failed to appear at what she considered the proper time she would fume and fuss. Then, at his ring, she would whisk into the front vestibule with surprising agility and, poking her head out of the door, berate him.

"You're getting later and later, Mail Man. Yesterday it was nine o'clock. Today it's almost half-past."

Mail Man was a chromic individual, his grayish hair blending into the grayish uniform above which his grayish face rose almost indefinably. He was lopsided from much service. "Well, everything's late these days, M'z. Payson. Since the war we haven't had any regular—"

"Oh, the war! You make me tired with your war. The war's over!"

Mail Man did not defend himself further. Mailmen have that henpecked look by virtue of their calling, which lays them open to tirade and abuse from every disappointed sweetheart, housemaid, daughter, wife, and mother.

"Expecting a letter from Miss Lottie, I suppose?"

"Yes. Have you—"

"Don't see it here this morning, M'z. Payson. Might be in on the eleven o'clock mail. Everything's late these days since the war."

They confidently expected her in December. In December she wrote that it would be January. The letter was postmarked Paris. In January she set the date of her homecoming for February and it was that letter which contained the astounding news of the impending French orphan.

The two old women stared at each other, their mouths open ludicrously, their eyes wide. Mrs. Payson had read the letter aloud to Aunt Charlotte there in the living room.

"A French child—a French orphan." It was then that Mrs. Payson had looked up, her face as blank of expression as that of a dead fish. She plunged back into the letter, holding the page away from her as though distance would change the meaning of the black letters on the white flimsy page.

"Well," said Aunt Charlotte, the first to recover, "that'll be kind of nice, now Jeannette's gone and all. Young folks around the house again. It's been kind of spooky. French child, h'm? That'll be odd. I used to know some French. Had it, when I was a girl, at Miss Rapp's school, across the river. Remember Miss Rapp's s—"

"Charlotte Thrift, you're crazy! So's Lottie, crazy. A French orphan!" Another dart at the letter—"Why, it's a baby—a French baby. One of those war babies, I'll be bound . . . Where's Belle? I'll get Belle. I'll telephone Belle." Later, at the telephone—"Yes, I tell you that's what it says. A French baby and she's bringing it home. Well, come here and read it for yourself then. I guess I can read. You telephone Henry right away, d'you hear! You tell him to telegraph her, or cable her, or whatever it is, that she can't bring any French baby here. The idea! Why! Girls nowdays! Look at Charley . . . Excited? Don't you tell me not to be excited, Belle Payson! I guess you'd be excited—"

Henry cabled. He agreed with Mother Payson that it was a little too much. Let the French take care of their own orphans. America'd furnish the money but no wet-nursing.

Winnie Steppier had returned from France in December. To her Mrs. Payson appealed for information. "Did you know anything about this crazy notion of Lottie's? Did she say anything to you when you were together there?"

"Yes, indeed. I saw her."

"Saw who?"

"The baby. The French baby. She's awfully cute. Fair . . . No, they're not all dark, you know . . . Well, now, Mrs. Payson, I wouldn't say that. It's a nice humane thing to do, I think. All those poor little things left fatherless. Lots of Americans are bringing home . . . You have? Well, I don't think even that will change her now. She seems to have her mind made up. Maybe when you see it—"

"But where'd she get it? Where did she find it? How did she happen—"

Winnie Steppier explained. "Well, you know, after St. Mihiel, when the Germans were retreating and our boys were advancing, the Germans took prisoner all the young French men and women—all they could lay hands on. Regular slavery. They took parents from their children, and all. This baby was found in a little town called Thiaucourt, all alone, in a kind of cellar. They took care of her, and sent her back to the American relief."

"But the father and mother? They may be alive, looking for her."

"The father was killed. That's proved. The mother died—"

It was at this point that the accumulation of family eccentricities proved too much for Mrs. Payson. The "faint feeling" mushroomed into a full-sized faint from which they thought she would never recover. Aunt Charlotte had come upon her younger sister seated saggingly in a chair in the living room. Her face was livid. She was breathing stertorously. They put her to bed. For a long time she did not regain consciousness. But almost immediately on doing so she tried to get up.

"Well! I'm not staying in bed. What's the matter! What's the matter! Don't you think you can keep me in bed."

Followed another attack. The doctor said that a third would probably prove the last. So she stayed in bed now, rebellious still, and indomitable. One could not but admire the will that still burned so bright in the charred ruin of the body.

So it was a subdued homecoming that Lottie met. When she stepped off the train at the Twelfth Street station with an unmistakable bundle in her arms, Belle and Henry kissed her across the bundle and said, almost simultaneously, "Mother's been quite sick, Lottie. You can't keep her at the house, you know."

"Mother sick? How sick?"

They told her. And again, "You see, there can't be a baby in the house."

"Oh, yes," said Lottie, not in argument, but almost amusedly, as though it were too ridiculous to argue. "Don't you want to see her?"

"Yes," said Belle, nervously. And "W-what's its name?" asked Henry.

"I think Claire would be nice, don't you?" Lottie turned back the flap of the downy coverlet and Claire blinked up at them rosily and caught this unguarded opportunity to shoot a wanton fist in the air.

"Why, say, she's a cute little tyke," said Henry, and jiggled her chin, and caught the velvet fist. "Claire, huh? That isn't so terribly French."

Belle gave a gasp. "Why, Lottie, she's so little! She's just a tiny baby! Almost new. You must be crazy. Mother's too sick to have—"

Lottie replaced the flap and captured the waving fist expertly, tucking it back into warmth. "She's not little. She's really large for her age. Those are all my bags, Henry, and things. There's a frightful lot of them. And here's my trunk check. Perhaps you'd better tend to them. Here, I'll take this, and that. Give them to the boy. Perhaps Belle and I had better go ahead in a taxi while you straighten out the mess."

She was calm, alert, smiling. Henry thought she looked handsome, and told her so. "War certainly agrees with you, Lottie. Gosh, you look great. Doesn't she, Belle? Darned pretty, if you ask me, Lot."

Belle, eyeing Lottie's clear fine skin, and the vital line of her shoulders and back and a certain set of the head, and a look that was at once peaceful and triumphant, nodded in agreement, vaguely puzzled. "I thought you'd be a wreck . . . What do you think of Charley? . . . Oh, well, and now Mother. And here you come complicating things still more. How did you happen to do such a crazy thing, Lottie?"

"I'll tell you all about it on the way home." Later, in the taxi, the heaving bundle fitting graciously into the hollow of her arm: "Well, you know, after St. Mihiel, when the Germans were retreating and retreating and our boys were advancing, the Germans took with them in their retreat all the young men and young women they could lay their hands on. Prisoners, you know. They meant to use them for work. Well, often, parents were taken from their children. Babies were left alone. When our men got to Thiaucourt—that's a little town of about three hundred—in September, it was a deserted ruined heap of stone. They were right up on the retreat. And there, in what had been a kitchen, without any roof to it, was a baby. They sent her back, of course, to us."

"Yes, but Lottie, perhaps the—"

"No. The father was killed in the war. They traced the mother. She died in November. I adopted her legally—"

"You didn't!"

"But I did."

"Claire—what?"

Lottie looked down at the bundle; squeezed it with a gentle pressure. "Claire Payson, I suppose, now."

Chapter XIX

The girls all came to see the baby. They exclaimed and cooed and *ah*'d and *oh*'d. "Of course it's wonderful and all. But it is a big responsibility, Lottie. How in the world did you happen—"

"Well, you know, after St. Mihiel, when the Germans were retreating and our boys were advancing—"

She was asked to lecture before some of the women's clubs but declined.

Beck Schaefer, grown a trifle too plump now in the role of Mrs. Sam Butler, insisted on holding the struggling Claire. "I never can tell whether I like a baby or not until I've held it—her. 'Scuse. Though this one certainly is a darling. Come to your Aunt Beck, sweetie. Oh, Lottie! Look at her! She put her little hand right up on my cheek! S'e is a tunnin' ol' sin, izzen s'e!" This last addressed directly to the object of her admiration. "Sam and I want to adopt a baby. That's what comes of marrying late. Though I suppose you heard about Celia. Imagine! But he looks just like Orville. Good thing he's a boy. I don't see why you didn't take a boy, while you were about it. Though, after all, when you've brought up a girl you know where she is, but a boy! Well! They leave you and then where are you! They don't even thank you for your trouble. And girls are such fun to dress. Oh, *what* did you think of Ben Gartz marrying a chorus girl! Didn't you nearly die! I saw her in the Pompeiian Room with him one night after the theatre. She's a common-looking little thing and young enough to be his daughter. She was ordering things under glass. Poor Ben. He was awfully sweet on you, Lottie, at one time. What happened, anyway?"

Against the doctor's orders and the nurse's advice and maneuverings, Mrs. Payson had insisted on seeing the baby immediately on Lottie's entering the house. They prepared Lottie. "It can't be much worse for her to see you—and the baby—now than not to see you. She's so worked up that we can't do anything with her anyway. But don't argue; and don't oppose her in anything. Lie, if you have to, about sending the baby away."

"Away! Oh! no!"

"But Lottie, you don't understand how sick she is. Any shock might—"

Lottie had scarcely divested herself of hat and wraps when she entered her mother's bedroom, the child in her arms. Mrs. Payson's eyes were on the door—had been from the moment she heard the flurry of homecoming downstairs. As Lottie stood in the doorway a moment, the sick woman's eyes dilated. She made as though to sit up. The nurse took the child from Lottie as she bent over to kiss her mother. Then, suddenly, she dropped to her knees at the side of the bed. "Oh, Mama, it's so good to be home." She took one of the flaccid hands in her own firm vital grasp.

"H'm. Well, that's some good come of your leaving, anyway. You look handsome, Lottie. How've you got your hair done?"

"Just as I always had it, Mama."

"Your face looks fuller, somehow. Let's see the young one."

The nurse turned and leaned over the bed. But at this final test of her good nature, Claire, travel worn, bewildered, hungry, failed them. She opened wide her mouth, lurched in muscular rebellion, and emitted a series of ear-piercing screams against the world; against this strange person in white who held her; against that which stared at her from the bed.

"There!" exclaimed Mrs. Payson. "Take it away. I knew it. Don't you think for one minute I'm going to have any foreign baby screaming around this house, sick as I am. Not for a minute. I hope you're satisfied,

Lottie. Running an orphan asylum in this house. Well, I've still got something to say."

But strangely enough she had little to say, after that. She showed small interest in the newcomer and they kept the baby out of the sick room. The little world of her bedside interested the sick woman more. She fancied them all in league against her. She would call Lottie to her bedside and send the nurse out of the room on some pretext or other that deceived no one.

"Lottie, come here. Listen. That woman has got to go. Why, she won't let me get up! I'm perfectly well."

"But perhaps you haven't quite got your strength, Mama. You know it takes a while."

"I'll never get my strength back lying here. Was I ever a person to stay in bed?"

"No, Mama. You've always been wonderful."

"A lot of thanks I've got for it, too. Now, Lottie, you see that I get another doctor. This man's a fool. He doesn't understand my case. Palavering young hand-holder, that's what he is."

"Don't you think you'd better try him a little longer? He hasn't had time, really."

"Time! I've been three mortal months in this bed. You're like all the rest of them. Glad if I died. Well, I'm not going to please you just yet. You'll see me up tomorrow, early."

They had heard this threat so regularly and so often that they scarcely heeded it now; or, if they did, only to say, soothingly, "We'll see how you feel by tomorrow, shall we?"

So that when, finally, she made good her threat, the nurse came in early one morning from where she slept in the alcove just off the big front bedroom to find her half-lying, half-sitting in the big chair by the window.

She had got up stealthily, had even fumbled about in bureau and closet for the clothes she had not worn in months. In one hand she grasped her corsets. She had actually meant to put them on as she had done every morning before her illness, regarding corsetless kimonoed women with contempt. She must have dragged herself up to the chair by an almost superhuman effort of will. So they found her. A born ruler, defying them all to the last.

Charley came home for the funeral. She was not to rejoin the Krisiloff company until its arrival in Chicago for the two-weeks' engagement there. "If ever," said Henry Kemp privately to Lottie. "I don't think she's so crazy about this trouping any more. You ought to have heard her talking about the fresh eggs at breakfast this morning. I asked her what she'd been eating on the road and she said, 'Vintage oofs.'"

Mrs. Carrie Payson's funeral proved an enlightening thing. There came to it a queer hodgepodge of people; representatives of Chicago's South Side old families who had not set foot in the Prairie Avenue house in half a century; real estate men who had known her in the days of her early business career; Brosch, the carpenter and contractor, with whom she had bickered and bartered for years; some of the Polish and Italian tenants from over Eighteenth Street way; women in shawls of whom Lottie had never heard, and who owed Mrs. Payson some unnamed debt of gratitude. Lottie wondered if she had ever really understood her mother; if the indomitability that amounted almost to ruthlessness had not been, after all, a finer quality than a certain fluid element in herself, in Aunt Charlotte, in Charley, which had handicapped them all.

Aunt Charlotte mourned her sister sincerely; seemed even to miss her tart-tongued goading. No one to find fault with her clothes, her habits, her ideas, her conversation. Lottie humored her outrageously. The household found itself buying as Mrs. Payson had bought; thinking as she had thought; regulating its hours as they had been regulated for her needs. Her personality was too powerful to fade so soon after the corporeal being had gone. More easily than any of them, Aunt Charlotte had accepted the advent of the French baby. To her the sound and sight of a baby in the old Prairie Avenue house seemed an accustomed and natural thing. She had a way of mixing names, bewilderingly. Often as not she called Claire "Lottie," or Charley "Claire." She clapped her hands at the baby and wagged her head at her tremulously, and said, "No, no, no! Auntie punish!" and "Come to Auntie Charlotte," exactly as she had done forty years before to Belle. Once she put the child down on the floor for a moment and Claire began to wriggle her way down the faded green stream of the parlor carpet river, and to poke a finger into the sails of the dim old ships and floral garlands, just as Lottie and Belle had done long ago.

There was much talk of selling the old house; but it never seemed to amount to more than talk. In proper time Claire was cutting her teeth and soothing her hot swollen gums on the hard surface of Ole Bull's arms, just as Belle and Lottie had done before her. This only, of course, when Aunt Charlotte was holding her. Lottie and Charley both put down the practice as highly unhygienic.

"Fiddlesticks! You and Belle did it with all your teeth. And you're living."

Charley came daily—often twice daily—to see the baby. She was fascinated by her, made herself Claire's slave, insisted on trundling her up and down Prairie Avenue in the smart English pram, though Lottie said she much preferred to have her sleep or take her airing in the back garden undisturbed. Charley and Aunt Charlotte opposed this. Charley said, "Oh, but look how ducky she is in that bonnet! Everybody stops to look at her, and then I brag. Yesterday I told a woman she was mine. I expected her to say, 'And you so young!' but she didn't."

Aunt Charlotte said, "This new fad of never talking to babies and never picking 'em up! It makes idiots of them. How can you ever expect them to learn anything? Lie there like wooden images. Or else break their hearts crying, when all they want is a little petting . . . Her want her ol' Auntie to p'ay wis her, yes her does, doesn't her?" to the baby.

Claire was one of those fair, rose-leaf babies, and possessed, at eight months, of that indefinable thing known as style. She was the kind of baby, Charley said, that looks dressy in a flannel nightgown. "Those French gals," Charley explained. "Chic. That's what she's got. Haven't you, *ma petite? Ma bébé*—or is it *mon bébé*, Lotta? I get so mixed." Charley's was the American college girl's French, verbless, scant, and faltering. She insisted on addressing Claire in it, to that young person's wide-eyed delight. "*Tu est mon chou—ma chou*—say, Lotta, you're a girl that's been around. Do they really call each other cabbages over there?"

One of the big bedrooms on the second floor had been cleared and refurnished as a nursery. Here, almost nightly at six o'clock, you found Lottie, Charley, and Aunt Charlotte. The six o'clock bottle was a vital affair. It just preceded sleeping time. It must be taken quietly for some dietetic reason. The three women talked low, in the twilight, watching Claire in her small bed. Claire lay rolling her eyes around at them ecstatically as she pulled at the bottle. She exercised tremendous suction and absorbed the bottle's contents almost magically unless carefully watched.

This evening the talk centered on the child, as always. Trivial talk, and yet vital.

"She's growing so I'll have to let her hems down again. And some new stockings. The heels of those she has come under the middle of her foot."

"Look at her Lotta! She's half asleep. There, now she's awake again and pulling like mad. Swoons off and shows the whites of her eyes and then remembers and goes at it again. Now she's—I never saw such a snoozey old thing. Sleeps something chronic, all day and all night. What good are you, anyway, h'm?"

Aunt Charlotte grew reminiscent. "Time you and Belle were babies, you wore long dresses—great long trailing bunchy things, and yards and yards of petticoats—flannel and white. It used to take the girl hours to do 'em up. Nowdays, seems the less they put on 'em the healthier they are."

Charley was seated cross-legged on the floor, her back against a fat old armchair. "How about the babies in France, Lotta? I suppose they're still bundling them up over there. What did the Coot have on when they found her, h'm?"

Lotta rose to take the empty bottle away, gently. Claire's eyes were again showing two white slits.

Aunt Charlotte, in the window chair, leaned forward. Her tremulous forefinger made circles, round and round, on her black-silk knee. "Yes, Lotta. Now what did she have on, poor little forlorn lamb!"

"Why—I don't remember, Aunt Charlotte." She tucked the coverlet in at the sides of the crib firmly. Claire was sound asleep now, her two fists held high above her head, as a healthy baby sleeps. Lottie stood a moment looking down at the child. The old, old virgin in the chair by the window and the young girl seated cross-legged on the floor watched her intently. Suddenly the quiet peaceful air of the nursery was electric. The child made a little clucking sound with tongue and lips, in her sleep. Charley sat forward, her eyes on Lottie.

"Lotta, do you remember my five—my five—" she broke off with a half-sob. Then she threw up her head. "I'll have them yet."

It was then Aunt Charlotte put into brave words the thought that was in the minds of the three women. "Don't you want to tell us about him, Lottie? Don't you!"

For one instant, terror leaped into Lottie's eyes as they went from Aunt Charlotte's face to Charley's. But at what they saw there the terror faded and in its place came relief—infinite relief. "Yes."

"Well, then, just you do."

But Lottie hesitated yet another moment, looking at them intently. "Did you both know—all the time." Aunt Charlotte nodded. But Charley shook her head slightly. "Not until just now, Lotta . . . something in your face as you stood there looking down at her."

Lottie came away from the crib, sat down in a low chair near Aunt Charlotte. Charley scuttled crab-wise over to her across the floor and settled there against her, her arm flung across Lottie's knee. The old Prairie Avenue house was quiet, quiet. You could hear the child's regular breathing. Lottie's voice was low, so that the baby's sleep might not be disturbed, yet clear, that Aunt Charlotte might hear. They could have gone downstairs, or to another chamber, but they did not. The three women sat in the dim room.

"We met—I met him—in Paris, the very first week. He had gone over there in the beginning as a correspondent. Then he had come all the way back to America and had enlisted for service. He hated it, as every intelligent man did. But he had to do it, he said. We—liked each other right away. I'd never met a man like that before. I didn't know there were any. Oh, I suppose I did know; but they had never come within my range. He had only a second-lieutenancy. There was nothing of the commander about him. He always said so. He used to say he had never learned to 'snap into it' properly. You know what I mean? He was thirty-seven. Winnie Steppier introduced us. She had known him in his Chicago cub reporter days. He went to New York, later. Well, that first week, when I was waiting to be sent out, he and Winnie and I—she met me in Paris, you know, when I came—went everywhere together and it was glorious. I can't tell you. Paris was being shelled but it refused to be terrorized. The streets and the parks and the restaurants were packed. You've no idea what it was, going about with him. He was like a boy about things—simple things, I mean—a print in a window, or a sauce in a restaurant, or a sunset on the Bois. We used to laugh at nothing—foolish, wonderful, private jokes like those families have that are funny to no one outside the family. The only other person I'd ever known like that was a boy at school when I went to Armour. I haven't seen him since I was eighteen, and he's an important person now. But he had that same quality. They call it a sense of humor, I suppose, but it's more than that. It's the most delightful thing in the world, and if you have it you don't need anything else. . . . Four months later he was wounded. Not badly. He was in the hospital for six weeks. In that time I didn't see him. Then he went back into it but he wasn't fit. We used to write regularly. I don't know how I can make you understand how things were—things—"

Charley looked up at her. "I know what you mean. The—the state of mind that people got into over there—nice people—nice girls. Is that what you mean?"

"Yes. Do you know?"

"Well, I can imagine—"

"No, you can't. The world was rocking and we over there were getting the full swing of it. It seemed that all the things we had considered so vital and fundamental didn't matter any more. Life didn't count. A city today was a brick heap tomorrow. Night and day were all mixed up. Terror and work. Exhaustion and hysteria. A lot of us were girls—women, I mean—who had never known freedom. Not license—freedom. Ordinary freedom of will, or intellect, or action. Men, too, who had their noses to the grindstone for years. You know there's a lot more to war than just killing, and winning battles, and patching people up. It does something to you—something chemical and transforming—after you've been in it. The reaction isn't always noble. I'm just trying to explain what I mean. There were a lot of things going around—especially among the older and more severe looking of us girls. It's queer. There was one girl—she'd been a librarian in some little town up in Michigan. She told me once that there were certain books they kept in what they called 'the Inferno,'' and only certain people could have them. They weren't on the shelves, for the boys and girls, or the general public. When she spoke of them she looked like a librarian. Her mouth made a thin straight line. You could picture her sitting in the library, at her desk, holding that pencil they use with a funny little rubber stamp thing attached to it, and refusing to allow some schoolgirl to take out *Jennie Gerhardt*. She was discharged and sent home for being what they called promiscuous . . . I just wanted you to know how things were . . . He got three days' leave. Winnie Steppier was in Paris at the time. I was to try for leave—I'd have gone AWOL if I hadn't got it—and we three were to meet there. Winnie had a little two-room flat across the river. She'd been there for almost a year, you know. She made it her headquarters. The concierge knew me. When I got there Robert was waiting for me. Winnie had left a note. She had been called to Italy by her paper. I was to use her apartment. We stayed there together . . . I'm not excusing it. There is no excuse. They were the happiest three days of my life—and always will be . . . There are two kinds of men, you know, who make the best soldiers. The butcher-boy type with no nerves and no imagination. And the fine, high-strung type that fears battle and hates war and who whips himself into courage and heroism because he's afraid he'll be afraid . . . He hated to go back, though he never said so . . . He was killed ten days later . . . I went to Switzerland for a while when . . . Winnie was with me . . . She was wonderful. I think I should have died without her ... I wanted to at first . . . But not now. Not now."

Stillness again. You heard only the child's breathing, gentle, rhythmical.

Aunt Charlotte's wavering tremulous forefinger traced circles round and round on her knee—round and round. The heavy black brows were drawn into a frown. She looked an age-old seeress sitting there in her black. "Well." She got up slowly and came over to the crib. She stood there a moment. "It's a brave lie, Lottie. You stick to it, for her. A topsy-turvy world she's come into. Perhaps she'll be the one to work out what we haven't done—we Thrift girls. She's got a job ahead of her. A job."

Lottie leaned forward in the darkness. "I'll never stand in her way. She's going to be free. I know. I'll never hamper her. Not in word, or look, or thought. You'll see."

"You probably will, Lottie. You're human. But I won't be here to see. Not I. And I'm not sorry. I've hardly been away from the spot where I was born, but I've seen the world. I've seen the world . . . Well . . ."

She went toward the door with her slow firm step, putting each foot down flat; along the hall she went, her black silk skirts making a soft susurrus. Lottie rose, opened a window to the sharp spring air. Then, together, she and Charley tiptoed out, stopping a moment, hand in hand at the crib. The nursery room was quiet except for the breathing of the child.

About the Authors

Edna Ferber was born in 1885 in Kalamazoo, Michigan. After a short career in journalism, she turned to writing novels, short stories, and plays. She won the Pulitzer Prize in 1925 for her novel, *So Big*, and subsequent works went on to become best-sellers. *Giant*, which she published in 1952, became the basis of the hit film starring Elizabeth Taylor, Rock Hudson, and James Dean. She died in 1968 at the age of eighty-two.

Kathleen Rooney is a founding editor of Rose Metal Press, a publisher of literary work in hybrid genres, and a founding member of Poems While You Wait, a team of poets and their typewriters who compose commissioned poetry on demand. She is the author, most recently, of the novels *Lillian Boxfish Takes a Walk* and *Cher Ami and Major Whittlesey*. Her latest collection, *Where Are the Snows*, winner of the X. J. Kennedy Prize, was released by Texas Review Press in September 2022, and her next novel, *From Dust to Stardust*, will be published by Lake Union Press in the fall of 2023.

CPSIA information can be obtained
at www.ICGtesting.com
Printed in the USA
JSHW081410120223
37532JS00002B/2